THE WORLD FORGOT

Also by Martin Leicht and Isla Neal

Mothership

A Stranger Thing

The World Forgot

BOOK THREE
OF THE EVER–
EXPANDING
UNIVERSE

Forgot

MARTIN
LEICHT
& ISLA
NEAL

SIMON & SCHUSTER BFYR

New York   London   Toronto   Sydney   New Delhi

SIMON & SCHUSTER BFYR

An imprint of Simon & Schuster Children's Publishing Division
1230 Avenue of the Americas, New York, New York 10020

Text copyright © 2015 by Lisa Graff and Martin Leicht
Jacket photograph copyright © 2015 by Ali Smith

For information about special discounts for bulk purchases, please contact
Simon & Schuster Special Sales at 1-866-506-1949
or business@simonandschuster.com.
The Simon & Schuster Speakers Bureau can bring authors to your live event.
For more information or to book an event, contact the Simon & Schuster Speakers
Bureau at 1-866-248-3049 or visit our website at www.simonspeakers.com.
Jacket design by Lizzy Bromley
Interior design by Hilary Zarycky
The text for this book is set in Electra.
Manufactured in the United States of America
2 4 6 8 10 9 7 5 3 1
Library of Congress Cataloging-in-Publication Data
Leicht, Martin.
The world forgot / Martin Leicht and Isla Neal. — First edition.
pages cm. — (The ever-expanding universe ; 3)
Summary: Teen mom Elvie Nara searches the universe after her daughter
has been kidnapped.
ISBN 978-1-4424-2966-6 (hardback) — ISBN 978-1-4424-2968-0 (eBook)
[1. Science fiction. 2. Teenage mothers—Fiction. 3. Human-alien encounters—
Fiction. 4. Kidnapping—Fiction.] I. Neal, Isla. II. Title.
PZ7.L53283Wo 2015
[Fic]—dc23
2014024001

FIRST
EDITION

For Lena and Bob

How happy is the blameless vestal's lot!
The world forgetting, by the world forgot.

—Alexander Pope, "Eloisa to Abelard"

PROLOGUE

Some days I sleep. Some days I pace. Some days, the days when they decide we have no need for light, I sit in absolute darkness.

Today I have no idea where I am. I haven't known much of anything for as long as I can remember. Since they brought me here. They moved me or didn't, and I simply can't remember. I can't seem to remember much of anything. Can't even remember which things I forgot and which things I never knew to begin with.

Today I do not know where I am.

It's loud. I know that much. Blaring horns, like an alarm or a whatdayacallit. Signage? Siphon?

It's loud. There are flashing lights. On and off and on again.

Siren. I remember the word. Siren, that's what's making so much noise.

A siren means something is wrong.

The others don't seem to care that something is wrong. Most of them are sleeping. Some of them, the ones who just came back from their tests, are sleeping the most soundly. You're always the most tired after a test.

After a while, I don't know how long, I drift off to sleep too.

More time passes.

I wake up.

I pace.

I sit in the darkness.

The door hisses and clicks, and suddenly everyone's at attention. Everyone always wakes up when they open the door.

The white light that streams in when the door is opened is blinding. Two black silhouettes in the doorway.

"Number Twelve!" the first guard barks out. I don't know his name. Or maybe I just don't remember.

I rub a sore spot on my shoulder. I don't know why it's sore. I don't think I've taken a test recently. Around me I hear whispers, more shifting of weight.

"Number Twelve!" the guard shouts again.

There is a sharp poke in my back. *"That's you,"* one of them hisses at me.

"Oh!" The wheels click together in my brain. "Oh." I squint into the whiteness of the light beyond the door. "That's me," I tell the guard. My voice is hoarse, cracking. I guess that's what happens when you're stuck in one dark room after another—you stop talking so much, and then your voice goes hoarse.

Or maybe my voice was always like that. I can't remember.

The guard jerks his chin downward, a sharp nod.

"Come with us," he says.

I step out into the light.

As my eyes adjust to the brightness, I take in the guard who leads me by the arm—with swift, sure strides—and, four steps behind him, the other, shorter guard. I recognize him. I think I recognize him. He is young. Short blond hair, sharp blue eyes. And I think I remember that he is friendlier than the others.

"Hi," I greet him quietly.

"No talking," the first guard snaps at me. He yanks me forward with such force that I stumble, almost fall. The second guard steadies me.

I turn to thank him, to offer him a smile at least, and I see that he is turned away from me. He will not accept my gratitude.

Still, I think, *I will remember this small kindness.* I will try to remember.

I am led to a room. White, sterile, silent. There's nothing here that's memorable, and yet when we walk into it, I'm flooded with memories. I can feel the sore spot on my shoulder. I can hear crying. But it's not me. A baby? A baby's cries? I . . . had a baby once—didn't I? Thoughts whirl through my brain, and I can't remember which are real and which are imagined. The white walls blur into one another in my memories. The friendlier guard leads me to a high table, and he helps me hop up to sit on it. The taller, gruffer guard stays in the hallway to confer with someone else. I take my opportunity to talk. Use my voice.

"Why did the siren go off, before?" I ask. I'm pleased that I was able to remember the word before I got to ask.

The guard's eyes dart to the door. No one is listening.

"There was a breach," he tells me. I don't know what that means. It's a word I've forgotten, or never learned. But I don't want him to know I can't remember. I want him to think I'm the kind of person who knows what words mean. "But it's okay. We're safe now."

We talk no more after that, and he doesn't look at me. But I sit up a little straighter. Brush the tangles out of my hair when I think he isn't looking.

The person who enters the room next is not the first guard but an older man. A doctor, maybe? He wears a white coat, carries a lap-pad. I may have met him before. He glances down at the lap-pad. "Number Twelve," he says, reading.

"Yes, sir," I respond. *I know that I am Number Twelve*, I think proudly. I remembered.

"How have you been feeling?" the doctor asks me.

I try to remember. "Fine," I say.

"Aches or pains of the joints?"

"No," I tell him. I think that's right. "Oh! My shoulder is sore." I rub the spot again. Tugging at the neck of my tunic, I can make out a mark there—one short line that intersects another at a right angle, like a capital *L*. I rub at it again, but the mark will not go away.

The doctor ignores my observation. "Any stomach cramping, abdominal pain, chest flutters?"

"No."

"Disturbing dreams? Thoughts?"

"Thoughts? No. Would that be bad?"

"Could be. Psychological stresses could introduce unknown variables into the testing."

Tests. It's my turn for a test. What are the tests for again? I always get so sleepy after and forget. I glance back at the friendly guard. He gives me a small smile when the doctor is focused on his lap-pad. I smile back.

I remember how to do *that*, at least.

"I don't have any dreams," I tell the doctor.

The doctor nods, pleased with my answer. "Just one final question," he tells me, "and then we can begin the testing." I sit up a little straighter, waiting. "Do you remember anything from before your time here began?"

"Remember?"

"Yes. For instance, your name? Do you remember your name?"

I open my mouth to answer—such a simple question— and find that I can't.

"I . . . ," I start. A jumble of words circle frantically in my brain, but I can't quite grab at any of them. I look at the friendly guard. He's frowning. I want to tell them, *Yes, I know my name. I can remember things. I'm good at knowing things and remembering words. I remembered the word for the loud noise before. Didn't I? Surgeon?* "I can't remember. I'm sorry." I hang my head, ashamed.

The doctor smiles a kind smile at me and sets down his lap-pad. "Don't be sorry. Let's get you into the lab so we can begin testing."

I nod. I'm tired. That must be why I can't remember. I

turn to the friendly guard, who puts a guiding hand on the small of my back. "This way," he directs.

I have disappointed him. And after the testing I'll be even more tired. And I'll remember even less.

I allow the guard to lead me to the door, while I still search my mind. There must be *something* there. I probe the furthest corners, grab at the tumbling thoughts.

Until, finally, I reach one.

"Britta," I say quickly, spinning around to face the doctor. "That's my name. Britta McVicker." They both look stunned, but I know this is correct. *I know something.* I am elated. I smile at the friendly guard.

But he is not smiling back. He takes in a deep breath. I *feel* it, as though he has taken in the air I needed to breathe.

And I don't know why, but the skin on the back of my knees begins to tingle.

I face the doctor again. He is frowning.

"That's right, isn't it?" I ask him, even though I am sure of the answer. "My name is Britta McVicker?" How have I disappointed them with my remembering?

"Sir?" the guard says to him, as though to confirm something.

The doctor is poking around inside a drawer, looking for something. "Unfortunate," he tells the guard. "We do not have time for these setbacks." He does look up now, but not at me.

The doctor is holding something long and thin in his hand. What do they call it? A needle. I think that's the word. The doctor clasps the needle tightly in his gloved hand.

I don't remember when he put on the gloves.

"Sit back down, please," the doctor tells me. His voice is cold. "Hold her down." That he says to the guard.

Suddenly I feel sick. A cold feeling—dread—runs through me. It's as if in finding my name I have turned on a switch, and now light is creeping slowly through a dark room. A room like where they were holding me. With the others. All the others. *The others.* Oh God. I remember. I know.

"Just relax," the friendly guard says. He's trying to smile as he holds my shoulders down, but his eyes are sad. "This won't hurt at all. You'll feel sleepy, and when you wake up, everything will be fine."

I look at his face, then the doctor's. I watch the needle go into my arm. And I know that he's lying.

Chapter One

IN WHICH WE ATTEMPT TO HIT THE GROUND RUNNING

Come on, already. Is it too much to ask for a little time to myself for once?

I spot Cole on the other side of the deck, where he slouches over the rail, staring out at the water. For a split second I consider turning around and heading back belowdecks, but Cole spots me before I make up my mind. He gives me a quick nod, then turns back to the water and takes a slug from a silver can. He makes no movement toward me, leaving me in the unenviable position of having to either be an antisocial jerk and ignore him or choose to hold an actual conversation.

You'd think that chatting with Cole would be easy enough, despite our current dire situation. I mean, we did conceive a child together. That kind of thing doesn't happen when you're communicating solely by semaphore. But after the realization I had back in Antarctica that I'm changing in really unexpected ways while Cole, for better or worse, is pretty much always going to be, well, Cole, I've been having a hard time acting normal around him. The fact that Cole's testing to see if I'll approach him is proof enough that even he has picked up on this.

I take up a spot about an arm's length away from him along the ship's railing and follow his gaze out to the horizon. The wind is superbrisk, but thanks to my Enosi hybrid genes, I adapted to the chill long before we even disembarked.

"Where's Ducky?" Cole says to me, still not looking in my direction.

"He's down in the bathroom. Barfing again."

"I'm surprised you're not down there holding his hair," Cole says. "You've barely left his side since we set sail from Cape Crozier."

"Cole, I've been with Ducky because Ducky's been with Marnie, and Marnie's been the one taking care of my dad. Remember? Harry Nara, middle-aged, out-of-shape engineer-slash-world's-oldest-and-most-chuteless-skydiver?"

Cole takes another long drag from his nondescript tin can, then hurls it overboard. I want to chastise him for being an ocean litterbug, but I somehow manage to stop myself. I guess I'm growing as a person. Cole bends down and pulls two more cans from a crate at his feet on his other side.

"You'd think he'd have his sea legs after two weeks at sea," he says, offering me one of the cans.

I don't take it. "He's spending twenty hours a day in a medical gel bath recovering from frostbite, hypothermia, and more than a few broken bones, Cole," I reply, more than a little rankled. "I hardly think sea legs are his biggest—"

"I meant Ducky."

"Oh. Well, I think he was hoping that Oates's contact would come pick us up in a fancy spaceship or something, instead of an old oil tanker. But I guess beggars can't be choosers when it comes to which smugglers aid in your escape from prison." I do take the can from him then, but I don't open it. It's shiny and silvery smooth, like a can of peaches with the label pulled off. I play with the pop-top, lifting it slightly up and then letting it snap back onto the lid. "Besides, I'm sure Ducky'd barf in a spaceship, too. I've yet to discover any form of transportation gentle enough for his world-class motion sickness."

"At least Oates had friends out there who could pick us up," Cole says. "Even if they are kinda shady. After those pricks on the elevator platform left us stranded."

"Well, the elevator was kinda sorta completely destroyed," I remind him. "Those guys didn't have any way to send a transport to pick us up before they left."

"They could have left us *something*," Cole argues. "Instead of scrambling back home with that weak-ass excuse about a 'communications blackout.' If it weren't for Oates's pals, we'd still be stuck in the snow."

I look at Cole's profile, a beautiful silhouette against the white sunlight. There are things we need to be talking about. Another conversation entirely.

I'm not sure I'm ready to have it.

"They're still fighting down there," I say, darting my eyes down to the deck below, where all the Almiri and Enosi trapped with us in Antarctica have been battling it out for the past several days. They stop only for meal breaks. "Oates is doing his best to referee, but no one's seeing eye to eye on the whole let's-go-back-to-Almiri-headquarters-and-hug-this-out plan we've got going."

"Well, probably because it's a shit plan," Cole says.

"It's the only option we have."

Cole turns and looks at me. "Elvs, the hybrids are never going to be okay with going to HQ. We Almiri have been huge dicks to them for centuries. And I don't see that changing anytime soon just because we all took a boat ride together."

"The Jin'Kai invasion is coming," I say, and I hate to admit it, but even I can hear the hint of desperation in my voice. "Marsden said as much. A fleet of those Devastators is on its way to Earth. Our only hope is to make sure everyone who calls Earth home—Almiri, Enosi, human—learns to play nice and form a unified resistance."

"That's all well and good to say," Cole says, "except that's not why you want to go back to HQ. You think Byron knows how to find Olivia."

"Yeah," I snap back. "And so what if that's my reason? You act like wanting to find my daughter is some sort of crime."

She stole her. My own mother kidnapped my daughter, right out of my hands, and handed her over to Dr. Marsden.

"*Our* daughter," Cole says, and when I give him a funny look, he bores his stony eyes into me. "You said 'my.' You keep forgetting that Olivia's my daughter too."

I do. I do keep forgetting that. Probably because Cole hasn't been acting much like a parent lately. Probably because he's been acting more like a whiny, entitled baby, sulking on the deck when he should be helping Oates to get everyone to play nice like I've been doing for two weeks straight. Suddenly I feel butterflies climbing into my throat. I haven't felt butterflies, not truly, since I was home in Ardmore, before any of this alien invasion craziness was a thing. A million years ago, in my bedroom in Ardmore, when Cole touched my hair, and I looked into his eyes, and he kissed me for the very first time.

Those were very different butterflies.

"I think we should break up," I say softly. The words hover in the air between us like they're in a cartoon speech bubble. Cole barely reacts at all, but I notice the corner of his mouth twitch. For several seconds the only sound is the crashing of the waves against the hull of the ship. I wait, as patiently as I can, for the explosion of feelings that's probably welling up inside him right now.

"Whatever," Cole says finally.

Not exactly what I was expecting.

"*Whatever?*" I snap back.

"What do you want me to say, Elvs?"

"Something more than 'whatever.' We have a *child* together, for Christ's sake."

"*You're* the one who just said you want to break up!"

I'm at a loss. I want so badly for Cole to understand. I want to tell him that he'll always be my first true love, that he'll always be the father of my child, and that there will always be a special place in my heart just for him. That I'll always want him in my life, but that I'm growing into a different person from who I was when we met, and that I need to figure out who this new person is going to be. I want to tell him I'm sorry.

"Fine. Whatever, then," I shoot back at him.

My mouth feels like I've been chewing on cotton balls. I crack open the silver can and take a huge sip, only to immediately spit it back out in a glorious spray over the bow of the ship.

"Jesus, Cole! What in the hell is this?" I run my finger along the lip of the can, picking up the thick white liquid. "Have you been drinking *condensed milk*?"

"It was all they had in the galley!" he shouts. "And, hey, I don't have to explain myself to you, because *we just broke up*!"

With that, he storms away, brushing past Captain Oates, who is walking toward us. Cole doesn't break his stride and starts running as he gets farther away from me. Oates looks back at him before turning to me with a concerned look on his face.

"Miss Elvie?" he asks. "You're crying."

"It's nothing," I say, holding up the can of syrupy milk. "Just went down the wrong pipe."

"Ah." Oates settles in right beside me and looks out at the water. I can tell he doesn't believe me, but he's way too British to let on. "It's quite lovely, isn't it?"

"Yeah," I say, sniffing.

"It's been too long since I've been on the water. I hadn't realized how much I truly missed it."

"Well, seems like you could have called your buddies here to escape from prison anytime you wanted to."

"I broke the law of my people, even if I felt that law to be unjust. If I wanted my actions to mean something, I could not run away from their consequences."

"I didn't realize extra hanky-panky was such a weighty

subject for you," I say. Seriously, I've always thought the Almiri "code" was a bit bogus—deciding who a dude gets to sleep with, and then locking him up indefinitely if said dude can't keep it in his pants—but my buddy Oates has taken things to a new level of bogusitude.

Oates looks me dead in the eye. Now I've done it. I should just keep my mouth shut for the rest of the trip so that I don't piss anyone else off.

"These sailors who aid us in our journey home . . . ," Oates begins.

"The smugglers? What about them?"

"They are not smugglers. Well, they are, but not in the manner that you suppose. They are freedom runners. They transport the, shall we say, recently liberated, to safer harbor."

"You mean like escaped convicts?" I ask.

Oates shrugs. "Perhaps, sometimes. But not always. They have been making their covert runs for centuries now."

"They're Almiri?" I'm stunned. I mean, I guess they were handsome enough dudes, but with this entire alien race war being such a sausagefest, I've been getting kind of immune to hot guys.

Oates nods. "They have helped to transport freed slaves. Illegal prisoners of war. And even men and women like yourself."

"Enosi," I say, slowly beginning to understand. "You mean they've helped hybrids escape from Almiri camps. But how did they . . ." And then it dawns on me, full force. "You!" I turn to face Oates straight on. "Cape Crozier wasn't originally for Almiri Code-breakers with extra ants in their pants, was it?

The Almiri held Enosi captive there, back when the continent was unexplored. And you . . . your trip to the South Pole in the twentieth century . . . you were *freeing* them."

Oates is way too classy a dude to even acknowledge his own heroics. He simply rubs the palms of his hands along the cool rail. Me, being not so cool or classy, I slap him on the arm.

"Why didn't you ever say anything? You helped rescue, what, a hundred Enosi prisoners? A thousand? You need to tell them that! They need to see that not all Almiri are raging prejudiced asshats."

"The time may very well be at hand," Oates agrees. "I am equally concerned with convincing the Almiri Council that they have been, as you put it so poetically, 'asshats.'"

"So you, what? Stayed in the prison as a statement to Byron and the others?"

"I did. And it has already had some positive effects."

"Such as?"

"Well, your grandfather sent you to me, did he not?"

Byron, aka James Dean, aka my grandfather. Who would have imagined that sending your granddaughter to an Antarctic prison could be considered a *relaxed* position in the whole Almiri-Enosi conundrum?

"So he sent me to you to keep me and Olivia safe," I say.

"That was the idea. God laughs at all our plans, child."

I feel the tightness in my chest that comes whenever I allow myself to think about my daughter. "Byron will help us get Olivia back, won't he? I mean, I know the world is coming to an end and everything, but . . ."

"We will find your daughter. I gave you my word. But you

must be patient. There are many developments that we must account for now, not the least of which is the imminent Jin'Kai invasion."

I clench my teeth and say nothing. I mean, I know he's right, that there are bigger things going on right now. That I need to be patient.

But that doesn't mean I can do it.

I grip the railing and smell the salty air as a frigid breeze blows across the deck of the rickety old boat. There's a bitter taste in my mouth, which can only be blamed in part on the milk residue on my tongue.

"How did you know?" I ask.

"Miss?"

"You stayed trapped for so long, because you thought it was the right thing to do. How did you know when it was time to free yourself?"

"We are all captains of our own destiny," he says, putting an arm gently around my shoulders. "When the time comes, you just know."

And for some reason that starts me bawling, crying like some sort of girl. I press my face into Oates's coat, letting it absorb my tears. He pats my back.

"There, there, Miss Elvie," he reassures me. "Everything's all right now. You're almost there."

And as I look out at the water, I can almost allow myself to believe it.

Hold on, I think to my daughter, wherever she may be. *Just hold on a little longer. Mama's coming for you.*

Hold on.

Chapter Two

IN WHICH THINGS ARE SEEN THAT CANNOT BE UNSEEN

"Wait," Ducky says as we walk down the narrow hall toward the med bay. "You *broke up* with Cole? Like, 'broke up' broke up?"

"Let's not make a thing about it, please," I say. "Let's file it under 'Old News.'"

"Old news? It happened, like, three seconds ago. And need I remind you that you've been swoony over that guy since you first laid eyes on him?"

"Seriously, Duck. Focus. We're almost home. Well, to the Poconos, at least. One short helicopter trip away from the Poconos."

Ducky clears his throat. "Helicopter. Goodie."

"Duck, you can barf out the window, okay? Nut up. We've got to be ready to leave as soon as we dock. And I've got one more Dad-shaped piece of luggage left to pack up."

We reach the med bay, and I knock gently on the door. There's no response, so I knock again and finally receive a very weak "Come in" from inside. Ducky and I enter quickly, closing the door behind us in order to give Dad some privacy from the hustle and bustle out in the hallway.

"Dad, everything's nearly ready to— *Oh my God!*" I spin around away from Dad and try to grab the door but instead smash head-on into Ducky.

Ducky slaps a hand over his eyes, but it's too late for him. For either of us. "Mr. Nara! I'm so sorry. Marnie told us you were almost ready to, um, go."

"Elvie, Donald, for heaven's sake, what's the matter?" Dad asks, his voice thin.

"Scarred. For. Life," I tell my father, emphasizing each bit of punctuation so that I really make my point clear. I push myself against the door, leaning my forehead against the cool metal surface. There's a hideous sloshing behind me, but I don't dare turn around again for fear of being subjected to the horrific sight another time.

"Dearheart, please don't be so dramatic," Dad scolds.

"Dramatic?" I shout, rather dramatically. "Did it ever occur to you that if someone has the decency to knock before entering that you should try to sink *below* the goo line if you're floating naked in a tub?"

"It's a medical recuperation bath, Elvie, and this 'goo' is healing my wounds. It's not like I'm in here enjoying a leisurely soak."

"That doesn't mean you should reenact *Welcome to My Dingle* for your daughter," I say. "Goo line. Get under it. I'm begging you."

Ducky still has a hand over his eyes, which is making it

difficult for him to find the doorknob and escape. "I just . . . I just . . ." He gives up and slithers to the floor, back against the wall, eyes still shut tight. "Don't mind me," he says. "I'll be over here. Not looking at anything."

"Dad, for God's sake, you've broken Ducky," I say.

"Please tell me you're not here to make me drink more of that vile tea," is Dad's only reply. His voice is wavering between legitimately enfeebled and playing the martyr. "Donald, tell your girlfriend her tea stinks."

Ducky manages the incredible feat of becoming even more flustered. With his eyes still squeezed shut, his face turns a crimson red, and he begins sputtering like a backed-up faucet. "She's not my girlfriend," he gets out at last.

"Dad, Marnie told me she was getting you out of the tub." I shield my eyes with my hand, in case Dad hasn't found the good sense to shift deeper into the goo yet, and turn to speak to him more directly. "It's almost time to leave."

Dad sloshes a bit in the tub, making a sickening *slorp!* sound. I try to keep down the little bit of food I managed to eat today. "I'd never make the trip, Elvie," he says, laying it on even thicker than the liquid he's currently marinating in. "Not in my condition."

"*Dad.*" I roll my eyes, which is a mistake, because the ceiling is reflective. "Marnie says you're more than capable of making the helicopter journey. And in any case, you don't have a choice. I'm not about to leave you here."

Dad's response is quiet. "I'm not well, dearheart."

I sigh the dramatic sigh a million girls have used on a million fathers before me. But the truth is that even though I'll probably have my father's disturbingly pudgy image burned into my brain until death or a severe head injury releases me, I'm really glad to still *have* a father who is able to flash me. And I totally get why he's hesitant to go back out into the elements. I mean, he was frostbitten *before* we had to bail out of that exploding space elevator car, and the blisteringly cold air and the whole semi-crashing into the snowy fields of Antarctica didn't do him any favors.

"We'll make sure you're all bundled up," I say. "The warmest suit we can fi— Dad, *seriously*, can't you, like, cover yourself with a washcloth or something?"

"I mean, we've never used the words 'girlfriend' or 'boyfriend' before," Ducky says, clearly off in another world that does not involve a buoyant parent in his birthday suit. "We were prisoners together, so we were bound to be close. But now that we're not in Antarctica anymore, I figure . . ." He trails off.

"Ducky," I tell him lovingly. "You adorable, idiotic dillhole. You and Marnie are totally boyfriend-girlfriend. You're practically joined at the hip. I'm surprised you don't break out in a rash when she eats fresh fruit. Now can we please focus on my father?"

"I don't know," Ducky says, eyes still squeezed shut. "I can't help thinking that this whole time I've just been her special camp friend."

Suddenly there's a new voice at the door. "Wha's this all about, then?" I turn to see Marnie, arms akimbo, wearing a very disapproving look on her face. "Dinnae I tell ye to get clear of that stuff twenty minutes ago?" she asks my father.

"I'm not *well*," he reiterates.

"Oh, ye poor wee bairn," Marnie says, the sarcasm slicing through her thick Scottish burr. I notice that she really lays into her accent when she's annoyed.

She pulls a thick bathrobe from a cabinet along the far wall. "Now come on outta there, and let's get the goop off ye," she says. "Hello there, Donald."

Ducky replies with little more than, "*Yeep!*"

Dad is still pleading his case. "I shouldn't be moved in my condition," he says. He's really working it now, all coughs and groans. Fortunately, and perhaps in an attempt to prolong his stay in the tub, he has submerged himself so that everything from the chin down is safely below the surface. I open my mouth to scold him, but Marnie holds up her hand, stopping me.

"Very well," she says, handing me the robe. She heads back over to the closet and starts rummaging through the now pretty bare supplies. Dad peeks over the edge of the tub to catch a glance at what she's up to. "I think I know why ye've been feeling so uncomfortable, Harry," Marnie calls over her shoulder. "Ye've been rolling around in that regenerative enzyme bath fer days now, and yer healing quite nicely, but there are . . . side effects."

"Side effects?" Dad asks squeamishly. His chin is resting on the edge of the tub, his eyes boring holes in Marnie's back as she digs out what she was looking for.

When she steps back from the closet, she is holding a large green synthetic cloth pad, a box of latex gloves, and what looks to be a small baby's bottle. "Yer stopped up, ye poor love," she says. "Constipated. Ye haven't moved yer bowels since we got ye in here, have ye, Harry?"

The goo makes another *slorp* sound as Dad moves to the far edge of the tub. "My . . . bowels?" comes his thin, worried voice.

"'Tis nothing to be ashamed of, Harry. We all get plugged up now and again. We'll just be givin' ye a wee enema to get things moving, and then ye'll feel much more able to move about."

"*Enema?*" Dad says, his eyes wide as, well, really wide eyes.

Marnie snaps a latex glove over her slender hand. "Of course, if that doesn't work right away, we can always try digital extract—"

The *slorp* turns into a *fwa-plop* as Dad practically levitates out of the tub and lands with a thud on the micro-tile.

"No need, no need!" Dad cries, suddenly sounding a *lot* less feeble. "You know, I'm actually feeling pretty mobile after all." As if to prove his point, Dad starts swinging his arms and legs around like he's getting a good stretch in after a run. Which, in case it weren't obvious, is *not* helping any with the whole buck-naked-Dad situation I'm having. I can only imagine the long-term trauma inflicted on my cerebellum by watching my father twist and flex while green ooze sloughs off his rotund nude body.

"What's happening?" Ducky cries, hand slapped over his eyes again. "What's going on?"

"Come on, Duck. Let's give Dad and your 'special camp friend' a little alone time," I say, and I yank him to his feet so we can hightail it out of the room as quickly as possible. Marnie gives me a quizzical look as we head to the door, and I realize I might have tipped Ducky's hand a little bit, which makes me feel bad. But not bad enough to stick around to explain myself.

"Dad, I'll be out here!" I call to my father. "Don't come out till you are *completely dressed!*"

With any luck, maybe someday I'll get kicked really hard in the head.

As modes of transportation go, helicopters most definitely rank in the top-ten loudest. That plus the invention of repulsor tech has really made them pretty obsolete. Before succumbing to a much needed nap, Dad subjected us to a mini-lecture on the copter we currently found ourselves riding in. A retrofitted Dragonfly 20 with magnetic stabilization, it was apparently one of the last helicopters ever mass-produced, back in the '50s. Originally a military craft, the only ones left in circulation tend to be used by emergency relief organizations with limited funds to transport personnel and/or supplies to destitute regions such as Africa, Eastern Europe, and Detroit. The thing is roomy enough that it easily houses half of our Antarctic contingent—Dad, Cole, Ducky, Marnie, yours truly, and the rest of the Enosi—while Oates flies on a second copter with the Almiri.

Of course, the novelty of flying on such a relic is somewhat muted by the Fantastic Barfing Twins huddled together over a bucket near the back of the copter.

"*Blaaaaaaargh!*" goes Ducky, face stuck in the bucket, hands tightly gripping the sides. Cole shoves him in the shoulder.

"Quit hoggin' it, Donalll . . . ," he slurs. Clearly, at some point between our little chat on the tanker and now, Cole managed to get into something quite a bit stronger than condensed milk. He tugs the plastic bucket toward him with the sloppy urgency that only the truly inebriated possess. The contents of the bucket slosh around as Cole envelops it in a nauseated bear hug.

"Oh God, Cole," Ducky gasps. "Please, give it back. I'm gonna . . . Oh, *blaaaaaaargh!*" He manages to grab the bucket just in time, but even as he's still yakking, Cole steals it back and shoves Ducky more forcibly, causing him to lose his balance and tip over.

"Hey, you leave him alone!" I have to scream to be heard over the whirring of the helicopter's blades.

"You don't get to tell me what to do anymore!" Cole screams back. "Because you *arnamygirfren!*"

"What?"

"You," Cole says more deliberately, staring daggers at me. "Arna. Mygirfren."

"They're quite the pair, aren't they?" Marnie muses. I'm sitting on the ground next to my snoozing father. (How he can sleep with all the racket/barfing is a true mystery.) Marnie sits on the other side of Dad, her back to the dueling vomiteers, and gives me a smile. She checks Dad's forehead with the back of her hand.

"Good," she says. "No fever. He's going to be fit to bring down a bear sooner 'n not."

"He was lucky to have such a good nurse," I tell her.

"Eh, give credit where it's due. The man has a will on 'im."

"Still," I say. "Thank you."

Marnie shakes me off. "So, I hear ye've called it quits with the cologne model, is that it?"

"Word gets around fast."

"Ducky's spoken of naught else since ye told him. He really loves ye, that one."

"Ducky?" I feel my cheeks getting red.

"No, the other lad who's followed ye around yer whole life," she says with a wink.

"Ducky's the best," I say. And I mean it.

"Can I ask ye somethin'?" Marnie looks back at the boys over her shoulder. "That thing ye said earlier. About 'special camp friends'?"

"Oh, that," I say, exhaling a breath I didn't realize I was holding. "I was just, um, having a go at Ducky."

"About what? About me?" Marnie arches her eyebrow, and I am reminded that she could probably judo toss me out of the helicopter in one fluid motion if she doesn't like my answer.

"Yes, but, I mean, not *about* you. I mean . . . How to put this? I think Ducky's afraid that, now that we're free and heading home, you're going to find him less compelling than say, some rugged Enosi freedom fighter from your past."

"Is that the truth, now?" she asks, smirking. She turns back to the boys. "And what if I'm afeart there's someone else he'll fancy now, seein' as how they're available?"

"Um, I don't know what you—"

"Donald Hunter Pence!" Marnie screams suddenly, rising up. Ducky snaps his head at the sound.

Marnie strides across the platform to where Ducky and Cole sit. Instinctively I leap up and follow her.

"Am I to understand that now that yer options are improvin', ye plan on castin' me aside, ye two-timin' rake?" Marnie fumes. Her blue eyes are wide with indignation, which—don't ask me how—seems to make her hair look redder.

"What?" Ducky asks, shock overwhelming his nausea. "Rake? Who? What? Don't speak so Scottish. I can't—"

"I'm onto ye, lad, and yer womanizing ways." She slaps him on the arm for emphasis. "Did ye enjoy yerself, anyway? Playing me heart like a bloody fiddle?"

"Who said? What? Who? What?" Ducky looks like he's being attacked by invisible mosquitoes all around his head.

"I'm yer special camp friend, izzat it?" Marnie continues. She's laying into the poor guy with everything she's got. Her eyes are wide, her finger's a-jabbing, and her brogue is turned to high. "Oh, ye've got all the time in the world for plain old Marnie when yer locked away in the blizzards. But with our Elvie being a single lass again, now that yer bloody soul mate is yers for the pluckin—"

"I knew it!" Cole interrupts, through a queasy burp.

"Elvie, what did you *say* to her?" Ducky asks me, shielding his face from a barrage of slaps.

"I may have said something about 'special camp friend,'" I admit with a cringe. "But that's it. I didn't mean to imply—"

"You've been after my girl the whole time!" Cole slurs at Ducky, lunging toward him awkwardly. Ducky dodges easily, and Cole crumples to the ground.

"Marnie, I swear," Ducky says, scrambling to his feet, "that's not what I meant."

"So you dinnae fancy Elvie, then?" Marnie asks.

"I was telling Elvie that I was afraid *you* didn't feel the same as me."

"And how izzit that ye feel, Donald?" Marnie says, looking him square in the eye.

"I . . ." Ducky looks around, possibly considering a head-first dive out of the helicopter to avoid answering. "I . . ." The rest of his words are mumbled into his chest so that I can't hear.

"Wha's that?" Marnie asks.

"I fancy you," he says, slightly more clearly.

Marnie's stern gaze immediately breaks, and she bursts out laughing.

"Do ye really think I'd be messin' with ye, prison or no, if I dinnae fancy ye back, ye nidderrodded dunce?"

"Um, I . . . ," Ducky says. "No?"

"Of course not." She grabs at his chest and clutches his shirt, pulling his face close to hers.

"Careful," Ducky says. "I smell like puke."

"And no doubt ye taste like it too." With that, Marnie plants a hard wet kiss on Ducky. "How's that fer a 'special camp friend'?" she says, before going in for a second smooch.

Cole turns to me, equal parts confused and queasy. "So, you didn't break up with me because of Ducky?" he asks.

I roll my eyes. "No," I tell him honestly.

"So, you really just don't like me at all?"

"Cole, I—"

A hand grabs at my sleeve. "Dearheart?"

I turn and look at my father. He's as white as a sheet. And not some ordinary run-of-the-mill sheet either. I mean like a really, really noticeably white example of sheetiness.

"What's the matter, Dad?" I ask, worried. "You feel sick?"

"You can have the bucket if you need it, Mr. Nara," Cole offers.

"No. Elvie. We've arrived."

"We're in the Poconos already?" Time sure flies when you're fighting with a vomiting comedy duo. "Do we need to send them a signal or something, to let them know we're coming in? I don't know if they have defensive laser mounts embedded in their lodge-stronghold thing or not, but better safe than—"

"Elvie, it's gone," Dad says.

I feel a sudden pit in my stomach. They can't have left. I need Byron. He's the only one who might be able to help me track down my baby. "How can you be sure?" I am reaching panic levels again. *Hold on*, I repeat to myself. To somewhere-Olivia. *Hold on. Mama's coming.* "Have you tried to radio them? It's the middle of the night; maybe they're all asleep."

"Elvie," Dad says again, the concern practically exploding all over his face. "It's gone."

"The lodge?"

"The Poconos."

All I'm aware of is how warm my face feels. Like a million red-hot needles were all carefully inserted into my skin at the same time. I rush to the long window along the side of the helicopter and look down at the ski resort town below. There are no lights for as far as I can see, save for the dim orange glow of a dozen fires.

The Poconos are burning.

Chapter Three

WHEREIN OUR MERRY GANG ONCE AGAIN FINDS ITSELF IN A PICKLE

"Try it now, dearheart," Dad says, his butt sticking out from under the console. Seeing the site of all our hopes for humanity's salvation ablaze has given the man an unexpected burst of energy, and now he's on his hands and knees, attempting to reconnect power to the lone computer system that seems to have survived the devastation.

One computer terminal. That's what we've found in the still-smoking rubble of the Almiri ski lodge headquarters. One—count it, *one*—computer on the second floor that was only nominally scathed by whatever took place here. Everything else in the area has been completely decimated. An entire town annihilated. Once we tuned in to local news broadcasts, we got reports of an apparent catastrophic overload in the town's power grid that had caused a cascade of electrical fires and explosions. The area has been evacuated for the time being while folks try to figure out the safest way to proceed.

But the second we landed at the skeletal remains of the lodge and saw the concentration of damage surrounding it, I knew what had happened here. Perhaps the power grid overload in town was used as a distraction, but the damage to the lodge is different, specific, and familiar. The energy burns on the building façade. The pinpoint destruction of crucial support structures. This wasn't a power surge. This was the Jin'Kai.

But which Jin'Kai? It couldn't be the invasion. It wouldn't make sense for them to target this one spot and then disappear. No, when they do hit, they're going to hit hard and fast, and they won't go anywhere once they're finished. This hit and run has Dr. Marsden written all over it. His splinter group must have found a way to locate the Almiri and target them. But why? Were they looking for something, or just trying to eliminate an adversary when the adversary wasn't expecting it? With the Almiri gone, what hope do I have to track my baby now? It's taking everything I have to not melt into a puddle of tears.

Hold on, Olivia, I think again. But the voice in my head is growing weaker by the minute. *Hold on.*

There's a slight hum as the power turns on and the monitor in front of me flickers to life. Barely, but there's a flicker.

"It worked!" I shout. From underneath the console comes Dad's trademark "Hmmph" of triumph.

The victory, however, is short-lived. I let out a frustrated sigh as I take in the black cursor, blinking against a totally white screen. I punch the screen with the bottom of my fist. The already cracked display rains little shards onto the console.

"What is it, dearheart?" Dad asks, shimmying awkwardly

out from underneath the console. He rises up on his knees to take a look.

"The operating system's been wiped," I tell him. Through the empty blown-out window frame I gaze at where the two helicopters rest in the snow. *Hold on, Olivia.* "Completely erased."

"There must be something here to salvage," Dad says. "We'll run some recovery software, or . . ." But he trails off without even finishing the thought. We both know that Apple probably doesn't make any software compatible with an Almiri mainframe server.

When Cole enters the room with Ducky and Marnie, I decide, just for the moment, to pretend like I am okay. I steady my breathing. Straighten my back.

"Any luck?" I ask them. The gang's been searching the rubble and the surrounding grounds for survivors. But as soon as I see their faces, I know the answer. Ducky, for one, looks like he has just vomited. And not from motion sickness.

Marnie puts a protective arm around Ducky's waist. Cole's face is ashen.

"We found them," Cole says, and it's obvious he's been experiencing the world's worst sobering-up. I'm hoping somehow that he won't say what he does next, but of course he has to. "They're all dead."

The ice in my chest plummets into my stomach. "All of them?" I ask.

Cole merely looks at the ground.

"They were still in their rooms," Marnie says. "It looks like they were locked in. They couldnae get out when . . ." She trails off and motions with her eyes at the burning debris surrounding us.

"Oh God." I sink to the floor.

Cole is the one who sinks down to comfort me. "We'll find her, Elvie," he tells me.

I bury my head in my arms. "Will we?" I ask.

"We have to."

Hold on, Olivia.

"Byron might still be alive," Dad says, rubbing my shoulder. "He seems like a more than capable fellow. Perhaps he was able to—"

"Shhh," Ducky says suddenly.

"What d'ye hear?" Marnie asks.

Ducky shakes his head—he's not sure. When he points to the blown-out window, I quickly rise and make my way over.

I hear it now too.

Voices. Outside. I peek my head out to look.

Down below, our friends Rupert and Clark, along with a handful of other Almiri and Enosi, are near the first-floor rear entrance, most likely searching the perimeter of the grounds.

"They're talking to someone," I whisper to the others, holding a hand up for them to stay back away from the window. "I can't tell who."

"But who could be—" Cole starts at full volume, before Marnie leans down to slap a hand over his mouth. I strain to listen to the conversation thirty meters away.

"We belong to the cooperative that runs the lodge, officers," I hear Rupert say. "We were only trying to survey the damage."

"In the middle of the night?" comes the gruff reply.

Cops. Damn. They must have seen the helicopters landing. Or perhaps the local authorities left a small detachment to patrol the mountain. Either way, dealing with a squad of clueless policeman could get real complicated real fast. How exactly are we supposed to explain who we are or what we're doing here?

"Sir, I'm going to need you to keep your hands where I can see them," one of the officers barks.

Rupert's hands are up near his chest. Even I can seem them. "What we have here is a simple misunderstanding," Rupert says. He sounds like he's trying to be playful, so I can only imagine that the police officer is handsome. Still, Rupert, not the time. "We didn't realize the area was off-limits. Don't you think we can discuss this like two—"

"Hands *up*," the officer growls again. Honestly, I'm surprised by the guy's tone. I've yet to meet anyone, male or female, who can resist Rupert's charms when he decides to crank the sexy up to eleven.

"Dearheart," Dad whispers. He comes over to tug on my arm. "Get away from the window."

But my eyes are fixed on the scene below.

As Rupert takes a step back, the main cop he's been dealing with comes into view.

Strong jaw.

Five o'clock shadow.

"*No!*" I shriek at the top of my lungs. But it's too late, because before Rupert or any of the others can even register who's screaming about what, the Jin'Kai in police garb pulls out his ray gun and fires. Rupert takes the blast straight through the chest and collapses backward in the snow, dead. It's instant pandemonium as the other Jin'Kai raise their weapons and open fire on the remaining Almiri and Enosi. Clark, stunned by the sudden execution of his best friend, is a half second late in reacting to a shot in his direction. He catches the blast in the shoulder and spins full around before falling face-first into the snow. I scream again, which distracts Clark's assailant just long enough for Clark to jump back up and swipe the guy's legs out from under him. I don't see the rest, because my screaming has drawn the rest of the Jin'Kai's attention, and all at once shots are perforating what's left of the wall around me.

Marnie pulls me down away from the window. "We've got to get out of here!" she yelps.

"But the others . . . ," I start.

"There's no time. We haven't any weapons. We must leave. Now!"

And for once I think maybe I'll listen to someone's advice.

Marnie, Cole, Ducky, Dad, and I book it out of the room. We're halfway down the hallway before we realize we don't have the faintest clue where we're going. More shots ring out from below, followed by confused shouts as the Jin'Kai make their way into the building and take aim at our remaining comrades.

"There's no way to get to the helicopters," I pant as we run. Way to state the obvious, Elvie. "They probably have all the entrances blocked." Maybe when I'm done with all the running, I can go back to school to get my PhD in dur.

"Is there any other exit?" Marnie asks. "A service entrance, or a garbage chute, perhaps?"

Oh dear Lord, not another garbage chute.

Cole suddenly gets a look on his face like a lightbulb just went off. Which, honestly, is not a look I've ever seen on him before.

"This way. Follow me!" he barks. He directs us down the left hallway, around a sharp turn, and toward a flight of stairs. For the first time since we hightailed it off the *Echidna*, he actually looks like the commando that barged his way onto a ship full of baddies to rescue me. I didn't realize quite how much I missed that Cole until just now.

We're racing down the hallway, when suddenly the floor breaks away beneath Dad. He lets out a startled squawk, and his right leg disappears. Just vanishes into the floor, all the way up to the knee. Ducky and I swarm on him as quickly as we can and try to hoist him up, but he's too heavy.

"The knee!" he grunts. "Why is it always my knee?"

"Cole, help!" I call ahead of me. The sounds of our impending doom are growing louder behind us. Stomping. Chasing. Jin'Kai barking orders to one another. But no more screaming. No more shots. For all I know, everyone else is dead already.

Cole slides to a halt and doubles back to us.

"Step back, Elvie!" Dad says, before letting Cole grab him underneath the arms. "The whole floor is completely unstable." Cole lifts Dad easily, and together they start back down the hall. Cole stops, though, when he realizes I'm not following them. Instead I'm kicking at the hole Dad fell through, filling it with clouds of debris and splintered wood.

"Elvie, what are you doing?" Cole shouts.

"Only be a minute!" I holler back, still kicking. It's not

until I hear our pursuers around the far corner that I turn tail and run toward the others. Ducky is waving his arms in a windmill motion, urging me on.

That's when the "cops" turn the corner and open fire.

Ducky flinches as the shots fizzle around him. "Just go!" I shout. He obliges, turning and making his way up the stairs where the others are already racing out of sight. A few more shots whip by me as I follow. At least my efforts to not be blasted to death are aided by the wreckage the Jin'Kai have already produced. The hallway is so trashed that I have to zigzag around the mess, which probably makes me a slightly more difficult target to hit.

I'd also like to think that my time in Antarctica helped me shed most of the baby weight.

"Hurry, Elvie. They're getting closer!" Ducky calls from the top of the stairs.

That's exactly what I'm counting on.

The weakened floor gives way under the hot cops' stomping feet, and I whirl around just in time to catch the results of my considerable kicking skills. The first two dopes fall completely through and crash to the floor below. The third manages to grab the edge of the newly gaping hole, but all that serves to do is rip the edge of the floor away even further, which sends him and number four—who had managed to stop just short of the fall—tumbling after their buddies, who have landed in a heap of douche bag below us.

I catch up to the others, pretty pleased with myself.

"Congrats," Marnie says drolly. "Ye've bought us ten seconds. After costing us twenty."

I frown. There'll be time later to be annoyed with Marnie for being right. Hopefully. For now I run.

Cole, with my father in tow, leads us down the new wide hallway toward an atrium, where the high glass ceiling has completely shattered to the ground. The cold night air rushes in around me as we run to the far door, slushing our way through beads of safety glass. I'm trying to figure out why Cole is leading us *up*. I'm really hoping he isn't planning on all of us leaping off a balcony, having forgotten that not everybody can survive a twenty-meter jump.

But when we come out through the door onto the balcony, suddenly I wish that jumping had been Cole's plan all along.

"You've got to be flipping kidding me," I say.

"You got any better suggestions?" Cole asks as he races to the battery console against the far railing, where he rips off the front panel with one hand. "Mr. Nara, could you?" He is still holding my father.

"I suppose I could," Dad says, sliding out of Cole's arms and doing a pretty weak job of holding himself up as he bends down to inspect the panel's wiring. After a single moment of consideration, he shifts his gaze across the expanse beyond the balcony. "Although I'm not quite sure I *should*."

The balcony on which we currently find ourselves is a massive covered wooden structure where the Almiri probably had secret tea parties or something. Despite the blast damage to the surrounding lodge, this place has stayed relatively intact. (Good thing, or we'd be toast right now.) Each beam has been carefully engraved, and if I were super into woodcraft—or, you know, if I weren't in the process of fleeing for my life—I'd probably spend more than a millisecond taking in the intricate details of the wildlife scenes carefully carved into the wood: squirrels climbing trees, wildflowers and bunnies, cute baby deer, that sort of thing.

Right now, of course, I'm more focused on the goons behind us.

And, oh yeah, the *giant gaping chasm* below.

Because this is not just any artsy-fartsy balcony Cole has lead us to. Oh no. It is, in fact, the base of a chairlift that stretches horizontally across the peaks of two neighboring mountains.

"Are you kidding me with this crap?" I say to no one in particular. "Why is this a thing? Tell me, why do the Almiri have a ski lift with no safety net just dangling over the edge of Splatter Mountain? Were they kamikaze snowboarding in their spare time?"

"That's, uh, a really big drop," Ducky says as he looks out over the ledge to the slope below.

Marnie looks too, then glances behind us. I have a feeling she's thinking the same thing I am: Are we safer attempting to cross a two-hundred-meter drop when there's a band of angry aliens behind us with ray guns, or might we be wiser to, you know, *not* do that?

"We could try to slide down the slope," Marnie interjects.

Dad's still fiddling with the lift's operating panel. "That's about as straight a drop down as you could ask for," he says.

"Why would you ever ask for that?" I mutter. The drop reminds me of the Death Torpedo waterslide on the board-walk down the shore. Except instead of merely chafing your thighs and shooting you into a pool with a nose full of water, this one would knock you across an assortment of jagged rocks and leave you a giant jelly smear at the foot of the mountain.

"All set!" Dad cries, slapping a triumphant hand on the control panel.

"So," I say, glancing down the side of the mountain once more, then back to where the Jin'Kai—and our certain doom—quickly approaches. I grab tight hold of the nearest chairlift. "Me first, then?"

I slide into the chair, and Ducky sits down beside me. At first I'm surprised he's chosen to plummet to his death next to me and not his girlfriend. But then, of course, I notice that Duck's skin is ashen gray, and despite the cold, he's sweating bullets. He probably could've sat down next to Dr. Marsden and not have noticed. I try to get ahold of myself, in order to help Ducky get ahold of *him*self.

"Ducky," I say in as soothing a tone as I can muster, while Cole helps my father settle in next to Marnie in the chair behind us. "You can do this, Duck. It's just a chair. You sit in chairs all the time. All you have to do is sit and not look down." Ducky nods vacantly and pulls down the front safety rod (like a single strip of metal half a meter from our stomachs is *really* going to save us in the event of an emergency) and grabs hold of the bar beside him like it's a limited-edition Jetman figurine. "There you go," I say. "You can do it."

Ducky lets out a whimper.

"Ye'll be fine, love!" Marnie shouts from behind us. "Be a brave lad, yeah?"

And is it just me, or does Ducky sit up just the tiniest bit straighter after that?

As soon as Dad and Marnie are safely tucked into their seat, Cole dashes to the control panel and smacks the go button. The lift comes to life and starts us with a jolt across the gap. I turn around just in time to see Cole ripping the control panel away from the console and punching it through with his fist, sending sparks flying and assuring that the Jin'Kai can't simply hit reverse on us. A moment of real commando can-do from Cole.

"Nice thinking, Cole!" I shout at him.

"Feel bad for dumping me yet?" he shouts back.

"Let's discuss it at a different time, shall we?"

Ducky moans.

My feet dangle beneath me as the lift moves rapidly forward, swaying slightly back and forth. Our destination is obscured, and the cable disappears ahead of us into the dark. Ducky's breathing is raspy, and when I turn to him, I see that he has not followed my instructions at all and is in fact staring directly down at the gaping maw of death.

"Elvie, I'm not gonna make it," he says, voice trembling.

"You'll be fine, Duck," I tell him. "Just look ahead."

"No." Ducky shakes his head weakly. "No, I think . . . yeah, I think I'll pass out now."

And before I know it, Ducky has begun *sliding out of his seat*. His butt's almost off the bench before I manage to clutch at his jacket.

"Ducky!" I scream. One hand still tight on his jacket, I release my grip on the bar beside me and slap Ducky's face with everything I've got, to try to rouse him. But his eyes just roll around blankly.

"I'll be fine, Elvie," he mumbles. At this point I'm not even entirely sure he's conscious. "Just let me pass out for a little whi . . ." His voice trails off and he slides even farther. I grab him with both hands—one wrapped awkwardly around his back and the other clutching the material under his armpit—but he's far too heavy for me, and apparently he has far too great a death wish. His butt slips right off the seat, and his weight jolts my arms at the sockets and yanks us both full-force into the safety rod.

Which turns out to be a good thing, since the laser blast fired from behind us zips by directly where my head used to be, and singes the hood of my jacket. Several more shots zip by, all off target, which makes me think we must be far enough into the misty darkness that the baddies can't see us clearly. But the shots aren't far enough away to make me *not* want to totally crap my pants.

"Help!" I scream as Ducky's dead weight slips in my weakening grasp. His chin is on the safety rod at the moment, and I *might* be worried that the thing were cutting into his jugular, if it weren't currently the only thing holding him up. As for me, my gut's smashed so hard into the bar that I am *this close* to puking, but I'm keeping it together because Ducky has saved my ass more times than I can count. I'm a little peeved that this is the moment he decided to let me return the favor, but I suppose we can discuss that later.

At least the Jin'Kai seem to have ceased firing. Who cares why.

Suddenly I hear a clanging, and the chair begins to sway as the cable jostles violently. It takes me a long second to realize that the movement is *not* due to Ducky plummeting to his death below me but rather something moving on the cable above. With my grip still as tight as I can get around my bestie, I crane my neck as far as I am able, and to my surprise I see a figure *climbing toward me on the cable.*

"Ducky!" I scream. "Ducky, *wake up!* They're coming! They're—"

I look up again. It is not a Jin'Kai making his way hand over hand across the length of moving cable.

It's Marnie.

Holy shit, that girl's a badass.

"Make room!" she orders one second before swooping down to land beside me, where Ducky was once sitting. Thankfully, I managed to dart my head to the side just a few centimeters, avoiding a boot to the nose. As she squats in the moving chair, Marnie reaches down and manages to find a better purchase on Ducky's jacket. Together we haul him up, both of us grunting in equal parts exertion and frustration. Ducky is mumbling incoherently, making every attempt to slide out of our grips to his death, but after some tricky maneuvering and arm repositioning, Marnie raises the safety rod and we pull him safely back into the seat. I've got him by the feet, his upper body stretched across Marnie's lap. He looks for all the world like a napping baby.

"Remind me to murder him later," I tell Marnie.

"Not if I get 'im first," she replies.

I don't know if the cable has been jostling this whole time and in my concern for Ducky I simply didn't notice, but suddenly I am once again aware of lots of tugging and bouncing.

"Is that the Jin'Kai?" I holler at Marnie over the wind. If *she* can climb across on that cable, Lord knows those hunks of alien evil can do it too. I wrap my free arm tightly around the bar beside me and do my best to see what's causing the movement, but the fog here is thick.

"Probably Cole with yer da'," Marnie tells me. Sure enough, as soon as she says it, I can make out Cole, moving hand over hand across the cable just like Marnie did. Except that Cole's got my father hanging around his neck like a kid who's way too old for a piggyback ride. Dad—to put it mildly—looks freaked. I let out a breath of relief. "The Jin'Kai are comin' up behind them," Marnie goes on. "They'll be on us in minutes."

Looks like I sighed a little too soon.

"What do we—" I start. But Marnie's too quick for me.

"I've got a plan," she says, then without any warning pushes Ducky's full weight into my lap and stands up once more in the chair. We rock and clang and sway, and if Ducky were awake, I'm positive he would full-on motion-sickness-barf right in my face.

I cling to him more tightly.

"What are you doing?" I shout up at Marnie.

But she's got no time for me. She's gazing back at Cole and Dad. "Archer!" she shouts. "Gan, catch the chib!" And she pulls a slender knife out from the small of her back. How she kept it hidden from the Almiri this whole time is a mystery for another time—like, say, a time when she's totally not thinking of doing what I'm pretty sure she's thinking of doing.

She tosses the knife to Cole, who—despite the fact that he

is *clinging from a moving cable with a full-grown man on his back*—catches it one-handed.

"Cut the line!" Marnie shouts at him.

"Are you crazy?" I scream, eyes bulging.

She glances down at me. "Ye oughtta lower that safety bar," she says. Then she glances back at Cole again, apparently with just enough time to save us all from his deathly stupidity. "*Behind* ye, ye daft bampot!" she screeches. "Cut the line *behind* ye!"

Even from here I can hear Cole's sotto voce "D'oh!"

I slap down the safety bar and hold on for dear life.

Whatever type of blade Marnie's been packing must be the Ginsu's burlier cousin, because within seconds I hear the thick metal cord above us *twang*. I feel just the slightest of jerks—the cable beginning to snap.

As quick as lightning, Marnie squeezes herself back into her seat.

A second *twang*! And we jerk again.

"Donald, love," Marnie says to the boy in the fetal position between us. Ducky's eyes flutter open and roll lazily in her direction. "Remember that story ye were gabbing on about in such detail a ways back, to pass the time?" She reaches over to pet his head gently. "The one with the archeologist, carried a whip?"

He's waking up. "Um, yeah?" You can practically see him trying to make his way through the brain fog with a lantern.

Twang!

"Ye recall that bit in the middle?" Marnie goes on. "With the bridge and the mingin crocodiles?"

45

Ducky's eyes grow slowly but steadily larger, to the point where I think they might expand and take over his entire face. He rouses enough to reach back and grab hold of the arm of the lift chair, easing my burden considerably.

"Oh, sweet Mama Jama," Ducky exhales.

"That's it, dove," Marnie coos, leaning back in her seat to watch Cole slicing. She turns back to us. "Hold on ti—"

That's when the last cord breaks away, and the cable swings down, and we are immediately flung forward. Behind us I can hear the screams of the Jin'Kai as their end of the cable swings back toward the lodge. It's a very short-lived relief, since, you know, we're hurtling toward the side of a mountain at an increasingly alarming speed. I slide in my seat, but the inertia of our swing plus Ducky's mass keeps us both from falling out.

I'm going to have to apologize to that safety rod for mocking it earlier.

As we swing lower and lower, the snowy slope ahead of us comes into focus.

"Wait fer it!" Marnie calls over the whipping wind. How she can even manage to form words in this chaos is beyond me. "Hold . . ." We're a few dozen meters from the slope when she releases my buddy the safety rod and kicks off the back of the chair.

"*Now!*" she screams.

I drop below the chair and feel the seat whip over my head.

For a second it feels like I'm flying, but really what I'm doing is falling sideways, Ducky still clutched to my chest. The snow comes up at us, and I hit it with a *whompf!* losing hold of Ducky in the process. I hear the impact of the others in the snow as well, but I can't see them, because I'm busy rolling backward down the slope, head over heels, without any way to get my bearings. I roll around and around and around, until the large tall dark object I'm fast approaching reveals itself to be a giant tree, and I twist to crash back-first into it, which sends another shower of snow down on top of me.

As I start to lose consciousness, I wonder why I can't ever find myself running for my life somewhere like the Bahamas.

Chapter Four

IN WHICH HOPE, HAVING BEEN DASHED, MAKES A SURPRISING REAPPEARANCE

When I come to—seconds later? minutes? I find myself still beneath the tree, looking up at the lightly falling snow. I decide that I must not have been out too long. Otherwise someone would have found me.

Assuming that they aren't all jelly stains on the mountainside.

"Dad? Ducky? Cole?" I call out weakly. "Marnie?" I get no response. I manage to sit up, my arms aching from the strain. I can feel what I imagine are some world-class bruises forming already. I look around in the dark, but all I see are the shadows of more trees. I rise slowly, unsure of what's making me so wobbly: my legs or my head. I wonder if I'm concussed. If that's the worst that comes out of falling off a kilometer-high ski lift and crashing into a mountain, then I suppose I'll count myself lucky.

There's a *shushing* sound out in the dark, coming toward

me. The dancing shadows are too much for my wonked-out vision to process, and I can't see who, or what, is moving in. As the *shushing* grows closer, I am able to determine that the rapid, synchronized footsteps are coming from farther down the slope. And they most definitely don't belong to my hobbled father or my extremely uncoordinated best friend.

I make a beeline away from the sound in a straight line, neither up nor down the hill. As soon as I start running, I hear the shushers change course in their pursuit. The snow isn't terribly deep, but the slope is steep enough that I am continuously losing my footing as I go. Ahead of me is a thick bramble of trees, and I move toward it, hoping to find cover among the pines.

"There she is!" one of them calls from behind me. In my panic my foot slips out from under me and I tumble, sliding on my ass through the dense tree coverage. I twist and turn in a series of comical contortions to avoid the trunks as best I can, and honestly I think I'm doing a pretty spectacular job of not smashing to death against an evergreen. I would probably give myself an A+ in Not Smashing, and that's not even grading on the curve. But I guess I've been too concerned about the trees and not enough about *huge honking boulders*, because suddenly one of those appears in front of me as though out of nowhere, and it's absolutely too late to move out of its way.

Well, we had a pretty good run there, Life.

I brace myself for the inevitable broken bones, praying I will somehow make it through the wreckage. . . .

And collide with the boulder with a dull *thud*.

A dull thud?

Sure enough, this particular boulder ends up being *soft*.

And warm.

And . . . furry?

"All right, human scum," says one of the three Jin'Kai I now find looming over me, ray guns pointed at my noggin. "Stand up, girl. Hands where we can see them."

The boulder behind me rumbles, and I smile at the suddenly confused looks on my attackers' faces. "Okay," I say. I rise from the ground, hands up over my head, and step to the side. "But before we go any further . . ." I nod toward the rumbling lump behind me. "Have you met my friend Drusilla?"

With that, the "boulder" rears up on its hind legs, revealing itself to be none other than Lord Byron's ursine companion, roughly 150 kilograms of bear-hurt. Drusilla is on top of the first Jin'Kai before he knows what's mauling him—pinning him to the ground and swiping at him with her massive paws.

The other two Jin'Kai open fire on the bear, and the smell of burned flesh and fur immediately fills my nostrils. I whip my head around to discover several large wounds they've opened in Drusilla's side. "No!" I cry out, throwing myself at one of the bastards. He merely tosses me aside, turning his gun on me.

But before he can fire, a flash of fur knocks his arm to the side, sending the shot astray. It takes me a second to realize that *this* lifesaver isn't Dru—she's still busy crushing her original prey, seemingly oblivious to the scorched wounds on her side. No, instead there are two dogs attached to my former assailant, and even in the commotion I recognize them as Thunder and Boatswain, Byron's pet pooches. They've got their jaws locked on the guy's forearm and crotch, respectively.

And the third Jin'Kai? Well, he has maybe a nanosecond to process the *When Animals Attack!* special unfolding in front of him before something smashes him in the back of the head and he drops to the ground, out cold.

Now, I spent a lot of boring days in Mrs. Kwan's English Lit class, daydreaming up elaborate scenarios in which Charles Dickens ran a cat orphanage, and D. H. Lawrence teamed up with Samuel Pepys in a traveling aerial burlesque act. (I was not, for the record, Mrs. Kwan's favorite student.) But I never, not even in my wildest imagination, pictured the poet Lord Byron and his menagerie of furry critters *performing kung fu in the snow.*

Where is my phone when I need to vidcap something?

Byron leaps into the air and sails over my head in what looks like a flying double roundhouse kick from Jetman, then punts the dog-entangled baddie square in the chest, sending the dude flying backward into the snow. The dogs fall back, perfectly content to let their master do the heavy lifting. They bark vociferously as Byron engages the Jin'Kai in mano a mano combat. It's a ballet of fists and knees and headbutts, complete with Byron's cocky carefree quips as they tussle.

"Have at thee, Mankin! Ha-ha-ha!" Byron spits.

Whatever it is Byron is talking about is totally lost on me — although I suspect it might make Mrs. Kwan chuckle.

The Jin'Kai retreats a step and reaches behind his back. But as he brings the weapon to bear (har, har), Drusilla's massive jaws clamp down on his arm, causing him to shriek. So the Jin'Kai might be superhuman alien killing machines, but it's nice to know that a good bear-chomping will still give them pause. The dude flops around like a rag doll as Drusilla whips him back and forth over her head, then finally flings him several meters through the air into a tree. When he lands, Byron is on him with several well-placed socks to the jaw.

"The great object of life," Byron tells the dude as he Hulk-smashes him, "is sensation." *Smash, smash, punchity-punchity, smash.* "To feel that we exist, even though in pain." He finishes off the dazed Jin'Kai with a spinning kick that forces the dude's head quite literally into the tree trunk, so that his suddenly limp body dangles from his anchored noggin.

"Feel that?" Byron asks.

There is no reply. All three Jin'Kai are out of commission, one with some pretty permanent reminders to never wrestle a bear.

"Hello, young Elvie!" Byron exclaims. "You look well."

"Uh, hey, Gramps," I reply. "By the by . . . what the hell is going on?"

Instead of answering me, Byron gives me a surprise shove down into the snow, which I appreciate in retrospect as a ray gun blast sizzles into the tree in front of me. I flip over onto my back to look down the hill, where I spy what appears to an entire platoon of Jin'Kai running straight for us, firing at will. Byron draws two firearms of his own from behind his back.

"This, sweet child? Why, this is the counteroffensive! Death and glory!"

As his dual-wielded blasters put an exclamation point on his battle cry, from over my head I hear several large electrical claps in response. At first when I look up, I'm not quite sure what it is I'm looking at. It just looks like moonlit sky, but somehow more . . . shimmery. I can make out the sparks from heavy weapon fire appearing from out of nowhere, raining down laser-y death on the Jin'Kai, who dive for whatever cover they can find. The shimmering effect above suddenly becomes more agitated, and the sky disappears and it's not the moon above me but a hovering ship.

A ship with a stealth cloak.

"Elvie!" Ducky cries from overhead. "I'm in a spaceship!"

"I can see that, Duck!" I scream back, super-relieved that he's still alive.

A cable lowers, dangling from a round porthole in the underbelly of the ship about half a meter in circumference.

"Elvie!" Byron shouts. "Connect me!"

Frantically I snatch the cable and search Byron for some kind of latch. I find it on his back, lock the catch into place, and then tug on the cable for good measure.

"Now grab hold, darling girl!"

I do as I'm told, wrapping myself around Byron in a big hug, with my arms placed securely under his so as not to obstruct the ass-whoopery he's still doling out. All at once the cable jolts, and we're flying up toward the porthole, which is sliding closed even as we hurtle its way. The Jin'Kai scatter in the face of suddenly uneven odds.

"Remember the Poconos!" Byron shouts as we pass into the ship. The porthole seals under our feet, and we land on the metallic surface with a *thunk*. Byron punches an intercom on the wall. "We're aboard. Now gather the animals and make haste!"

"We've got them, sir!" comes the response. I can feel the ship shift course.

"Well, aren't you a sight for sore eyes?" Byron says, looking down at me.

Slowly I release my death grip on Byron's chest. Looking around, I spy Ducky, Marnie, Dad, and Cole, each one with a bigger grin on their face than the last. "So I take it you're the cavalry?" I ask after finally taking a breath.

"This quaint little carriage?" Byron replies, unlatching himself from the cable. "No, dear." He accesses a vidscreen next to the intercom and brings up an image that I assume is a replica of the ship's main view screen. We are speeding away from the ground, already nearly a kilometer above the surface. The view is wavering with the now familiar shimmer of the Almiri stealth. Out of thin air an entire squadron of spaceships appears, a large command ship at the center of the formation.

"*There* is your cavalry."

"You've been building a fleet?" I ask, incredulous.

"'Fleet' implies a scale we have not attained," Byron says as he leads us through the hallways of the command ship toward the bridge. "We began construction a few years ago after the realization that the Jin'Kai might pose a serious threat. Our efforts had to be carried out in secret, of course. Mankind might have become a wee bit paranoid if advanced starcraft had suddenly appeared in the skies above them."

"You mean like in the way they did just now?" Ducky points out.

"Well, the situation has changed, hasn't it?" Byron explains. "The Jin'Kai have escalated things to another level altogether. They didn't just hit us, Elvie. Hundreds of humans, maybe more, died down there in the Poconos when they struck."

"It was Marsden," I say as we pass through a second hallway.

"We cannae ken such a thing fer sure, Elvie," Marnie chimes in.

"I *do* ken," I tell her. "Er, know. I know it. The computers at HQ were wiped. Not just destroyed. Wiped. And Marsden left one terminal operational for me to find. He's trying to tell me that I won't be able to find them."

"Yer sounding a wee paranoid, Elvie," Marnie says.

We come to a sealed door, and Byron flashes a card across the wall sensor.

"Access granted, Commander Byron." The door slides open onto a large command bridge. The room is a hive of activity, with Almiri officers buzzing about intently at work stations and running around to who-knows-where.

But the only person I see is Captain Oates.

"You didn't think a little gunfire could stop me now, did you?" he says as he absorbs the full brunt of my face-first bear hug.

"Of course not," I say, trying to suck the tears back into my eyes before anyone else sees them. "What about the others?"

"Clark is fine. A few others you probably don't know. We lost eight in all. Including Rupert."

Byron takes his place in the command chair at the center of the bridge and taps aimlessly at his arm console. "I'm sorry for your loss, old friend," he tells Oates earnestly. "I wish we had arrived sooner."

"That you arrived at all is the only reason any of us still draw breath, Commander," Oates says. He says it without a hint of malice—just a simple statement of truth.

"Elvie," Byron says to me. "You said Marsden was trying to send you a message? You personally? Why would he do that?"

"They have Olivia. My daughter. Your great-granddaughter. Marsden took her, with my mom."

"Your mother?" Byron says. He stops tapping and gapes at me. "Zee? She's alive?"

"Oh, right, yeah." I give Gramps the quickest version of "Previously: On Elvie's Shit Life" I can muster. "My mom faked her death after she gave birth to me and is actually one hundred percent alive. Hurray."

A glimmer of something flashes across Byron's face. Something like sadness? Regret, maybe? It's hard to tell with him, seeing as he's so melodramatic all the time regardless.

"This Marsden took her and your daughter?"

I almost don't have the heart to tell him.

"No," I say. "Zee's . . . with him. She sold out the Almiri at Cape Crozier, stole Olivia from me, and took off with Marsden to wherever it is evil douche bags go after daring aerial escapes."

Byron takes a moment to let the news of his estranged daughter's betrayal sink in. His eyes close and he tilts his head back, letting out a long sigh.

"Anyway," I say. I can feel a poem coming on, and I'd like to nip that in the bud if at all possible. I don't have time for self-pity from a guy who loves to hear himself talk. Not right at the moment, at any rate. "We came back to the ski lodge hoping you could help us track them down. Which is when we found the whole town barbecued."

"I warned them," Byron says, his head hanging. "But they weren't inclined to listen to me at that point."

"How'd ye ever make the slip out from such a hackit mess?" Marnie asks.

"I was not at the lodge for some time before the attack occurred."

At that, Cole chimes in for the first time. "Sir?" he asks. "Why not?"

"The Council has . . . seen fit to relieve me of my duties as commander."

Color me stunned. "You mean you're not the Head Almiri in Charge anymore?"

"My lenience with regards to the Enosi—and certain individuals within that larger group—caused me to fall out of favor," Byron tells us. "Rather quickly, by our standards. The Council allowed me to retain my rank, but my voice on policy matters has been somewhat muted for the time being." He looks at me, a wistful look in his eye. "My opponents had me stripped of power within a week of my shuttling you away to safety. Or what I thought was safety. My comrades aboard these vessels are the remaining few who still follow my orders."

Suddenly he pounds his armchair and jumps up with the theatrical flair you'd expect to find in a community production of Shakespeare in the Park.

"Curse my stunted vision! This is all my fault. Your mother. The base. All of it. I should have listened to you, Titus, from the start, and worked harder to reconcile the Almiri and their Enosi offspring. But no, I was the consummate politician, wasn't I? Compromising my morals into a vapor. Talking when I should have acted! The exact antithesis of the great Titus Oates! And now my own daughter, siding with the enemy, because of my failings. 'The thorns which I have reaped are of the tree I planted. They have torn me, and I bleed.'"

Please, please don't let this dovetail into twenty minutes of iambic pentameter or something. I think I'd rather fight the Jin'Kai again.

"We all find our conscience," Oates says. "You did what you thought was right. As you always have."

Dad steps in too. I guess it's not every day that you get to console your alien father-in-law. "We must live in the present, not the past," Dad tells him. He's using the voice he used to with me when I would sulk over a bad test grade. "It was quite fortuitous that you happened across us back on the mountain."

"Fortunate? Yes. But not a coincidence," Byron says.

I cock an eyebrow. "What do you mean?"

Byron reaches to the outer right side of his command chair and taps a sensor, which opens a small compartment. Several electronic devices rest inside. (I half-expected it to be a beer mini-fridge, but maybe that's on the other side.) Byron pulls out a long, flat device that looks almost like a bent Ping-Pong paddle, with an angled grip attached to an LED screen. It is beeping at a fairly rapid rate.

"What is that?"

Byron approaches me, and as he does, the beeping grows even faster. He hands me the device, and I look at the display. The majority of the screen is a faint blue, warbling around the edges with a slight purple distortion. But dead center is a bright flashing yellow dot, and in the bottom right-hand corner is a series of numbers. No, not just numbers.

Coordinates.

"Elvie?" Cole says, looking over my shoulder. "What is it?"

"This is me!" I gasp. "You've been . . . *tracking* me?"

Byron nods. "Since I sent you to Titus."

"How? Why?"

"I knew I needed to get you as far away from the Council as I could, at least until I could figure out a better course of action. I figured a remote, little-known location would be ideal, with Titus being the perfect guardian. I still wanted to be able to keep tabs on you, however, just in case. So I placed a tracer in you."

"You stuck something inside me without my knowledge or permission?" I ask. "You Almiri, man, you have some real issues."

"I didn't do anything so quaint," Byron says. "I wanted to be able to track you, but I also wanted to be the only one with such capabilities. A physical tag could be spotted too easily. A mutation, however . . ."

"This isn't going to end anywhere good, is it?" I say. I already feel sick to my stomach.

"To be blunt, my dear," Byron replies, "I altered your DNA."

"You did *what?*" I shriek. "What did you *do?*" I begin frantically searching my arms, like I'm going to, I don't know, spot a new mutated tracer mole or something. "Wasn't I hybrid enough for you before?"

"It wasn't anything serious. I promise. I simply gave you a little tweak to assign you a specific membrane potential—an electrical signature on a cellular level—that I would be able to detect even from great distances using the device you're holding."

"So leaving aside the great invasion to my rights as an individual and my serious *disgust* at the intrusion for just a second," I begin, and Byron nods, "you're saying that you picked up this signature of mine and knew I was headed to the Poconos . . ."

"And we doubled back, yes," Byron finishes for me. "We would have been here sooner, had we not first followed the other signal out into orbit."

"Other signal? What other signal?" My eyes go wide, and I can feel my ears do that weird thing where they move backward on my head without my having to touch them. "You put this genetic tracer mutation in Olivia too, didn't you?"

"Yes," Byron says. "The device tracks both frequencies on separate channels. When Olivia's signal began to move independently, I grew concerned. We lost the signal out in the Rust Belt. We would have continued the pursuit, but then I saw you headed for the Poconos, and into the Jin'Kai's waiting arms, so we doubled back."

My body turns to ice. "What do you mean, you lost the signal?" I say. "You couldn't track it anymore or . . ." I can't even bear to finish the sentence. I feel a hand on my shoulder. It's Cole. I shrug him off.

"The signal dissipated," Byron tells me. "We believed that to be due to interference in the belt, although of course we can't know for sure. That's why, when we saw your signal, we—"

"You *left* her," I finish for him. "You left her with *them*." Half of me wants to punch my grandfather in the kisser—for turning away when Olivia needed him most, for violating both of us for our own protection (because one must never forget that the high and mighty Almiri always know what's best for *everyone*). But honestly the other half of me wants to give him a big old kiss on the mouth—this horrible violation might be my only fighting chance at finding my daughter. I shake my head free of confusion. Focus on what's important. "What are we waiting for?" I ask him, pointing to the tracker in his hand. *Hold on, Olivia.* "Why aren't we heading back there this second? Let's go find her!"

"The fact remains that we have no point of trajectory to use as a locus for a search," Byron says, dousing my hope with a bladder full of buzzkill. "A full-scale sweep of the entire sector would be necessary."

"Well, then that's exactly what we're going to do!" I tell him. "Let's put all this flipping advanced alien tech to use for a change, for something other than your own selfish purposes!"

Byron looks at me with a stern expression. It's not quite angry, but we've entered into no-nonsense territory. It's like I can feel him winding up the hammer, ready to bring it down on all my remaining conviction.

"We simply don't have the manpower for that, Elvie, given our current situation. The Almiri—nay, the world, is under direct assault. The enemy has dealt the first blow, and we must regroup. My modest strike force alone cannot hope to repel the invaders. We must rally the forces of men and Almiri alike for the coming—"

"I want my daughter back, you son of a bitch!" I scream, flying at him. He doesn't flinch as I fall on him, slapping at his face and clawing at his shirt. Some of the crewmen on the bridge move to grab me, but Byron waves them off. It's Oates who puts his strong hands on my shoulders. He doesn't pull me, or wrap me up. He just holds me until I calm down. The tears are racing down my cheeks and dribbling off the edge of my nose. I'm sure I'm quite the sight, but I don't care. That's kinda the point.

"My dearest child," Byron says softly. "I promise you, when the time is right, I shall move heaven and earth to help you find your daughter. But we must focus on the bigger picture for now. We must force the Council's hand by making ourselves known to the leaders of Earth. And there are mysteries to be unlocked which may be our only hope of surviving the coming storm."

"Yeah, whatever," I say, wiping my nose. "You do that."

Byron turns to one of his crewmen. "Ensign, would you please take our guests to the quarters we've made up for them? You should all rest. We'll reach the rendezvous point with the rest of my men shortly. From there we will discuss how to proceed."

"Lord Byron, or, should I say, Commander," Dad says, stepping forward. "I would like to offer my services to you in any way possible. I know the Almiri are a race of superintelligent beings, and I don't want to toot my own horn, but I am probably the smartest person I know."

"It would be my honor to have you on our team, Mr. Nara," Byron says.

Dad wraps me up in a big hug and kisses my cheek.

"Get some rest, dearheart. I'll come see you shortly."

I don't answer, just return his hug. He pulls away and looks at me, sadness on his face.

"We must make our plans according to the problems before us," Dad tells me softly. I can see the pain in his eyes. "We'll find her," he says. "I promise."

"Sure," I say, and I even manage a nod. I turn back to Byron, the tracking device still in my hand. "Is it all right . . . if I hold on to this for now?" I ask. "I know she's not going to suddenly reappear while I'm napping, but . . ."

"Of course," Byron tells me. "There's no harm in holding out hope." He nods to his ensign, and the young crewman leads me, Ducky, Marnie, and Cole back out into the hall. The whole way down the corridor, Ducky's got his arm around me, and I rest my head on his shoulder.

Hold on, Olivia, I think. *Just hold on.*

"These quarters aren't so bad," Ducky says, bouncing his butt on the cot a little, taking in the 1970s-era sci-fi blandness that the Almiri let pass for décor. He nudges me in the arm. "I mean, considering we just spent a month underground at the South Pole."

"Yuh-huh," I say absently. In truth, I'm not paying attention. I'm counting in my head.

"I cannae imagine what yer goin' through," Marnie says. "But rest assured that when the time comes, I'll help ye find yer bairn. If she's been taken to the Rust Belt, the Enosi have contacts there. Folks that go unnoticed, and therefore notice everything."

"What's a Rusbell?" Cole asks from his bunk across the room.

"The Rust Belt," Marnie repeats. "Tha's where all the low-pin space stations are and all tha'. Cruisers, beat-up ships, lots of rubbish, mainly."

"Guys," Cole says to me and Ducky, "is it just me, or is Marnie talking gibberish?"

I attempt to act as translator. "The Rust Belt," I say. "You've been there, Cole. It's where the *Echidna* was stationed."

"Oh, the *Rust Belt*," Cole says. "I thought Marnie said 'Rusbell.' And I was like, 'Where's the Rusbell? I've never heard of that place.' And then the other part of me was like, 'Yeah, I don't know. Better ask.'"

"Thanks for that glance into your inner monologue, Cole," I say. I turn my attention to Ducky. "How long do you think it's been since they left us here? Five minutes?"

"Probably closer to ten," he replies. "Why?"

Without answering I spring up off the mattress and open the door.

"Elvie?" Cole says as I pass him into the corridor. "Where are you going?"

I look both ways down the hall. Empty. And why wouldn't it be? We're not prisoners anymore. We probably have free rein to go wherever we please on Grandpop's party boat in the sky.

Well, almost anywhere.

I'm already halfway down the hall toward the lift when the others realize I'm not merely stretching my legs. The three of them come bounding after me, and catch up just as I enter the elevator and hit the down button. They squeeze themselves in with me before the doors slide shut.

"Mind filling me in, Elvs?" Cole asks as we travel down to the bottom deck.

"Let the boys up there enjoy their explosions and heroics and other boring derring-dos," I say. "The Almiri can have their little race war. I'm getting my daughter back."

"Yer going to track down Marsden?" Marnie asks. "How?"

I wield the tracker. "With this." The elevator doors slide open, and we're down on the hangar level. I make a beeline for the sealed bay doors.

"Elvie, you heard the commander," Cole says. "That thing won't be able to penetrate whatever interference is mucking up the signal. You'd have to be, like, right next to Olivia for it to pick her up."

"Then I guess we have a needle in a haystack to find," I say. "Marnie, your contacts in the Rust Belt. Where can we reach them?"

"We've eyes 'n' ears on several installations," Marnie says. "I'd start on New Moon, the ozone refinery station."

"Very well, then. We'll start there. Maybe your guys have heard about some unsavory types lurking about, hiding with the rest of the floating garbage up there."

"And how do you propose we get there?" Ducky asks. "Swim?"

"If it wasn't already clear, I'm stealing a spaceship," I say. "One of those neat little numbers with the stealth shield."

Ducky slides in front of me, bringing me to a halt. "Elvie, you're not thinking." He turns and points at the bay doors. "Unless you've suddenly jumped several ranks in the military service of the aliens who *don't even like your kind,* you don't have the clearance to open those doors, let alone launch a ship."

"True," I say, twirling my grandfather's security clearance card around in my hand. "But Byron does."

"How did you get that?" Ducky asks.

"You son of a bitch!" I fake-cry as I pantomime slapping Ducky in the chest. I burst into a great big smile.

"Aren't ye the canny lass," Marnie says, a grin spreading across her face.

"When the need arises," I say. "Always have a plan."

"Even if you can get the ship started up," Cole counters, "they'll spot it and shut the outer doors down."

My smile only broadens as I turn to Cole. "Then I guess I have some pretty extraordinary hacking to get started on." *Hold on, Olivia. Mama's coming.* "Let's get to work."

Chapter Five

IN WHICH COMMUNICATIONS BEGIN TO BREAK DOWN

Not to brag or anything, but if they gave out medals for stealing invisible ships and piloting them away from your alien grandfather undetected, yours truly would grab the gold, easy.

"Okay," Ducky says after we've successfully broken away from the Almiri strike force and plunged into the blackness of space. His face is green, naturally, because we are moving, and he grips the armrests of his seat tightly. "So, like, *now* what?"

To that I have absolutely no response. But at least someone else does.

"We're thirteen-point-three-thousand clicks from the Rust Belt," Marnie tells us. The chick's been standing over my shoulder for the past fifteen minutes or so, watching me work the controls, and it's making me mildly claustrophobic. "New Moon is near the center of the densest cluster of ships. Tricky flying, but this ship's slight enough that we shouldnae have much trouble."

"What are spies doing sitting in the middle of an orbital

ghetto?" Cole asks, fiddling with the tracker. He wanted something to do so I let him hold it, but I'm getting worried he's going to break it.

"Cole!" I snap as he bangs the tracker with the heel of his hand. "Be careful with that."

"They're na' spies," Marnie tells him. "More as like they're untapped fonts of information."

"How much info can you get sitting on a defunct space station with the dregs of humanity?"

"Where d'ya reckon undesirables go when they want to do business?" Marnie says. "They go where they think no folks are watching. So, what better place to watch?"

"I'm confused as to why you would need contacts like that in the first place," Cole asks, still banging the tracker.

"We can't all be as selective about our friends as the Almiri," Marnie says.

"Ha-ha," Cole says. He flips another switch on the tracker, and it starts frantically beeping. "Holy shit, Elvs! I got it working!" He's waving the tracker around like a maniac. "Olivia's here! She's, like, two meters away or something!"

I roll my eyes. "Cole, any chance you switched it to frequency one again?"

He checks, then presses his lips together, all chagrinned-like. "Um . . . ," he says slowly. "It's possible, yeah."

"*I'm* frequency one," I tell Cole for, like, the four-billionth time. I grab the tracker from him to flip the switch back to stop the inane beeping. "Our daughter is frequency *two*."

"It's hard to remember," he says by way of defense as he takes the tracker back.

"Try to make up a mnemonic," Ducky calls from his chair. And he doesn't even need to turn around to sense that Cole is staring at him blankly. "A memory trick," he clarifies. "Like . . . 'Frequency two, which rhymes with 'coo,' which is what babies do.' So two for Olivia."

"Or how 'bout 'eejit,'" Marnie chimes in. "Cuz there's two *E*s in 'eejit,' and if yer so daft ye cannae remember that, then that's what ye are."

"I'll remember," Cole says.

"So," I say, turning my attention to Marnie. "To the Rust Belt, then? To find this contact of yours?" It's the best—sorry, *only*—plan any of us have had so far, and if anyone can give us information that leads to Olivia, I'm all for it. "All agreed?" I ask.

Marnie gives an emphatic "Aye!" Cole on the other hand . . .

"Guys!" he shouts. "I found her! I found our daughter! She's, like, two meters aw— Oh, wait. Frequency *two*, right?"

And that's when Ducky barfs on the floor.

Clearly, Marsden and his cronies don't stand a chance.

The station, designated New Moon A-1138 according to my navigational readouts, looms large in front of us as I bring the ship in closer. Did I say large? I meant *uge*, as in so huge that there isn't any room left for the *h*. I've been to New York City only twice, once on a middle school field trip to the Museum of Pretentious Art and once when Dad took me and Ducky to see *2 Fast 2 Furious* on Broadway for my eleventh birthday, so I don't have a great sense of the actual size of the island of Manhattan, but if I had to guess, I'd say it's roughly the same as the floating hunk of metal that I'm currently steering toward.

"Look at the size of that thing!" Cole whistles from behind me.

"Cut the chatter, Red Two," Ducky says, half-snorting.

"Red what?" Cole asks.

"It's just . . . It's from . . . Forget it. Hey, but, guys, I was thinking. We're working a reconnaissance mission, right? Gathering intel?" Ducky is still green, but it's an *excited* green. I can tell he's about to nerd out on all of us. "Don't you think we should all be incognito? Like, with secret identities and stuff? I've been working on mine." He sits up a little straighter. "Alfred Sniggle, new junior sanitation engineer. Thoughts?" He looks expectantly to the rest of us.

I am not the only person concerned with things besides Ducky's nerd fantasy, apparently.

"This thing's getting even wonkier," Cole says. He's still messing with the tracker. "Now *both* frequencies are buzzing in and out."

"It's the debris from all the derelict craft in this sector," Marnie tells him. "Radiation, magnetic fields, et cetera. Chops up yer signal, makes it cockeyed."

"You sure it's not just broken?" Cole asks, aiming the tracker at his head. No signal *there*, obviously.

"Cole, give me that thing," I say, attempting to snatch it from him with one hand while the other operates the ship's controls.

"Best leave it aboard, act'ly," Marnie tells me. "A precious object like tha' won't be safe where we're going. It'll get pocketed an' sold less than five minutes off the ship."

"I'll hide it somewhere *really* safe," I promise.

"Trust me," Marnie says. "Ye could hide it up yer own arse—those thieves'd have it off ye 'fore you even noticed they pulled down yer drawers. Much safer here."

"Hard to believe this isn't more of a vacation destination," I mutter. But I know Marnie's got a better sense of this place than I do. The tracker will stay on board.

Hold on, Livvie, I think as the station looms ever larger before us.

"I've never seen a station this big before," Cole says.

"Or so . . . gross," I add.

Even from this distance it's easy to tell that New Moon has seen better days. I didn't realize you could see rust from kilometers away, but if that's not what I'm looking at, then whatever it is is doing a pretty good rust impersonation. The blotchy brown patches on the hull of the station must be several hundred meters in diameter, at least, and from what I can see, they snake all over the surface. There are cracks, holes, and just plain shoddy construction running the entire length of New Moon from start to finish.

"It's amazing that thing doesn't break apart," I muse.

"Why in the heck do they call it New Moon?" Cole asks.

"That's no moon," Ducky begins. "It's a space—"

"Ducky, enough," I tell him.

"*Alfred*," he insists. "I'm Alfred Sniggle now. Don't forget. You'll blow my cover."

I roll my eyes. "Okay, then. Enough, *Alfred*. Now listen to this." And I begin reading the information from the heads-up display the console is feeding me. "According to the description here, New Moon is the largest orbital station ever constructed, and the second largest satellite of Earth after the actual moon. Built in 2043, it has been home to an ozone processing refinery, the only ever off-world supercollider, and for a brief period in the sixties served as the headquarters for the Psychedelic Tofreegan Collective before they were all committed. Now everything's gone except the refinery."

"Well, if you ask me," Cole says, "New Moon is the biggest hunk of crap I've ever seen."

"Can't argue with you there," I say.

"*That's* a first," Cole replies with a snort.

I sigh. I'm getting more than a little fed up with Cole's attitude. Sure, he agreed to steal a stealth ship with me and go flying off into the great unknown in an attempt to rescue our daughter, disobeying a direct order from his former Almiri supervisor, and potentially endangering the entire planet in the process, but he's been such a *drag* about it.

I flip the comm to an open channel as we begin our approach.

"New Moon control, this is, um, the U.S. . . . *Baby Chaser*," I say, shrugging at Ducky as he shakes his head at me. "Request permission to dock."

I leave the channel open, awaiting a response. All that comes back over the comm is static.

"New Moon control," I repeat, "this is—"

"Ye can save yer voice," Marnie tells me. "There 'nt a control to give clearance."

"Well, then how are we supposed to know where to dock?" I ask. "Not to mention avoid crashing into other incoming vessels?"

"I'll show ye where to land," Marnie assures me. "As fer the other thing, well, ye'll jes' have to show off some fine piloting skills, won't ye?"

Marnie does indeed seem to know her way around this place. She guides me past the prow, where I would have assumed the docking bay to be, and down along the seamy underbelly of the station.

"This is a really weird approach for a landing dock," I say. "How are you supposed to find it if you don't already know it's there?"

"Tha's the point," Marnie says.

"Well, at least there isn't any other traffic, so we don't have to worry about—"

On cue—because the universe absolutely adores using me as its straight man—three small ships come flying out of nowhere from underneath the station, screeching by so close that I can practically feel the paint scratching off our hull. For a moment I lose control and we swerve hard enough for Ducky to lose his footing at the console behind me. There is a violent *thud!* against the side of the hull as the last ship zips past.

"What the hell was that?" I shout, scrambling to regain control of the ship. "Did one of them hit us?"

"Negative," Marnie says, smiling a bit as she reads Ducky's display (Ducky being otherwise occupied, picking himself off the floor). "They jettisoned some rubbish out the back as they passed. It's nothin' to be afeart of. Jes' a friendly suggestion we watch ourselves."

"We should *watch ourselves*? Who where those jackasses?"

"O$_3$ Cowboys," Marnie tells us. "They take the ozone

bricks from the refinery and deploy them into the atmosphere, where they break down and revert to gas."

"They fly around in those little ships like that carrying ozone?" Ducky asks incredulously. "It's a miracle they don't blow up."

"They do, from time to time," Marnie says. "It's not the most stable career, to be sure."

I grunt in reply, but I have more important things to concern myself with than a bunch of alpha-apes. "Marnie, just show me where we're landing on this heap."

The docking hangar is long, wide, and decrepit. It seems like it might break away from the station and float off into space at any moment, which would be a real accomplishment for a structure that, technically, is just a hole in the side of the platform. It's from here that the cowboys have been disembarking, and the flow of small, possibly explosive transport crafts is steadier—but since I can see them coming now, it's far less nerve-racking. I approach at a low angle but don't waver on my course, letting these atmo-jockeys know that we belong. It wouldn't do to stick out like a sore thumb before we even land.

"Yer pretty good at the stick," Marnie says with a whistle. I try to suppress my smile as I angle us toward the nearest free landing pad. For some reason Marnie's approval feels incredibly rewarding, but I really don't want her to know that.

"It's not my first spaceship," is all I say. "Once I put her down, what's our first move?"

"Well, I dunnae about the rest of ye, but I could sure go fer a pint," Marnie says.

Typical Scot.

"Um, Marnie, honey"—and, oh my God, no one has ever said the word "honey" more awkwardly than Ducky just did—"none of the rest of us are twenty-one. So if they try to card us, we're screwed."

I can hear the smack as Marnie plants a big wet kiss on Ducky's forehead behind me.

"Ach, Donald. Yer a bonnie lad, aren't ye?" she says, and kisses him again. From the squelching noises Ducky's making, I can visualize the romantic Celtic headlock Marnie must have him in. Cole sits down next to me and gives me a look.

"You okay?" he asks me.

"I'm fine," I say, staring straight ahead out the viewport as we make our approach.

"You look . . . superfocused," he replies.

"Just making sure not to crash the ship and kill us all in a fiery blaze."

The kissing noises behind me stop.

So it turns out that landing a spaceship in a crowded hangar is a lot trickier than piloting it through the emptiness of space. It sure doesn't help that there's no landing guidance whatsoever to tell us where to go. The first pad that seems empty is apparently already spoken for by an incoming cowboy who decides to slip underneath us to sneak into the spot just as I'm about to engage the repulsors. Luckily I avoid crushing the maniac's tiny little ship as flat as a frat boy's used beer can. (Normally it wouldn't bother me to crush the guy, because I've always been of a mind that parking infractions should be punishable by death, but we're trying to keep a low profile here. Oh, and the whole thing where the guy might still have ozone bricks on board with him, which would've ended up with all of us in smithereens. Tiny details.)

Anyway, I'm finally able to navigate to a free space, although I do have to engage in a brief staring contest with a supply transport whose pilot seems just as weary of the etiquette up here as I am.

When the door slides open, it's all I can do to keep from gagging. In fact, it's more than I can do. I gag. I gag big-time. The stench on the docking platform is absolutely putrid, with the almost indescribable combination of oxidized metal, congealed grease, and something that smells like rotting possum but (one would hope) couldn't possibly be, all swirling together to form one of the most odiferous confections I've ever come across. I'd be hard pressed to ascertain when, if ever, this place had been sanitized.

"You look as green as I feel," Ducky whispers to me as we walk down the exit ramp.

"I don't think I've ever smelled anything like it," I say, choking back tears. "This must be where highway rest stops are born."

Marnie takes a deep breath and exhales gleefully as she traipses past us into the hangar. "Ye lot certainly are a bunch of delicate flowers, then, aren't ye?" she says. "Jes' remember, people live here. So dinnae be rude."

"Don't worry," I say. "We're not so dumb that we're going to go around shouting about how—"

"This place flipping reeks!" Cole shouts as he climbs down

the ramp behind us. More than a few heads turn to look at us.

I grit my teeth but choose to let Marnie give Cole the chiding glare this time. The truth is, even if Cole's lack of tact could probably get us stabbed with something seriously unhygienic, the dude's not wrong. I was prepared for this place to be run-down, but I have never, ever, seen anything like *this*. This place makes squalor seem like a resort spa.

We make our way hastily through the hangar, which is buzzing with activity. The place is packed to the gills with an array of raggedy ships, many of which look like they might be held together with staples and duct tape. People tinker on their vessels using equipment ranging in quality from automated repair drones to manual screwdrivers. One guy, I swear, is using a baseball bat to pound something into place. Our ship already stands out from the rest, since it's the only craft currently docked that looks like it could pass a legitimate safety inspection.

As soon as we exit the hangar, we find ourselves on a massive promenade, with cathedral-high ceilings and wide avenues snaking in every direction. The paths are congested with hundreds, if not thousands, of people who seem to be going nowhere in particular, but are rather just spinning about in random circuitous paths like atomic particles. Marnie has pushed well ahead of us, and were it not for her brilliant red hair, I would have immediately lost her in the gray-brown throng pressing against me on all sides. The metallic rotting smells of the hangar have made way for a far more organic but no less offensive stench. Warm bodies grind against me as I move forward, leading with my shoulder. I can feel the tangible grime from their clothes rubbing off on me as I go. From behind I feel something clutching at my shirt near my waist. Instinctively I twist around, expecting to see one of the pickpockets Marnie warned us about. But it's only Ducky.

"I'm trying not to lose you," he says over the din, reaching his hand out. I grab it and hold on for dear life as we keep moving.

"Where's Cole?" I ask without looking back.

"I'm here!" he calls, trailing well behind us. "Nobody worry about grabbing my hand! I'm just fine!"

"I'll hold your hand," Ducky says.

On either side of the path, barkers are hawking dilapidated wares. One olive-skinned old woman with a long crooked nose and only three teeth in her head jumps out and waves a dingy-looking length of woven cloth at me.

"Face-swath cheap's they come!" she spits, literally, in my face.

"E-excuse me?" I stammer, leaning away as far as I can.

"Wear's mask, use's scarf. Real wool synth. Five 'n' five ducks needs give!"

The woman shoves the gross cloth into my boob with one hand, while pulling forcibly on my arm with the other. Rattled, I shove her back, and she stumbles into the wall. Immediately three other vagrant-types are swarming me, shouting at me in their incomprehensible dialect and shaking their fists violently.

"Just back off!" I holler, feeling the heat rise in my cheeks. "I don't want your filthy rag." I feel Ducky and Cole flank me defensively. Just when I'm sure I've inadvertently ignited a brawl that will get us unceremoniously dumped out of the nearest air lock, Marnie strides through the crowd as if she were liquid metal seeping through the cracks of an old concrete wall.

"Cheap's they come?" she says, pointing at the cloth still clutched in the tooth-challenged woman's hand.

"Five 'n' five ducks," the woman replies from the ground.

Marnie sneers. "Two 'n' five's they lucky."

"Four's they go."

"Three 'n' five's we walk."

The woman lifts herself, using the already dingy cloth to push herself up off the even filthier floor. To my surprise she's laughing and smiling, putting all three pearly not-so-whites on display. She waves the dirty cloth in my direction again.

"I told you, I don't want—" I start, but instead of pushing me with the cloth, she drapes it over my shoulder and lets go, turning her cupped hand palm-up expectantly. Marnie drops three large coins and one smaller one into the woman's hand, which clutches the coins for dear life as they land. The other barkers are still shaking their fists, but now they're directing the gesture to the woman, who responds by shouting at them so rapidly that I have no shot at deciphering what she's saying.

"What in the hell was all that?" I ask Marnie as we start back through the crowd.

"'Grats, Elvie. Ye've jes' had yer first haggle," Marnie tells me.

"Haggle?" I say, staring down at the dirty cloth lying across my shoulder. "We bought this on purpose?"

"I know it can make ye a tad dizzy at first," Marnie says. "But yer instincts to push her off were good."

"Why do they talk like that?" Cole asks.

"Local patter. There's more than two hundred dialects that have been canoodling with one another up here fer decades. It takes the rules from each language and then ignores them all equally. Ye pick it up after a spell."

"And I thought you were hard to understand before," I mutter.

"C'mon, then," Marnie says, smiling. "Let's head down to one of the local watering holes. Good a place as any to start trolling fer information."

The promenade level where we first arrived is only one level of four, each stacked on top of the other and connected by magnetic elevators. Marnie ushers us into one of the elevators when it settles on our level, and we wait for the flood of people to pour off the platform around us before we're pushed forward by the throng behind us heading to the lower levels. I hold my grip on the railing and look down over the open-air car to the levels below.

"Ducky, do us all a favor," I tell him. "Don't look down." It's hard to estimate just how far down the station goes, but if I had to guess, I'd say you could drop the Empire State Building from the top and still have to wait quite a while to hear it hit the bottom. Even I can feel my knees wobble a little beneath me as I fathom the splatitude that would be the result of a fall from this height. At least I have this one creaky, hip-level metal railing to keep the two dozen or so other passengers from pushing me off the edge to my doom.

Safety was apparently not high on the station builders' list of priorities.

"Already on top of it," Ducky says, and when I look back, I see that he has covered his eyes with both hands like he's about to play the most death-defying game of peekaboo known to man. "And the *name*," he reminds me, "is Alfred Sniggle."

"Here, Alfred," Marnie says, slipping her arms around his waist from behind and snuggling against him. "Let me guide ye."

In this manner we make our way off the elevator, out to Level 1, and into what Marnie informs us is New Moon's classiest bar.

The whole place looks eerily like the cantina scene from *Star Wars*—after they yelled "cut" and the extras stripped out of their alien suits, revealing the pent-up funk of sweat and slime that results from spending twelve hours under hot lights while wearing a latex mask. Seriously, the room has a visible "stank smog" wafting around. If I vomited on the floor, it would be a marked improvement in hygiene.

"Go find yerselves a seat," Marnie urges. "And try to na' stick out too much."

"Us? Stick out?" I say, trying to coat my extreme nervousness in a hardy candy-coated shell of sarcasm. Marnie smirks and moves away toward the bar. Cole starts to follow her, when I grab his arm.

"Where are you going?" I ask.

"Don't worry about it, Elvs. You're not my girlfriend anymore, so you don't have to pretend to care what I do." And with that, he storms after Marnie toward the bar.

"Two days after our breakup, in the middle of a goddamn rescue mission in outer space, and he decides to go all Devin from *Martian Chronicles* on me," I seethe. Ducky leads me by the shoulder toward a booth in the back that has just opened up.

"Don't let it get under your skin," he says. "Let's sit down and wait to see what contacts Marnie still has up here."

We sit in the corner booth, which gives me a pretty good lay of the land. The clientele is markedly different from the mobs we found up on the promenade. It's mostly men, tough burly types that must all take turns sharing the same razor, because there's more than enough straggly facial hair to go around. They're loud and raucous, the kind of shouting where it's hard to differentiate camaraderie from the prelude to a knife fight. There's not much danger of any Jin'Kai types moving around incognito in here either. This is a decidedly unattractive group of dudes.

"I highly doubt we're going to find any useful information in a place like this," I say, raising my voice enough to be heard over the shouting coming from the next booth.

"You never know," Ducky says. "Marnie says tons of traffic comes through here. Being so far off the grid and all. Attracts all kinds."

"It's a shame it didn't attract any shower salespeople," I say. "I hope Marnie's right about this. I'd hate to have come all this way for nothing."

"Aw, wouldn't say nuffin, luff," says a broad, portly dude who seems to have just materialized in front of our table. "You've not had chances wif me weren't y'ere."

"Why don't you go peddle your sweet talk somewhere else, Romeo?" I reply, looking down at the table, trying to avoid staring at the creep's tooth-challenged mouth.

"Um, Elvie," Ducky whispers. He grabs my knee under

the table, and I look up to see that my scraggly suitor has three large friends with him. They're all wearing the same dirty gray coveralls, like a mechanic-themed boy band on an ill-advised comeback tour.

"Luff, seems we've launched with a bum rocket," the ringleader says. "Let's start again real nice, yeah?"

Without another word he slides gracelessly into the booth next to me, with two of his friends following after, shoving me into Ducky and nearly spilling Ducky onto the floor. Only one of them remains standing, hovering over Ducky.

"Look, f-fellas," Ducky stammers, "we don't want any trouble."

"Aw, son, none trouble here," the ringleader says. His breath reeks of heavy spices and vinegar, so strong that my eyes start watering. "Look at us to be the welcome wagon for you's new 'cruits."

The one standing over Ducky claps him on the shoulder and literally lifts him up out of the booth before resting him down on his feet.

"You's c'n be drinks," he says, sliding into Ducky's old spot. "New 'cruits be drinks, we's all friendly."

I look at Ducky with a slightly panicked expression that I'm hoping says, *Don't you dare leave me with these hairy mouth breathers.* In response Ducky furrows his brow and sticks his tongue between his upper teeth and lower lip, which clearly means, *Stay here while I go get Cole, or Marnie, or barring that, a whole bunch of drinks, and hopefully this lot will turn out to be more boorish than villainous. In the meantime, keep them busy, and try not to do anything to make them angry.*

What can I say? Ducky and I absolutely *kill* in charades.

"A round for the table, then," Ducky says, and disappears into the crowd, leaving me with my new friends pushing in close on either side.

"You's with the new bunch?" the ringleader asks, looking me up and down. He has the longest beard in the group, which may be how he got voted capo in the first place. "We's told they's Chinese." He squints at me. "You's Chinese?"

"Well, um, no," I say. Keep them busy. "But my grandfather was Japanese, though."

Long Beard looks to the fellow on his right—let's call him Scrungy Neck. "She's look Japanese?" he asks.

"Dunno she's look Japanese," Scrungy Neck responds. "Know she's look pretty."

Don't make them angry. "Why, um, thank you," I muster.

"Too pretty for gasworks."

Shit.

"Beg pardon?"

"Gasworks are for poor, dumb, desperate," says a third guy. Mr. Chip Tooth. "For those without another place. Look you's pretty white teeth. Listen to talk. You's no 'cruit."

"No, you're right," I say, trying to think on my feet. Or from my seated butt at least. "I didn't come here to work at the ozone refinery. I'm a, uh, pilot."

The fourth one, Stout N. Smelly, leans in with a deadly serious look on his face, so close that I'm afraid I won't be able to get the vinegar smell out of my hair for weeks. I wonder for a moment if he's going to clock me. But to my simultaneous relief and annoyance, he bursts into a fit of laughter.

"You's pilot! Ha-ha-ha!" Stout N. Smelly bellows, spittle wetting the whole side of my face. The others join in on the laughter. "Fellas, look it the lady pilot!" He calls to anyone within earshot, pointing at me. "Gov'ner must be dreggin' the mist if he's brung pretty things as pilot!"

The laughter is spreading, and it's getting under my skin. I keep telling myself to let it go and let these Neanderthals have their fun, but no one ever accused Elvie Nara of being without a temper.

"While I'm sure that would be funny if I had the slightest idea what it was you were trying to say," I say before I can stop myself, "I am a pilot. I flew to this piss bucket easy enough."

"Fancy pretty pilot with the mouf," Long Beard says, chortling. I give him my most condescending smile, the one I used to reserve exclusively for Britta McVicker.

"Smelly fat ass with the breath," I say. To my continued annoyance, my snark is simply making them laugh more loudly. And worse, I'm starting to gather an audience. Other bar patrons hover near the table, while my new would-be drinking buddies are crowding me on either side. I look around for my rescue, and as if on cue, Ducky parts the crowd and emerges in front of the table . . .

. . . carrying a tray of mugs.

"Hey there, guys," Ducky says sheepishly. "I, uh, didn't bring any credit with me, so, um, the bartender said he'd put it on your tab."

The table goes silent. Long Beard rises slowly from his seat directly across from where Ducky stands. His mouth has become tight and small, and his eyes seem to have grown to compensate. Ducky shakily puts the tray down on the table and lifts one mug in offering, with a look that says, *Please don't break my arms, cuz I'm really rather fond of them.* Long Beard reaches out—only, he doesn't take the mug. He grabs hold of Ducky's forearm and squeezes. His other hand shoots up and clasps Ducky around the back of the neck, and before I can move, he has pulled Ducky in toward him so that Ducky is leaning precariously across the table. Their faces are so close, I'm sure that the dude's breath is going to dissolve Ducky's corneas. Then, just when it appears the guy is going to make balloon animals out of Ducky's body, Long Beard lifts his head and plants a big wet kiss on Ducky's forehead.

"Luffly! Look, boys. Table serfice!" he bellows, and with that, all his cronies burst out laughing again, each grabbing a mug off the tray. Stout N. Smelly rises up, grabs Ducky roughly, and shoves him back into the booth next to me, slapping him on the back so hard that he nearly chokes.

"That went slightly better than I'd feared," Ducky says, checking his arms—to make certain they're still there, I suppose.

"I thought you were going to get help, not to actually get drinks," I hiss at him.

"I couldn't find Marnie anywhere," Ducky says. "She must have wandered off somewhere to find her contacts."

"Well, what about Cole?"

"He's, um, at the bar."

There's something in Ducky's voice that makes me think there's something going on with Cole that I definitely don't want to know about. So of course I tilt as far back in my seat as I can, so I can know about it.

"What the . . ." I start. Leave it to Cole to find the one woman in this entire bar and start hitting on her. Seriously, cliché much? He's leaning with one elbow on the bar, swishing a drink in his hand and making eyes at his new lady love. Although, I notice that every three seconds or so he darts his eyes my way, to be sure that I'm noticing.

Ducky puts an arm on my shoulder. "Just leave it," he tells me. "He's not doing any harm. Let's talk to these guys and wait for Marnie."

"Yeah," hoots Long Beard. "Speaks t'us, luff." He turns his attention to Ducky. "You's pilot, same?" he asks.

"Oh," Ducky says, startled. "Oh." He looks at me. I know he's trying to get me to read something in his face again, but I'm only half-paying attention. I'm focusing every ounce of control I have on *not* turning my head again to look at Cole "Dingbat" Archer, who's over at the bar *ruining our only chance of finding our daughter, in order to flirt with some chippie.*

"Uuuuuh," Ducky says, drawing the syllable out as long as possible. "Uh. Actually, I'm a sanitation engineer, myself. Not a pilot, not me." He lets out a fake laugh. "Ho, ho! That's a good one. Right, Wanda?"

I'm assuming I'm meant to be Wanda.

"Sure," I say. "Right." I take a quick swig of my beer, and immediately regret it. "Oh God, that's bad!" I choke, allowing half the mouthful to dribble out onto my chin. "Duck, what did you *order*?"

"My name is Alfred Sniggle!" Ducky shouts, *much* too loudly. "I'm twenty-one years old! I've never been to prison, and my favorite cheese is bleu!"

Oh dear.

"He specky, this one?" Long Beard asks me. He looks pretty concerned. So do the other guys, actually, and the half dozen or so other patrons who have decided to stop doing whatever it was they were doing before and stare at us instead. Way to fly under the radar, Duck.

"He's fine," I say quickly. "Sometimes he has episodes. Alfred, did you take your medication this morning?" Ducky hunches back in his seat and nods painfully. And I think the stench of this place must be infecting my brain or something, because before I realize what I'm doing, I've lifted the mug to my mouth again and—"Shit, that's *terrible!*"

Fortunately for us, the group of dudes in front of us seems to find the whole thing rather hysterical. Perhaps they've decided that Ducky and I are this evening's entertainment. Long Beard lets out the most raucous laugh of all of them. "Needs getting used to," he tells me.

I set the mug down on the table with a clatter. "I don't think I could ever get used to that," I reply.

"Pinchin noses helps," Stout N. Smelly tells me.

"And shuttin eyes," adds Chip Tooth.

"And stoppin breathin," says Scrungy Neck.

"Here." Long Beard lifts my mug out toward me. "Give her 'nother go."

Well, at least I've managed to divert their attention from the master spy technique of Alfred Sniggle. "Hey, now," I say in my coyest voice. I take the mug from old Long Beard and smile at him. "If I didn't know any better, I'd say you were trying to get me drunk."

"Oh, the luff knows good," Long Beard says with another laugh. The others join in. Next to me, my buddy Sir Sniggle is starting to relax just the slightest. I have a feeling these guys have finally decided we're harmless weirdos, and are doing their best to initiate us into their group. I'm actually considering taking another sip of the vile concoction, when—I swear not on purpose—I glance back over at the bar and get my first good look at the woman Cole is talking to.

She's no woman at all. She's, like, my age. Skinny little tart with straight black hair, like mine but sleeker (as though she somehow managed to lay her hands on some styling cream in this hellhole, which must've been a feat). Thick arched eyebrows, like mine. Seems Cole went out of his way to find my prettier doppelganger just to flirt with her right in front of me. He gives her his nothing-up-my-sleeves-but-my-killer-biceps move, and then darts his eyes my way again.

Which I guess would explain why I'm not really in the right headspace when Long Beard reaches over toward my boob and declares, "Ain't this suffin, then!"

In a gut-reaction move of self-defense, I flick my mug at Long Beard, shooting the entire contents directly into the very large fellow's very dirty face.

Chairs screech across the bar floor. Mugs slam down on tables. All conversation stops.

It is only then that I realize that my bearded companion was reaching not for my breast but rather for the raggedy facecloth still draped over my shoulder.

Oops.

"Way to blend, Wanda," Ducky whispers at me as he does his best to shrink into the wooden bench. There isn't a single person in this bar who *isn't* staring at us.

I am suddenly feeling like I played this very, very poorly.

Chapter Six

WHEREIN THE HITS JUST KEEP ON COMING

I've pulled a lot of chromer moves in my time. (Let's not even *discuss* the high-waisted shorts fiasco of '71.) But even I have trouble processing that I just dumped the universe's grossest beer on some dude the size of a yeti.

"Uh, sorry about that," I say lamely, making quick eyes at Long Beard across the table. I have no idea what the dude is thinking. Maybe he gets beers dumped on him every day and he thinks it's hilarious. Maybe he's contemplating how best to remove my head from my shoulders. What I do know is that I need to make this situation right as quickly as possible, or all our asses will be floating lifelessly out into space before Marnie can dig up any dirt, and then we'll *never* find Olivia.

"Everything okay here?"

And now here's Cole, who has ditched his hot date to come jump into the role of Elvie's manly protector. Like what we really need now is Cole using his righteous alien superstrength to punch some Neanderthal in the face, blowing our already shit cover for good.

"We're fine," I tell Cole. Long Beard is busy wiping his chin off on the hem of his shirt, and I still can't get a read on his face. His comrades are watching in stunned silence, presumably waiting for their leader to tell them precisely which grade of pulp we should be turned into.

"It's my fault," I tell Long Beard. "I saw you reaching out of the corner of my eye, and I just overreacted." I hand him my haggle rag so he can better mop his face. "I don't know what got into me. I'm an ass. Forgive me?"

Long Beard stares at the rag like I've just handed him a precious heirloom.

"No ass, luff," Long Beard says, mopping his face. He finishes and hands me back my rag like it's a lap-pad full of irreplaceable baby pics. "Things happen. We's move on."

Around us I can feel the energy of the bar shifting. People murmuring in begrudging acceptance. Even Ducky eases up a little on the bench. So kudos to me, I guess. Elvie, massager of awkward situations.

Perhaps unsurprisingly, however, Cole doesn't seem to get the memo re: chillaxing.

"You make friends wherever you go, don't you, Elvs?" Cole says.

"Wanda," I say, giving him a hard look. But Cole never was any good at charades.

"Wanda? What? What are you talking about? Why are you throwing drinks in people's faces?"

"It was an accident," I say. "You're not helping."

Cole's eye twitches. Oops. That must've been a chord I just struck.

"Not helping? What would you like me to do, then, Elvs? Should I start dousing people in cheap beer? Or maybe I should start a fistfight? Would that count as being helpful in your book?"

"Can you stop being you for just two seconds?" I ask.

"What's that supposed to mean?"

"If you weren't you, you'd know," I say. "Just . . . go away. Go flirt with your bar floozy some more."

"What do you care who I flirt with? I'm currently unattached, remember?"

"You are such an ass."

"I'm an ass? I'm. An ass. That's rich. Coming from the queen bee of asses."

"The queen bee of asses? Do you even formulate words in your head before you speak, or do random sounds just fall out of your mouth?"

Across the table Long Beard slowly rises to his feet. "Seems nuff from you's," he says, pointing at Cole. "Luff said sorry. You's do it now."

If I were Cole Archer, and a giant bearded redwood of a man were standing in front of me asking me to shut the hell up, I might think about obliging.

But Cole, as we know, doesn't have the sense God gave a mannequin.

"Apologize? She's the one who doused you with swill," Cole continues. "She's the ass, not me. In fact, I think I'm gonna write it on a cake. You'd like that, Elvie, wouldn't you?

You like cake. What if I have it written on a cake? 'Elvie's an ass,' in chocolate frosting." My eyes dart to Long Beard, whose face is dark and expressionless as he listens to Cole bluster.

"And I know what you're thinking too," Cole continues. "That I'm such a nimrod, I can't spell 'ass'? Well, how's this for nimrod?" He gets right in my face. "A." There is a bit of spittle on my left cheek. I bite my lip and pray for this whole ridiculous fiasco to end soon. Where the hell is Marnie? "S . . ."

Before he can get to the last letter, he up and gets cracked in the jaw with a beer mug.

"Whoops," says Long Beard. And I have to say, he's got Cole beat in the sarcasm department. "Guess 'haps I'm an ass too."

The crowd roars, dripping with joy. Ducky, for his part, looks like he's trying to melt into the bench and disappear completely. I'm pretty sure my eyes are frozen, watermelon-wide, in shock and terror.

And Cole?

"Ow," he says. With about the depth of feeling you might have if you accidentally drank orange juice right after brushing your teeth. Which is probably not the reaction the crowd was expecting from the dude who just broke a beer mug with his face.

"I mean . . ." Cole snaps a quick look at Long Beard, and then suddenly seems to remember that he's posing as a human and not a freakishly strong alien hunkazoid. "I mean . . . *ooooh-OW!*" he hollers, jumping completely to the other end of the pain spectrum. We're talking branding-iron-to-the-groin level. He collapses to the floor. "*Elvie, I think I'm dying! My jaw! He hit me so hard on my fragile human jaw!*"

I move to the ground next to Cole, although until I'm there, I don't know if I'm going to cradle his head or slap his face for making Ducky look like a world-class sleuth.

"What the bloody biscuits?" says Long Beard.

There is a chorus of agreement of that very sentiment.

"Do you think they bought it?" Cole whispers at me from the floor. He's clutching at his chin. "I'm acting hurt."

I tug him to his feet. Reach out for bench-Ducky, too. "I noticed," I say.

The skinny flirt at the bar, I see, has completely disappeared.

Not a terrible idea.

Or . . . not.

I don't take one step before Long Beard slaps a strong hand on my shoulder and forces me back into my seat. He doesn't look so interested in protecting my honor now. Neither, for that matter, do Chip Tooth or Scrungy Neck. Or really any of the other approximately four-point-eight-million people in the bar who are staring at us with more than a little curiosity. "Suffin fishy's startin ta rot," Long Beard says.

Understatement of the millennium, Mr. Beard.

"They's cahooting wif tha Guv'na!" someone calls out from the crowd.

And you know how you're not supposed to shout "Fire!" in a crowded theater because it makes everyone go raving nut bars? Apparently, here on New Moon, you shouldn't shout "Cahootin wif tha Guv'na!" in a cantina.

Major ruckus, that's what I'm getting at.

"We're not cahooting with anybody!" Ducky shouts over

the sudden chaos. Scrungy Neck has him by the collar and is probably trying to blind him with his vinegar breath.

Cole, who apparently would hold out approximately three seconds longer in a torture/interrogation situation than Ducky, shouts to the man at *his* throat. "I don't even know *how* to cahoot!"

For my part, I'm being pressed into the back of the booth by Long Beard's sausage of an index finger. "Luff, you bess tell us truths bout who yous is and what yous doing, or these lot might jess eat yous all, pretty or no."

"They're with me," comes a new voice from the crowd. A figure presses through, but when it reaches us, I have absolutely no idea who the person is. A man—no a boy, a teenager, probably not much older than me—with long dark hair and more than a bit of swagger in his step. "Hamish, ease up on them," this new mystery man tells Long Beard. "You don't wanna get involved, trust me."

Long Beard/Hamish darts eyes between his captives and the greasy-haired youth. "They's acting s'picious," he says. "Rousing in 'at."

"We're very roused!" calls one particularly loud local from the back.

Beside me Ducky is entering full-on panic mode, which is never a pretty sight. "I lied before," he tells Scrungy Neck. "About the cheese. My favorite's really ricotta. Please don't hurt me."

"Do what you will," Mystery Teen tells Long Beard. "But if you hurt them, Hux is gonna have your hide."

Well. You should hear the crowd go silent *then*.

Long Beard looks about as confused as I feel. "You's throw wit' Huxtable?" he asks me.

"Uh, yeah," I say slowly, following Mystery Teen's eyes as they dart sideways to Long Beard. He nods slightly: *Go with it*. And really, what have I got to lose besides my teeth? "Hux," I say. "We're, uh, working with Hux. For Hux. He's really gonna have your hide. Whew, boy."

Well, sign me up for CIA duty right now. I mean, I am *nailing* this shit.

Mystery Teen takes advantage of Hamish's confusion to reach out and tug me out of his grip. He does the same with Cole and Ducky, whose assailants aren't so thrilled about letting them go but grudgingly allow it. "Seems we should be going," he tells the crowd, and just like that, he pulls us from the fray.

It isn't until we reach the far less crowded corner of the bar that I notice Marnie, standing with her arms across her chest, shaking her head at us.

"Cannae take ye *anywhere*," she scolds. When Mystery Teen releases us into Marnie's custody, she offers him a peck on the cheek—and I *know* Ducky must be shaken up, because he doesn't even seem to notice. "Thanks, love," she tells him. Then she turns her attentions back to us. "Everyone, meet Dodge. Dodge, everyone."

Marnie's contact—and our new best friend—slides into the empty bench at the table Marnie has been guarding, and cocks his head to take us in, smirking. "Pleasure," he says. Then he turns back to Marnie. "I don't know what you're after, but the price just tripled," he tells her.

. . .

I'm staring at a plate of what I've been told is food, but you'd be hard pressed to convince me of that. If I'm being honest (and more than a little gross), I'd say this looks like something Ducky would bring back up after a particularly nasty trip in a space elevator.

"What is this?" I ask, poking the soggy lump of *something*. It's swimming in a thin blue-white liquid that I can only imagine unicorn tears must look like.

"It's a curry," Dodge says as he mops the substance up from his own plate with a hunk of rye. "Well, sorta. It's good if you sop up the juices with the bread."

I consider my own piece of bread, turning it over in my hand. A shower of crumbs falls onto my plate. I rip a piece off the edge and give it a munch.

"It's stale," I say, forcing it down.

"I know. Great, isn't it?" Dodge says. He slurps the soggy end of the bread in his mouth, sending the juices dribbling down his chin. "Usually you gotta pick out the maggots first, but we must've gotten lucky with the last shipment."

Marnie leans over to me. "Try it, Elvie," she says.

"I'm not all that hungry."

"Try it."

It's clearly not a suggestion. I look for sympathy from Cole or Ducky, but they're having their own curry issues at the moment. Cole is simply tilting the plate back and forth to watch the gelatinous substance slosh around. Meanwhile, Ducky looks like he's doing a pantomime of eating, complete with rubbing his stomach after each phantom bite.

"It's good," he says in a completely unconvincing voice.

Marnie's gaze has not left me, and now I realize that Dodge is watching me expectantly too. I take a deep breath, dip the hard bread into the slimy liquid, and take a tentative bite. Immediately my mouth is overwhelmed by the most pungent form of vinegar I have ever tasted. It spreads across my tongue like an electrical arc, making my eyes water. After the initial shock of the vinegar, I realize that my mouth is *on fire*. Like, fifty-two-alarm-chili level of spicy.

"Oh God!" I say, spitting the food out onto my plate and coughing. "What'd they do, drop a whole jar of devil peppers into this crap?"

"Elvie, fer Pete's sake," Marnie scolds.

"Oh, it's all right, luff," Dodge says, laughing. "I wouldn't expect a bunch of zoners to take to the seasoning right off the bat."

"What's a zoner?" Cole asks, using the question as a distraction as he clumsily pushes his own plate away.

"You lot," Dodge says. "Living planet-side, enjoying the little bit o' ozone we provide for you up here? Zoners."

"Why in the name of all that is holy would you eat this . . . *this*?" I ask.

"Bein' out here too long, your sense of taste and smell start to wane," Dodge explains. "After a few years you can't taste anything unless it's flavor-blasted."

"I think I'd rather eat that protein gel crap we had in Antarctica."

"Protein gel?" Dodge whistles. "Well, aren't we the fanciest of pants? You want protein here, best wait for the next bakery delivery and pray for maggots."

The conversation has turned Ducky a color not unlike the milky slop on our plates. He tries to mask a queasy burp as he slides his plate away, knocking my plate in the process and nearly spilling it over the edge onto my lap.

"Watch it!" I cry. "You think I want to smell like this stuff until the end of time?"

Dodge is laughing hard now. I guess watching others suffer amuses him? I dunno. He wipes tears away from his eyes and stands up from the table.

"Why don't I get you guys another round to wash the food down, eh?"

"That swill's not much better than this," I say. "Just thinner."

That gets Dodge laughing again, and he slaps my arm as he chortles. Marnie reaches into her pocket, but Dodge stops her.

"No, luff. This round's on me. For old times, yeah?"

He walks away toward the bar, still laughing and shaking his head.

"Well, he's a fun guy, isn't he?" I say. Ducky shrugs and uses the opportunity to dump his food onto Cole's plate.

"Hey!" Cole screams, shoving the plate toward Ducky.

I smirk at the boys' antics, but when I turn to Marnie, I drop the smile. To say that she's giving me the evil eye is to do a disservice to the evil eye, which is downright benign by comparison.

"What?" I ask. She doesn't answer me. I check the wall behind me to make sure I'm not sitting in front of a portrait of Pol Pot or something. But nope. It's just me. "What?" I ask again. "What did I do?"

When she replies, her voice is laced with barely sup-
pressed rage.

"Yer actin' like a wee rotten princess," Marnie replies dryly.

Cole and Ducky freeze their food spat and stare at us,
dumbfounded. Cole whistles through his teeth. Ducky tries
once again to become one with the bench.

"Excuse me?" I say.

"Ye've been naught but a spoiled bairn since ye arrived
here," Marnie says. "The lot of ye. I'm sick of it."

"I'm being *spoiled*?" I huff. "I'm being *spoiled*?" She
nods, all sassy-like. "Would you mind explaining to me how
traveling on a mission to find my kidnapped child makes me
spoiled?" I feel like my face might burst into flames. "Or,
no, wait. Maybe I got so spoiled after my mother *faked her
own death* and ran off with your lot. Is that the part you were
referring to? Or maybe it was the thing where I just, like, a
month ago figured out I wasn't even a friggin' human. So, I
apologize, *Marnie*, if with all that going on I'm having a hard
time feigning non-disgust regarding this failed science project
masquerading as food. It's hard to be polite sometimes when
your entire life is falling apart."

I may be a spastic lunatic of rage at this point, but Marnie
is nothing but calm. "No one denies yer in a bad spot, Elvie,"
she says. "And I feel sorry fer ye, I do. But ye've done nothing
but dismiss this place and these folk since we got here, and I
might remind ye that these folks"—she jerks her head toward
the crowd—"are most of them fine gents who've lived near
their whole lives in this spot that ye wouldn't lower yerself to
spit in. They work hard, they die quick, and fer what? So they

can spend their free time and the little money they make shooting shite with their friends. And that 'swill,' as ye so disdainful put it? It's costin' Dodge what would go fer a day's wage round here, so ye jes' think about that 'fore ye turn yer nose up at it."

I am starting to feel a little squirmy in my seat, but Marnie goes on. "And as fer learning about yer roots a month ago"— she leans forward on both elbows, never breaking her intense gaze—"I've been Enosi me whole life, which is how long I've been runnin' and hidin'. Cry me a river, ye ought. And even I wouldn't swap one day with one of these fellas."

I finally allow myself a breath. "Are you finished?" I say as she leans back in her seat. She gives me a look, daring a snarky comeback. Before I can speak, Dodge returns with a tray of beers. I can tell from the first sniff that this new batch is going to taste a whole lot like regurgitated sheep's feet.

"Here you go. These should be a little easier on your tongue than the last," Dodge says.

I take a mug from the tray. I can feel all eyes on me as I put it to my lips, tasting the bitter metal lip of the mug before the warm beverage fills my mouth. Yup. Sheep's feet.

"Thank you," I say quietly.

I look at Marnie, and she nods ever so slightly in my direction.

"Look, Dodge," Marnie says as Dodge settles back in at the table with his own mug. "We're in need of a favor."

"Anything for you, Legs," Dodge says with a wink. "I still owe you for the 'favor' you did me."

Ducky suddenly sits up as straight as an arrow in his seat. "Legs?" he asks no one in particular.

"Don't be crass," Marnie says. "Rake." Her freckles disappear into a sea of red blush, a development that is not lost on Ducky. "We're lookin' fer information."

"Who isn't, luff? Information on what?"

"There's a group of blokes, in deep with some bad bizzo. Nasty lot. Dangerous. Last place they were ken to be heading was up to the Belt."

"You just described everyone I know," Dodge says. "What're you after them for?"

"They took my daughter," I blurt out. Marnie gives me a quick sideways glance without moving her head. I think I detect the corner of her mouth tightening in a barely perceptible frown.

"Nappers, eh?" Dodge says, shaking his head with so much contrived sincerity that you'd think he was in a regional production of *Our Town*. "That's the worst. But again, not uncommon. Belt's a big place. You're going to have to give me more than that to go on."

"I dunnae that we are," Marnie says, narrowing her eyes. I give her a confused look, but she doesn't break her gaze away from our would-be informant. "Whaddya know, Dodge?"

I can feel my stomach twisting itself into a knot, and it's only partially the result of indigestion. Dodge grins at Marnie and gives her a wink, which does nothing to calm my nerves.

"Still read me like a book, dontcha?" he says. "Now that you mention it, I might know about some unusual goings-on, but aside from the beers, nuthin's free up here, luff."

"Dinnae take me fer a dobber," Marnie says. "We've got a line of credit, ye and I."

"But this here's delicate information, Red. The price is, oh, triple the old rate."

"Double," Marnie says, unwavering. Dodge takes a long draw from his mug. Without putting it down, he holds out his other hand expectantly. Marnie reaches into her pocket and pulls out a credits card. She slaps it down onto Dodge's palm. Before he can pull his hand back, she squeezes, pressing the card between their hands. She raises her eyebrows inquisitively, and he nods in answer. Only then does she release her grip. Dodge puts down his mug and pulls a card reader out of his jacket pocket. He swiftly swipes Marnie's card and plugs in an amount I can't see, before flashing the reader at Marnie for confirmation. She nods, and he pockets the reader, handing the card back to her.

"So, what do ye know, Dodge?" Marnie asks. "They hidin' in the outer shoals somewhere?"

"That'd be a grand place to lay low, to be sure," Dodge says. "But if you're looking for who I think you are, then you won't have to go nearly that far."

"How far, then?" I interject.

"Oh, maybe a dozen decks or so."

The information lands on the table like a bomb, as literally all of us fall back in our seats like we've been flavor-blasted.

"Dr. Marsden is *here*?" I gasp.

"Can't say I got names," Dodge says.

Marnie puts a calming hand on my forearm. "Let's slow down," she says, turning back to Dodge. "Awrite, what's yer tale?"

Dodge shrugs. "All I know is that a little while ago New

Moon got some new tenants downstairs. Secretive bunch. Set up shop in the unused facilities underneath the refinery."

"Jes' like that," Marnie says, a hint of disbelief in her voice. "That area's owned by the Federated Gas Minin' Conglomerate. And yer sayin' these bastarts waltzed in and took over the entire facility without any fuss?"

"Well, if all I'd done was seen 'em, I might've guessed they coasted by on their good looks," Dodge says. My heart is smashing into my rib cage. "But these guys are full bricks, yeah?"

"Full bricks?" Cole asks.

"They've got money," Marnie translates.

"That's the understatement of the year, luff," Dodge replies. "These guys have thrown so much money at the Governor, they can pretty much do whatever they please. They could be running around the ship taking anything they wanted, *if* that was what they felt like doing. But they've stayed out of sight, for the most part. Doing God knows what down there in those old medical facilities."

Medical facilities. Oh God. What are they doing to my poor baby?

"That's them!" I say a little too loudly. "It's got to be them. What are we waiting for?"

"Hold yer roll, Elvie," Marnie says. "Even if it is them, from what Dodge is sayin', they've got the protection of the local government."

"Calling it government, there's a laugh," Dodge says. "Just the Governor and his goons, really. Used to get by on squeezing whatever credit they could from the poor blokes living here. Now, with all the bricks comin' in from this new lot, they don't know what to do with all their wealth. Like giving a walrus a mandolin."

"They won't want anyone poking around their benefactors," Marnie says. "We best be dead careful, or we'll wind up stockaded."

"Or worse," Dodge agrees. "Having wealthy backers is making the Governor cocky. He was always a greedy, opportunistic prick, but times past he wouldn't rock the boat too much, for fear of interrupting his credit flow. Now, though, he fancies himself some kind of bloody kingpin. He's even pressing Huxtable a bit, hiring away some muscle."

"Who is this Huxtable guy?" Cole asks. But before he can get an answer, I stand up. This is a million times better than I even dared dream. Marsden's cronies, here, on this very space station? That places the odds that my baby is within crying distance at good to awesome. I reach into my pocket for the tracker, before remembering I left it on board the ship.

"What are we waiting for?" I ask the gang. All of my emotions are battling inside me—relief, fear, hope—and the adrenaline from it is making me shaky. I just hope I don't start bawling in the bar.

Marnie rises as well. "Best get back to the ship."

"Exactly," I say. "I'll grab the tracker. Then we'll be able to follow it to—"

"Elvie." Marnie offers me a sorrowful look. "We dinnae know fer certain that yer bairn is here. And even did we, we can't jes' go bargin' into a Jin'Kai stronghold, the four a us, no weapons. Tha's suicide."

I am confused. "But my *baby*," I say. I can feel my neck going rigid.

"I think I'm gonna leave you to it," Dodge says, taking in the rising tension around the table. "Marnie, always a pleasure, luff. Maybe next time you'll make a social call, yeah?"

He kisses her hand and disappears into the crowd so quickly that it's tempting to think he might never have been there in the first place.

"What does he mean by that?" Ducky asks.

"Forget about him," I say. "We need to find out how to get down to these secret facilities and rescue my daughter."

"What we need to do," Marnie tells me, "is head back to Oates and th' others, tell them what we learnt. Now we've found Marsden's base of operations, we need to inform someone who can do something about it."

"You want to abandon her here?" I ask in disbelief.

"I want to do what's in the greater good," she tells me. "And I want ye to wake up and do the same."

"But she's here!"

"Aye, and what do ye want to do about it? Blast yer way into a fortified base crawlin' with Jin'Kai? I thought we'd get a lead if we were lucky, something to point us in the right direction as we formulated a plan. We're not prepared for a rescue."

"I don't believe this bullshit," I say. I storm away from the table and head for the exit.

"Elvie, wait!" I hear Cole call from behind me. I stop and turn, to find him pushing his way toward me.

"What, Cole? You have something to add?"

"Only that, whatever you want to do, Elvs, I'm with you."

Finally, someone I can rely—

"Hey, handsome, you're not leaving so soon, are you?"

The chippie from the bar sidles up to us and puts an arm around Cole's.

"Excuse me," I say to her.

"You're excused," she replies, barely giving me a glance before turning back to Cole. "I didn't get your digits or anything," she tells him with a wink.

"Oh, um, hey," Cole says. He looks between me and his floozy hanger-on. "Um, this, um, isn't the best time right now."

I can barely muster an "Ugh!" as I storm away into the outer passageway. I'm halfway to the elevator banks when the gang catches up to me.

"Elvie, please, just think about this for a minute," Ducky says, panting.

I turn to my last and greatest ally. "Ducky," I say, "can you please explain to your girlfriend why we're not leaving here until we get what we came for? Thanks so much."

"Actually, Elvie, I, er . . ." Ducky trails off, rubbing his arm slowly.

"What?" I snap at him. "Afraid Marnie won't like you anymore if you tell her what you really think?"

"Elvie." Marnie's voice is soft. Sympathetic. "Yer the one he's afeart to tell."

I knit my eyebrows together. "What?" I say, looking back to Ducky.

Ducky is clearly hoping Marnie will do the talking, but when she only stands there, looking pointedly at him, he finally pipes up, his voice hoarse. "We have information now.

More than we could have hoped for. But Marnie's right, we aren't some kind of special forces strike force. We're just us."

"I was on a special forces strike force," Cole chimes in.

"And how'd that go?" Ducky counters. "Look, we can use this information. Give it to your grandfather. They'll know what to do."

"All they care about is the invasion," I say. "I need Olivia. If she's here, I'm going to find her."

"I'm sorry, Elvie," Ducky tells me. He sounds genuinely gutted. "I want to find Olivia too. I do. But this is the entire *world* we're talking about. These Devastator guys could literally *destroy the planet* if we don't act fast. When you weigh things that way . . . she's just one baby."

We are all silent, letting Ducky's words sink in.

"If we go back to Earth," Ducky says softly, placating, "we can tell people what we know. People who can do something. We'll get her back, Elvie. I promise."

She's just one baby.

"Don't you talk to me," I tell Ducky. My chest is frozen. "Not ever again."

She's just one baby.

Ducky reaches out an arm to try to make it up to me — leaving my baby in this place to die or worse — with a hug, I guess. But it's not happening. I give him a stiff arm, sending him stumbling back for Marnie to catch.

"C'mon, then," Marnie says. Her tone is conciliatory. "We'll go ahead and get the ship fired up. Give ye a few ticks to yerself."

"You do that."

Marnie heads off to the elevators, Ducky in tow. He turns and gives me a pitiful look, but I am in no way willing to feel sorry for that backstabbing creep right now. I hope his new squeeze is there for him the next time his infant is kidnapped by aliens, because if he expects me to lift a finger, he can just forget it. They get into the first open elevator and turn to face us.

"Archer?" Marnie asks. It's only then that I realize that Cole is standing right next to me.

"We'll catch up," Cole says. At this very moment I really wish that he'd put a strong, reassuring hand on my shoulder, like he used to. But he doesn't. He just stands dutifully beside me, like one of Byron's Newfoundlands. The elevator doors swish shut, leaving us alone with about four hundred other lost souls milling in and out of the bar.

"You okay?" Cole asks. The only way I know to answer him involves a lot of cursing or crying, so I say nothing. He turns to face me directly.

"Elvie, you say the word," he says. "You tell me what to do, and I'll do it. You just tell me the plan."

"What plan?" I say, the tears edging dangerously toward the corners of my eyes. "What are the two of us supposed to do against Marsden's whole gang? It's not like we can waltz in the front door."

"Actually," comes a voice from behind us, "it might be you could do exactly that."

I whip around to see Dodge leaning against a pillar several yards away from us, picking at something resembling slimy flat noodles from a flat square tin.

"Where did you—" I start to ask.

"I took off," he interrupts, walking up to us, "but I never left. Sometimes folks tell you a lot more when you're not there." He picks up one of the "noodles" from the tin and slides it down his throat like it's some sort of delicacy. He offers the tin to me, but I shake my head politely, because despite my tears, my nose still works. Dodge shrugs and closes the tin, then slips it into his jacket pocket.

"You must be a real ace mum," he says.

"Not yet," I say. "But I'll never get there without practice."

"Wish I'd had a mum like you. Mine sold me to the Conglomerate when I was ten, to pay off her debts. She's living somewhere planet-side now, rot take her."

"I'm sorry," I say. I'm not sure where this is going. "You said we could get in the front door? What do you mean by that?"

"Just what I said," Dodge answers. "These folks you're after, they're below the refinery, yeah? So the only way in is *through* the refinery. The security there is pretty tight—they don't want just anyone sneaking in and scampering off with any of their precious ozone bricks—but if you know the right scamp . . ."

"And you're that scamp," I finish. "We don't have any credits, Dodge."

Dodge waves me off like he's insulted. "Not everything's about money, luff." I give him a look. "Okay," he says, and smirks. "Most things are. Look, if I help you get your wee one back, all I ask is that you comp me a ride planet-side on your ship. If you're still feeling generous then, we can discuss further compensation later."

"Why would you help us like that?" Cole asks, suspicious.

"You know the going rate of a flight down?" Dodge asks. "I'm not talking a joy ride with any of these space jockeys, who are just as likely to blow up as get you anywhere. I mean an honest-to-goodness ride back to civilization? I couldn't afford it on ten years' scamming."

"You could have asked Marnie for a ride anytime you wanted," I say.

"Legs usually travels with that humorless bunch of sad sacks she calls her family. She's never had a proper ship. Like you."

"How did you—"

"Luff, this will go a lot faster if you just accept that I know a lot more than you think I should, without asking the why," Dodge says. "I've broken into the plant before. Ozone—even gas—fetches a fair price around here. I can get you in and out before your mates have even finished prepping the ship for takeoff. Whaddya say?"

Cole gives me a worried look, but when he sees my face, he must realize there's no use in arguing.

Hold on, Olivia, I think, the voice in my head growing louder by the second. *Just hold on.*

Chapter Seven

IN WHICH A PREVIOUSLY INCONSEQUENTIAL SOMEONE MAKES AN EXPLOSIVE REAPPEARANCE

"Here. Put these on," Dodge says, handing us two dirty pairs of coveralls. Not at all like the one I wore during my failed attempt to escape the *Echidna* in the trash compactor, or the ones the Almiri gave us when they first shuttled us onto the space elevator to the South Pole. No, these are decidedly . . . earthier. There's so much grease and assorted grime caked to the coarsely woven material that it feels crunchy in my hands as I unfurl it.

"Why?" I ask. Presently I am very unappreciative of my Enosi adaptive abilities. I would love to not be able to smell this jumper.

"Because you're a scrubber, remember?" Dodge replies. "We're being all sneaky-like."

"Oh," I say. "Right." I really wish people would leave the being-a-sarcastic-pain-in-the-ass thing to me.

"You too, pretty boy," Dodge tells Cole, who seems to be having similar difficulty in building the courage to slip the filthy cover over his own clothes. "You're going to stand out too much as it is, smooth little peach that you are."

"I am not a . . . peach," Cole says defiantly. But when he slips into the coveralls and zips the front up, he looks like a flat-pic superhero after a grueling but sexy battle in the mud, whereas I can only assume I look like a moldy prune someone dropped in a soggy trash can.

"Where's your disguise?" I ask Dodge.

"Disguise? Yours truly?" Dodge says, sounding sincerely and profoundly hurt. "My notoriety is a blessing here, my lufflies, unlike yours, should you be caught trespassing. Don't you fret. With ol' Dodge as your guide, we'll have you where you're headed in no time."

Once we're in our crunchy coveralls, we exit the terminal booth. The crowds are thinner down here than they were up on the promenade or residential levels, which suddenly makes me feel very naked in spite of the rumpled disguise I'm wearing.

"So remember," Dodge says as we walk, "you're new scrubbers fresh off the latest transport, came here thanks to a generous donation on my part toward the purchase of two tickets for said transport, and we're going to set up your debit wage, with a thirty-five percent cut going to yours truly."

"Thirty-five percent?" I say, incredulous.

"It's not for real, luff. Don't get caught in a spot over it. It's got to look legit for us to get inside."

"Somehow even fictional indentured servitude gives me pause," I say.

"That's nothing," Dodge says. "Wait till you see the convenience and processing fees. A weekly wage of seven hundred dollars usually leaves a new scrubber with a debit card of under three hundred."

"How can they get away with that?" I ask, honestly indignant. "There are labor laws for that sort of thing."

"Laws is for zoners, luff."

"But why doesn't anyone do anything about it?"

"And here I thought rich girls didn't catch the activist bug until uni," Dodge tells me. "Look, it's a bloody awful system, luff. But it didn't come from nowhere. That's why I'm helping you. We uncover this big bad you think you're after, why, that can't help but shine a light on some of the other unmentionable things going on here. Just so long as you don't forget about all this back planet-side."

"I won't," I say. "I promise."

"Right, then," Dodge says. "A few more blocks to the facility gates."

The front of the refinery complex looks like the terminal of a decidedly fourth-rate airport. There are several rows of plastic chairs back-to-back, forming narrowing channels toward a barrier, a twelve-meter-high silver wall with six gates—three checkpoints on the right marked by a blue light above each doorway, while the three to the left are marked by a red light. Hanging from the ceiling are three spherical surround-view cameras taking in enough visual data to create a fully manipulable, examinable 3-D image of the grand foyer.

"That's some fancy security," I say, nodding upward.

Dodge smiles but doesn't look up. "New toys the Governor had installed not too long back," he informs us. "Among others. Not exactly standard issue for this kind of plant."

"The kind of toy that'd come in handy if you wanted to keep extra close tabs on who was coming in and out," I say.

"You think it's Marsden?" Cole asks, looking straight up.

"Maybe," I say, resisting the urge to tell Cole not to point his face directly at the camera.

The other thing I notice as we approach the entry is that there is suddenly a large cluster of people hovering near one of the gates. They aren't wearing work coveralls, and they don't look like they are here in any kind of professional capacity. They look like the throng flooding the promenade level.

"What's with the crowd?" I ask.

"Payday," Dodge says.

His meaning is made clear as we reach the gate. The crowd flocks toward us, clutching at our sleeves as they plead in the assorted dialects of the upper levels.

Beggars.

As we approach, a tone sounds through the room. For a split second I freeze, fearing that we've been found out (although, technically, we haven't done anything illegal yet). That's when I see the men and women start to exit the complex through the red-light marked doorways. The beggars immediately tear away from us and fly at the workers just ending their shift—presumably with a weekly debit payment in their pocket. Many of the beggars extend small digital card readers toward the scrubbers, hoping for a charitable swipe of a few credits, while some of the less fortunate futilely hold their bare hands out, palms up, on the off chance that someone might be carrying an actual piece of physical currency. Having just been told how measly their working wage is, I'm surprised to see that more than half of the two or three dozen scrubbers pause on their way home to transfer a few dollars here and there to those unable to get work. The only people who don't break their stride are a group of men wearing completely different uniforms—dark, trim jumpsuits. Pilot attire.

"Come on," Dodge says, eyeing the scene with a bitter expression. "Stick close once we're inside, and follow my lead."

Cole and I follow Dodge closely. He passes through the far right blue-lit doorway without incident, but the door lets out two soft dings as Cole and I walk through.

"Don't fret," Dodge tells us. "It's just 'cause you don't have a pass card." On the other side of the silver wall, there is another lobby, just as drab as the outer foyer. Along the right wall is a small glass office space, from which two men exit at the sound of the pings. Dodge opens his arms in a grandiose gesture as they approach, a smile twice as wide as his face.

"Bricks, Potter, how are ya, mates?" Dodge greets them.

"What's ya there, Dodge?" the one called Bricks says, gesturing at us.

"Fresh offerings from the below," Dodge says.

Bricks looks us over, unimpressed. "Zoners, eh?" He inhales what sounds like an inordinately large block of phlegm from his left nostril.

"Not anymore, they ain't," Dodge tells him. "Got the scrubber bug."

"They're really dreggin' the mists with these lot nowadays, eh?" Bricks says, smirking.

"That's the second time someone's said that about me," I whisper to Cole. "I'm starting to think it's not a compliment."

"The less they think of us the better, right?" Cole says with a shrug.

"All right," Potter says to Dodge. "So what's yer cut, then?"

Dodge turns to us and barks, "You's wait while we discuss business." And with that he disappears into the glass office with Bricks and Potter, an arm around each man's grime-encrusted shoulder.

"So, um," Cole says, looking around to see if there's anywhere to sit, which there isn't. "Once we're inside . . . then what, Elvs?"

I merely shrug. "I'm assuming Dodge will know where to go."

Cole raises an eyebrow. "To find this supersecret place where the supersecret Jin'Kai who might not actually be working with Dr. Marsden are doing supersecret things?" he asks.

"Um, yep," I say lamely. But I guess I get defensive when I see the look Cole offers me then. "No one said it would be easy," I say.

"No offense, Elvs," Cole says, "but I'm used to a little more planning from you on stuff like this."

"You know what, Cole, if you didn't like the plan, then why'd you even bother to come with me?"

I'm not actually angry at Cole, of course. The dude could not be more right. I do usually plan these things better. If my dad isn't already disappointed in me for stealing Byron's ship and going rogue, he'll most assuredly be chagrinned by this half-baked baby-rescue mission.

To my surprise Cole gets right in my face, and he looks fierce. "Why'd I come with you?" he snaps. "She's my daughter too, Elvie."

I think the fact that I can feel my face go white as I stumble back a few paces is enough to inform Cole that he's got me dead to rights.

"I'm . . . sorry," I say slowly. God, it seems like I've had to say that a lot lately. But Cole is right, and I guess I'd sort of let that detail slip out of my brain for a while. No matter what he and I are to each other, he is Olivia's father. Always will be.

Cole nods slightly. "S'okay," he mumbles, staring at Dodge and those guys in the glass booth.

As far as I can tell, Dodge is still BS-ing. I can't hear anything they're saying, but Bricks in particular looks confused, whereas Potter looks more concerned as he peppers Dodge with silent questions. I wish I were a better lip-reader.

After a few minutes Potter nods, seemingly in agreement. Bricks looks through the glass at us again and smiles, revealing several gaps in his crooked set of teeth.

"What's happening?" Cole asks, staring back at the glass booth trio. Dodge clasps Potter's hand in a firm shake. "Is that . . . good?"

I honestly don't know how to answer. Dodge walks to the door before spinning around and doing an elaborate curtsy for the two men. They each give him an equally exaggerated gesture with their hands, then turn to look at us with shit-eating grins.

"I don't like it," I say, feeling my body tense. "Something's not right."

Dodge is through the door with a smirk on his face. As he approaches, he gestures toward the long snaking corridor leading into the facility. "This way, lass and lad," he says without breaking stride. "Let ol' Dodge guide you through the gates of Dis."

"What was that all about?" I ask, running to catch up to him as he passes through the first archway. "What was with all that smiling?"

"Elvie, my dear," he says, "I'm sorry to inform you that Bricks and Potter'll each be getting a five percent kickback on your wages for letting you on the rolls."

"After your cut, we'll hardly have enough to live off," I say. Then I break into a grin. "Nicely played."

"You bribed them with fake money?" Cole asks.

"Don't feel too bad for 'em, Cole old boy," Dodge says. "I'm sure they'll get by on the backs of some other poor saps."

The winding corridor leads us farther into the heart of the factory. The first thing that hits me right away is the smell. It smells like a pool. The chlorine stench is so strong that my vision actually goes a little blurry. The second thing is the cold. While it doesn't bother me nearly as much as the smell, it's noticeably frigid.

"Why is it so chilly in here?" I ask as we pass underneath a large robotic crane arm shifting pallets of equipment from the ground level to the open upper deck.

"Keeping the temp down reduces the chance that the ozone will combust," Dodge says. "This is nuffin'. Wait till we get into the processing chambers. That'll chip the nips right off ya."

"Charming," I reply. I feel a hand on my back. It's Cole, guiding me forward slightly faster than I'd like. I turn to give him the old what-do-you-think-you're-doing? routine, but then I see that the crane we just passed under has jammed and is whirring loudly under the strain of a pallet that hasn't quite reached its destination. A team of workers on the top level rush to the edge and reach out precariously with grappling rods to pull the cargo up. "It's a wonder this whole place hasn't blown up already."

"Tech is old, run-down, but it works. Mostly. Problem is injuries. Even with his new cash flow, the Governor ain't dropped a credit toward upping safety standards for the floor crew. Only place he's put in a little dough is the compressor system what presses the bricks 'emselves. Guess he don't want 'em going boom right under his own arse."

We pass into a cavernous room, twice as big as the machinery floor we just left, and sure enough, the temp is probably half what it was before. My breath can see its own breath in here.

"Your brights are on, luff," Dodge says with a smirk. At first I don't know what he means. Cole, looking embarrassed, gestures at the half-zipped top of my overalls.

"Thanks for the heads up," I growl, zipping the overalls up to my neck. Dodge clucks his tongue in what I think is disappointment.

"Not trying to be vulgar. I am a great admirer of the female form." He punches Cole in the arm jovially, but Cole just stares back at him.

"So, what goes on in here?" I ask, trying to change the subject, lest Cole start to get chivalrous on my behalf at the worst possible moment.

"Here's where the ozone gas is pressed into brick form." Dodge points at the long chain of machines whirring along the left side of the room. "The gas feeds in through the venting system there, where's it's purified. Then the temp goes down to -112 degrees Celsius through them pipes, and the gas goes gooey." He gestures to the series of massive tubing that stretches for dozens of meters toward a tall, boxy machine. The contraption stands close to thirty meters high and runs almost the complete length of the room. "The goo goes in there, and the temp drops even further, gets fashioned into the bricks. Each brick's about half a cubic meter, weighing about one metric ton, and if one o' them popped, you'd feel it on the far side of the station, that's how much wallop they pack. They drop through that shaft you see at the end there, straight down, and get delivered to the factory hangar, where they're loaded into the flyers so they can be deployed into the atmo, and you zoners can keep going to the beach without having to use SPF 200 sunscreen."

"You sure know a lot about how the sausage is made around here," I say.

"You gotta know how things work, luff," Dodge says as we come to a stop at the end of the compression room. He pulls a security card from his jacket pocket. "Everything and everyone. Once you get that wired, you've got a shot."

He gives me a wink as he swipes his pass card across the door's security sensor, but the panel honks—the card's been rejected.

"That's odd," Dodge says, raising an eyebrow. He swipes the card across again, and gets the same honking response. "This should be working." He tries again, with the same response from the security sensor.

"Knock it off. You're going to draw attention to us," I hiss. I look around nervously. Despite the lack of visible security cameras in this area, I still have the uncomfortable feeling that we're being watched. I look across the floor, but there's no one else around. I glance up to the catwalk in the cooling/ventilation system above us—nothing. It's empty. Way too empty.

"Is there another way in?" Cole asks. He's getting anxious as well.

"No," Dodge says. "I'm afraid this is it."

The sensor pings in the affirmative, and it takes me a split second too long to realize that Dodge didn't swipe his card. I try to get Cole's attention, but before I can speak, the door slides open and five men come pouring out. Four of them are large and rough, wearing the same uniforms Bricks and Potter wore. They quickly surround us. The fifth man is of medium height and maximum width. Seriously, he's sporting the kind of girth that demands that you find employment in a lowered gravity environment.

"So's you've deliverated as promised, eh, Dodge?" the man says, a crooked yellow grin on his face. His clothes are remarkably posh compared to anyone else I've seen on the station— pressed white dress slacks, a bright blue dress shirt, and a purple sports jacket with a single button. I even recognize his boots (which seem quite ill-fitted for factory work) from last year's Macydale collection. Despite the quality of the outfit, the man wearing it doesn't match. His greasy dome of a head sports a messy thin comb-over, while several days' worth of stubble spreads unevenly down his cheeks to his collar, which is stained with sweat. All of his clothes stretch with uncertainty around the man's massive frame, threatening to bust loose at any moment. His pants are dingy at the knees.

"Evenin', Guv'na," Dodge says with a wink. "Your delivery, as promised."

"You sold us out?" Cole blurts.

Of course he did. Flip me. Why didn't I see this coming?

"Sorry, mates," Dodge says, clearly not sorry in the slightest. "You seem all right for zoners, but you're worth enough to get me off this rickety bucket once and for all."

"You could have come with us," I say.

Dodge merely shrugs. "Okay, so you're worth a ride plus a little more, monetarily speaking."

"More 'n a little, boy," the Governor tells him. "You'll not be wanting fer much." He unwedges a wrinkled handkerchief from his pants pocket and drags it across his brow—which, despite the chilly temp in here, is dripping with sweat. Then he nods to one of the large thugs, who hands Dodge an envelope. Dodge opens it and examines the contents: a passport book, something that looks like a bundle of different travel tickets, and a green debit card.

"No offense, 'mate,'" I say to Dodge, "but I hope you choke on your thirty pieces of silver."

"A terribly cutting insult, to be sure, luff."

"Cole," I whisper, "now might be a time for some thrilling heroics."

"I don't think so," he replies, gesturing toward the thugs. They're all touting high-powered pistols, ready to give the Swiss cheese treatment to anyone feeling particularly escape-y. I glance back at Dodge, who gives me one of his charming winks and begins to whistle as he walks away from us back the way we came. As he passes behind us, he raises his hand, index finger pointed upward, in one last dismissive farewell gesture. I have to credit Cole for his restraint. Armed goons or not, if I had Cole's quickness and strength, I'd probably leap over and snap Dodge's finger off before doing horrible, horrible things to him with it.

"So, you are our new snoops, intrudicating upon my affairs," the Governor wheezes when Dodge has disappeared for good. He rubs the back of his neck with his handkerchief, then brings it back around and jams it into his pocket, a good three times grosser than it was before. "Now, how a couple of zoners would get curiatized as to the comings and goings upon this most gesticulated spacial institution, that would perforate me most greatly."

There's a long pause as the Governor waits, looking at us expectantly. Finally Cole leans over to me.

"Elvie, we're in luck," he whispers. "I think he's having a stroke."

The Governor harrumphs and begins pacing back and forth in a clearly rehearsed and hilariously miscalculated attempt to look intimidating. If it weren't for the mortal peril we currently find ourselves in, the visual of this zeppelin waddling like a duck and spouting nonsense would be worthy of an autotune vid upload for sure.

"My benefactorous business associates will be most enjoyed upon finding such illicitating trouble-makers brought to their attention. I believe a bonus to our fiduciary concordance will present itself . . . presently."

So Dodge ratted us out only to the locals, which means the Jin'Kai don't know we're here yet. Maybe that gives us a chance, if I play this just right.

"I really don't think you want to do that," I tell the Governor, trying to muster as much cool as I can.

"Oh, do expound upon such statements," he replies with a smirk. "Under what guise of treacherating deceitedness do you boast so?"

"Well, I know you're a big cheese up here and all that," I say. Cool, Elvie. Icy cool. "But I don't think our boss will be too happy to know that you've interfered with us."

"And pray tell, who is your employifier?"

"We're on a special assignment," I say with a shrug. "For Huxtable."

There is a sound of air escaping as the thugs seem to gasp in unison. Even the Governor's smug smile drops, and a new swath of sweat speckles his forehead.

"You work for Hux—Huxtable?" he stammers. He's uncomfortable even saying the name. So, good. The boogeyman works on this lot as well. "Dodge never said anything about that."

"Well, Dodge had no need to know of our affiliation," I say.

The overfilled bowl of saturated fat peers at me through narrowed eyes. "What verifying evidentials do you have?"

"Hey, if you need proof, you can ask the man yourself," I say. And sure enough, that seems like it might be working. The Governor looks around hesitantly at his men, who are busy murmuring to one another.

"I dun want no trouble wit Huxtable," one of them mutters. The others mumble in agreement.

"Das nuf," the Governor says, his mannered speech faltering, if only for a moment. He grabs one of the thugs by the arm. "Go grab Dodge, the little rodent, before he's fled."

The thug holsters his gun and trots toward the front of the facility. One armed assailant down; three to go. Gotta get the odds in Cole's favor.

"You're in over your head with these new 'friends' of yours, 'Guv'na,'" I say, stretching my back in an exaggerated gesture of calm. "You don't understand the people you're dealing with."

"And what would you know about who I'm dealing with?" he says. The handkerchief is back out of his pocket as he furiously mops up his flop sweat again. "They don't cause any trouble. Not one fisticutory disturbance."

"Do you even know what they're doing on your own station?" I ask, laying on the disbelief. "Do you know what you've gotten yourself into?"

"I've no informatives on their practitions!" the Governor says, his eyes bulging in his fat head. "If they've come at odds with Huxtable's dealings—"

"Oh, but they have," I say. "In a big way. And you don't want to make him any angrier than he already is, do you?"

"Boss, mebbe we should cut 'em free," one of the thugs says.

The Governor stands frozen, like the OS in his brain needs a reboot. Maybe, just maybe, this guy is chump enough to buy this bluff long enough for us to—

"No!" he shouts suddenly, his face collapsing into a scowl even less attractive than his normal expression. "Huxtable thinks he calls all the shots here? Not anymore. I have money now. I have muscle behind me. I am the caller of shots. I am the decider!" He pokes the nearest thug in the arm. "Shoot these dregs."

Um, so, bluff backfired. I'm at a loss for a response.

"Shit," Cole says.

That works.

"Boss?" the thug responds, confused. "You's want to war with Huxtable?"

"Huxtable ain't scare me no more! I got uppers on 'im! I'm the real weight around here now," the Governor replies.

"No argument here," I mutter. Which actually gets a snicker out of the thugs.

But snickers don't save lives.

The thug next to the Governor raises his handgun and points it right at Cole. "Hope you's know what you're doin'," he tells his boss.

"Elvie . . . ," Cole says. His muscles are coiled tightly, ready to spring into action. He could probably take the guy out—he might be able to take them *all* out—but he knows as well as I do that there's very little chance that I can survive a firefight unarmed and surrounded. I want to scream for Cole to just go, run, smash everyone's face and break into the Jin'Kai base, find Olivia, save Olivia, go run away and raise her on an island somewhere that doesn't have mosquitoes and make sure she's happy . . .

The first shot is so unexpected that I don't even flinch. There's just a flash and we all stand still for a moment. Then my brain registers what has happened. It occurs to the thug with his gun trained on Cole too. Probably because he's the one who just got shot.

"Run!" one of the others shouts as his comrade collapses, dead, to the floor. More shots rain down from the catwalk above us. I look up to see who's up there playing Rescue Ranger. The shooter is in the shadows, but the green crackle of the energy blasts has a familiar glint to it.

The thugs scatter and take cover in the doorway as the Governor trips over his own fat legs trying to backtrack to safety. He rolls more than falls to the ground, whimpering, as his men grab hold of his purple jacket and pull him inside the cover of the entryway.

"It's Huxtable!" one of them shouts.

"What are you waiting for?" the Governor yells. "Shoot! Shoot! Perforate the transgressitators!" The thugs comply, firing blindly up at the attacker.

"Is it Marnie?" Cole asks as we duck down behind a bulkhead to avoid the cross fire.

"I don't remember her bringing an Almiri ray gun with her," I reply.

A shot strikes one of the coolant valves above us, causing steam to burst out in a violent rush. The shooter moves out of the steam's path, into the light.

"What are you conks waiting for?" the shooter calls. Female. Definitely female. "You don't actually *want* to be dead, do you?"

I look up, but it's not Marnie on the catwalk. It's not even Ducky, reduced to a squealing soprano brought on by the stressful situation.

It's the cheap floozy from the bar that Cole was hitting on.

"Dude," I say to Cole. "Just how much time did you two have to 'chat'?"

"Elvie!" Cole shouts, grabbing my arm to pull me out of the line of another shot. "Gift horse. Mouth."

"The ladder!" the chippie shouts down at us. I look to where she's pointing. A service ladder about a dozen meters behind us, leading to the catwalk. The little tart with the ray gun sends several blasts toward the doorway, forcing the thugs to hide behind their cover. "Now would be a good time!" she screams.

Cole pushes me from behind the bulkhead, and then I'm running like crazy. As soon as I reach the ladder, I grab hold of the first rung, and before I even start climbing, the girl slaps a control panel on the wall above, and the ladder begins to retract up into the ceiling. I scramble to maintain purchase on the rung as I fly upward, but I lose my grip and have to catch hold with the crook of my elbow.

"Cole!" I scream as I rise far above him. The floozy lays down a suppressive cover fire for her new boy toy, and Cole takes off from where he's been crouching, leaping the several meters to catch the bottom of the ladder. He lands against me with a thud and holds me safely in place as we zip the rest of the way up to the catwalk. When the ladder locks into place with a jolt, Cole lets go and drops to the ground, catching me as I release my dodgy grip.

"Cole," the girl says.

(She would just say his name like that.)

"What are you doing here, Chloe?" Cole asks.

(I never really noticed before how dumb a name "Chloe" is.)

"Someone had to save your skins," Chloe responds. "Follow me, pretty boy."

(Not the time, Elvie. So not the time.)

With that, Chloe takes off down the catwalk toward a

coolant system service shaft. "This way," she instructs, like the world's most obvious tour guide. I mean, where else does she think we're going to go? Back down toward the guys trying to shoot our heads off?

"Chloe," Cole calls as we run, heads ducked low, through the shaft. "How did you know I was here? And what are you doing with a gun?"

"You want answers?" Chloe says, leading the way. "Or do you want to get out of here in one piece? A ship?"

"Was that supposed to be a question?" I ask.

"A ship," she repeats over her shoulder, her voice indicating that she thinks *I'm* the chromer in this group. "Do you have one?"

"Our friends have a ship," Cole answers. "They were prepping to leave when we snuck off."

"Well, with any luck we'll catch them before they head off without you," Chloe says. We come up to a magnetically sealed service hatch that requires a pass key.

"And how do you propose we get there?" I ask, pointing to the door.

Chloe smirks (which someone should inform her is not flattering for her face shape) and pulls a pass card out of her pocket. She swipes the access card, and the door *hiss-pops* open.

"It's called being prepared," she says.

If she weren't saving our lives right now, I'd soooo punch her in her stupid teeth.

The service shaft leads to the same processing room we passed through earlier. The scrubbers below us mill about unawares as we scamper overhead. I'm starting to think that we might be able to sneak quietly by, but then my eyes land on Dodge on the factory floor. The guard who had been sent after him is now dragging him by the collar back to the Governor, Dodge kicking and squirming the whole way, pleading his case. That's when he happens to look up, and we lock eyeballs.

"Don't you do it," I whisper under my breath. "You slimy little—"

"Up there!" Dodge screams, pointing right at us. The guard looks up just as his companions run in and join him from the other room. "There they are! It's thems you want, not poor old Dodge!"

"Guys . . . ," I say.

Chloe turns, sees our pursuers, and fires off several shots down in their direction, scattering the scrubbers, who scream while looking for the nearest exit.

"Chloe, what the hell!" Cole shouts, grabbing her arm. "The ozone! You want to blow us to smithereens?"

If Cole's lecturing someone on safety, then you *know* they've pooched it. Even the Governor's men know better than to open fire in this room. Chloe looks around for a split second, then smirks again.

"Good thinking," she says, and before you can say "stupidest idea ever," she takes aim at one of the compressor units that's pushing out bricks, and fires directly on the exhaust grill. The compressor and the ozone feeders connected to it detonate in a chain reaction, setting off a series of massive explosions. Dodge and the Governor's men are instantly evaporated. The force of the blasts knocks me off my feet.

Cole catches me with one hand, his other tightly gripping the rail for support.

"Are you insane?" I shout at Chloe, my hands clasped over my ears. But Chloe doesn't respond—she simply keeps moving across the walkway through to the next service shaft. Cole and I exchange a glance, then follow after her.

The factory is on alert now, sirens blaring, emergency lights casting the entire place in a get-the-flip-out-of-here crimson glow. When the catwalk comes to an end, we run down the wobbly metal stairway to the ground level, where we are met by hundreds of factory workers rushing into the long hallway to the facility entrance.

"Time to blend," says the girl who just fired blasts into exposed ozone.

Chloe, Cole, and I pour out into the inner lobby, mixing with the throng. Several guys who look more like guards than scrubbers are near the entrance by the glass office, trying to stem the tide, searching over the crowd as it floods toward them.

Searching for us.

I stay crouched behind Chloe as the crowd pushes us toward the entrance. With all the commotion, I hope it'll be hard to spot us. Once we're outside, it will be only a matter of getting to the elevators, out of the view of those fancy 360-degree cameras, and praying that Ducky and Marnie haven't decided to leave our asses here for good.

Chloe is the first out the doorway into the outer foyer. As I run to catch up, I spot Potter, spinning on his heels as he scans the area. I'm running right at him—nothing else I can do with the push of so many people behind me. Sure enough, he spots me as I come bearing down on him. Recognition crosses his face, and he reaches for something inside his jacket.

"Here's your cut!" I holler at him, plowing into his groinal area knee-first.

Potter's air escapes him in a high-pitched *woof!* and he collapses onto the ground with me on top of him. I feel Cole lift me by my coveralls with one hand, landing a knockout punch to Potter's face with the other. He doesn't even break his stride as he heads for the exit, dragging me along with him.

Once we're outside, we shift gears, doing our best to stride calmly rather than run. Emergency services are streaming toward the factory—firefighters, medics, etc.—to see to any wounded. Chloe guides us to a bank of lifts that I hadn't noticed before, around a corner and out of the way. A few dozen other scrubbers walk in the same direction.

"What level is your ship on?" Chloe asks me quietly as we ride up. She's tucked her blaster out of sight into the folds of her tunic, and she stands casually with her hand on her hip like she couldn't care less where she was headed or when she'll get there.

"The hangar," I tell her.

"Which hangar?" she presses, the impatience in her voice somehow heightened by her hushed tone.

"I don't know. The big one. Right off that promenade with the crazy marketplace."

"Right. Let's head there straight off. Hopefully, we'll catch your friends before they bail on you."

"They're not bailing on us," I say, annoyed for I don't know what reason. "Well, not really. Technically, you could say we bailed on them."

"Whatever." As Chloe watches the floor indicator above us, I notice her foot tapping unconsciously in time with the thrumming of the lift. I look down at my own feet and realize that I'm doing it as well. I stop and look straight ahead.

"You gonna tell us who you are and why you're helping us?" I ask. "'Cause if this is just a big gesture to get into Cole's pants, I can tell you for a fact that there are easier methods."

Chloe gives me a look that could be read as disgust, bemusement, or possibly gas.

"Let's wait till we're safely on your ship," she says, super-condescending-like. "Then I'll explain everything."

"I think you should tell me now."

"Look, do you want to get your daughter back, or what?"

Boom. A perfectly timed emotional uppercut successfully landed. But if this chick thinks she is going to KO me with one big punch, she hasn't danced in the ring with anyone like Elvie Nara before. I grab her shirt and slam her into the elevator rail.

"How do you know about my daughter?" I shout, inches from her face.

"I know where she's being held," Chloe responds, as calm as a cucumber. The elevator comes to rest and the doors slide open. "I can take you to her. But we need to get to your ship. Now." She removes my hand from her shirt and brushes past me out onto the promenade.

Who *is* this chick?

The promenade is bustling, but no more than it was before. I hear murmurs about an accident inside the ozone factory. As we make our way to the hangar, a name is whispered more than once in quiet, reverential tones.

Huxtable.

"Seriously, who is this Huxtable guy?" I ask, for like the umpteenth time.

"He's not important now," Chloe says. "I'd concern myself with your own situation."

My situation. Olivia. This girl can get me to Olivia. She's right. Nothing else matters right now.

Inside the hangar a PA speaker blares a muffled message.

"Attention. Due to a minor incident on the factory level, all outgoing traffic is suspended to allow emergency vehicles clear airspace. Normal takeoff procedures will recommence shortly. Attention. Due to a minor incident on the factory level . . ."

Seeing our ship still in dock makes me want to reach out and kiss the hull. The outer door slides open, and Ducky rushes out.

"Elvie!" he exclaims, surprise and concern mixed into a panic cocktail all over his face. Only, he's talking not to me but to Chloe, who gives him a small, insincere smile. Ducky does a full-body double take. "Sorry. I thought you were . . . You look a whole lot like . . . Who *are* you?" Then, taking in the announcement over the PA, he turns finally to me. "What did you do?"

No time to answer this one. "This is Chloe," I tell him instead. "She's coming with us."

"We're na' goin' anywhere," Marnie says from behind Ducky. "Thanks to whatever stunt ye two've pulled, the hangar is on lockdown until further notice."

I push my way into the ship and bulldoze my way to the bridge, Cole and Chloe not far behind.

"If they close that door, I'm slamming through it. We're out of here now, or we're never getting free." I sit down in the pilot's seat and start to initiate the takeoff sequence.

"Elvie, enough," Marnie says, placing a hand on my forearm to stop me from reaching the control panels. "Ye cannae keep flyin' off half-cocked."

"Some new information has come to light, so we're changing course. But the plan hasn't changed. We're getting Olivia back."

"Elvie?" I hear Cole squeak behind me. A persistent beeping lurks at the outskirts of my consciousness, but I'm too riled up to pay it much mind. I pull my arm free from Marnie, who simply reestablishes her grip.

"Yer not thinkin' straight, daft girl."

"Get off me, Marnie, or I swear to God . . . ," I start, rising up to go toe-to-toe with her.

"Elvie," Cole says, a little more forcefully.

"Why don't we all calm down?" Ducky says, trying—and failing—to come between me and his girlfriend.

"*Elvie!*" Cole shouts.

"Cole, what?" I say, still not breaking eye contact with Marnie.

"The tracker . . ." That's when I notice the beeping again. "It's going nuts," Cole says.

"For the last time, Cole, you've got to set it to frequency two! You're picking up my signal again."

"No," he says, and his voice is shaky, like I've never heard it before. "I'm not."

I turn to look at him. He is as white as a sheet. And when he holds out the tracker to show me, I see it.

Sure enough, the tracker is picking up a second signal.

"But how?" I say, the threat of tears crackling in my voice. "I mean, where . . ." My voice trails off as I follow the direction of the signal. According to the tracker, our daughter should be right in front of—

"*You*," I breathe.

Chloe stands there, just outside in the center cargo area, smirking at us, and suddenly I start noticing things—her thin, straight black hair, her upturned chin, and even the shape of her eyebrows. It can't be. But it is.

"Olivia," I say.

And then I notice something perhaps even more obvious about her.

"I'm afraid you're all going to have to come with me now," Olivia/Chloe says, her blaster aimed directly at me. "Dr. Marsden will want to see you right away."

Chapter Eight

WHEREIN OUR PLUCKY HEROINE COMPLETELY LOSES HER SHIT

Some days I sleep. Some days I pace. Some days, the days when they decide we have no need for light, I sit in absolute darkness.

Or perhaps it isn't even days. Perhaps I've been here for only a matter of hours and it only feels like an eternity, because I'm losing my mind.

Olivia, my mind wails as I slump against the dark, cold wall for who-knows-how-long. *My baby. What did he DO to her?*

My precious girl. Altered. Grown. Years ripped from her, ripped from me. And it's not even that I wonder *how* it's possible—I've seen Marsden's genetic experiments in action before, when we found Britta's friend's baby in the ruins of the *Echidna*. Bok Choy, an approximately two-week-old infant who looked like he was six years old.

But I wonder *why.* What could possibly possess a monster

like Marsden to take such a perfect, tiny girl like my Olivia and . . .

My thoughts are lost in a storm of wails.

I pound the walls with my fists. I kick the door until I'm sure I've broken toes on both feet. I press my head against the cold metal and I scream until I'm hoarse.

A day passes. Maybe more. Maybe less.

I sleep.

I scream.

I weep in the dark.

Then, after a while, I just lie there.

I'm woken by the door lock clicking and the door sliding open, filling the room with a blinding white light. I guard my eyes with one hand, but still I blink fiercely.

A silhouette appears in the doorway between my eyes and the light—a momentary sanctuary of shadow.

"Elvie?" the voice says, not unkindly. The owner of the silhouette pronounces my name with familiarity, but it is a voice I do not recognize.

I slowly rouse myself from the floor. I am only vaguely aware of the tangles of my hair, the crusts of tears at the corners of my eyes, my nose, my mouth. I am weak, my thoughts and my skin tingly, fuzzy—whether from malnourishment or delirium, I neither know nor care.

I blink up at the man. I can do no more than that.

"I need you to come with me," the voice says. "Can you stand?"

I blink again. No answer. I do not know if I can stand. It doesn't much matter to me.

Her first steps, I think. *I missed her first steps.* I'm not exactly sure what the noise that escapes from my mouth is. It could be crying, laughing, or just air pushing its way out of me in a nervous convulsion. Whatever it is, it gives my captor pause.

He stands still in the doorway for a long while, perhaps waiting for me to stop doing whatever it is that I'm doing.

"Here," he says finally. He bends down, offers his hand. "Let me help you up."

The man helps me up. Or he lifts me completely. I do not know. Not much penetrates the fog. Before I'm aware of it, we have left the dark room and are passing through a long white hallway. I squint as the man helps me along. I am still unaccustomed to the brightness. My feet work, they hold me upright. But only barely.

Where is she? I mean to ask the man. *Can I see her? I need to see her.* But I have forgotten how to speak, or perhaps I've become unable. I try again. *Where?* But the words do not leave my parched throat.

"Ssssh. It's okay, Elvie," the man tells me. "Just concentrate on walking. You're doing a great job."

Who is this man? I was not expecting kindness here. I don't deserve it—not when I've failed my daughter so miserably. My cheeks are wet. I'm crying again.

"Ssssh," the man repeats. He looks around the empty hallway, then softly rubs my back with one hand and, after a pause, begins humming into my ear.

It is a song I know.

I love you, a bushel and a peck.
A bushel and a peck and a hug—

A sob catches in my throat as I place the tune. I look up at the man's face for the first time.

"Hi, Elvie," Bok Choy says to me.

And I am wailing again, although I don't know why.

"Good morning, Elvie."

That's a voice I'd recognize anywhere. My stomach flops inside me as Bok Choy deposits me gently onto an examination table in the center of a white room—face-to-face with none other than the very man who stole my baby girl from me.

Marsden.

Instinctively all the strength in my body pools in my shoulder, and I slap him hard across the face.

He smiles at me.

I turn my head to whimper at Bok Choy, beg him to rescue me from this man, but he is out the door before I can remember how to form the words.

"I'm so glad you came to find me," Marsden tells me.

I think I fall asleep again. Maybe from exhaustion. Maybe I am drugged. I can't know for sure. I'm not sure I care.

"She lives!" Dr. Marsden says with a chuckle as I blink open my eyes again.

I am vaguely aware of a needle in my arm. Is the doctor taking blood from me? Giving me something?

My head droops on my neck, unable to hold itself up.

"We've got to stop meeting like this, Elvie," Marsden says. Which, when it penetrates my brain, makes me think perhaps this is not the first time I've been in this room, needle in my arm. Maybe there have been a dozen times. Maybe more.

How long have I been here? I mean to ask.

"Where?"

That is what I ask instead.

"Ah, so you do have a voice," Marsden says. "I was beginning to worry. You know, Elvie, I've been surprised by you. The others have adjusted to their surroundings quite well. And you, normally so feisty . . ." He clucks his tongue. "But I knew you'd come around." Again that fatherly smile, like he's *proud* of me. "To answer you're question, you are in my laboratory. Would you like to hear my mad-scientist laugh?" Another chuckle. "You can't know how happy I was to see you, Elvie. Apart from your general witty demeanor—these past several visits notwithstanding, obviously—I was in dire need of your DNA. After your mother—"

I have found my voice. "Where is she?" I croak out.

Marsden's face is a dark cloud. "That one? Run away. Gone. And good riddance."

That wasn't what I meant, I want to say. *Olivia. Where is my baby?*

But my words are caught in my throat again, and Marsden is back to his jovial self. "But let's talk about something more pleasant, shall we? It was so kind of you to bring me a plethora of DNA to add to my research. I can't tell you how unfortunate it was that my comrades failed to preserve any viable Almiri samples at the compound in the mountains."

"You slaughtered them," I say, slowly finding my voice. "The Almiri." *You're a monster.* But I don't have enough breath for the last sentence.

"Now with Mr. Archer here," he continues, ignoring me, "I have a small hope of isolating the gene I've been searching for." He pulls the needle from my arm. "So thank you again, Elvie, for that."

Cole. Cole is here. And perhaps the others, too.

"Where is she?" I ask.

This time the reply comes from the doorway.

"She's muttering," the voice says. "Want me to knock her out again?"

I turn, as best I can, and the small movement sends my brain spinning. When I steady myself and focus my vision, I take her in.

Chloe.

Olivia.

My baby.

I almost collapse to the floor. The other figure in the doorway—Bok Choy, I think—leaps to my aid and catches me just in time, righting me on the exam table. I try to reach out a hand to my daughter, but I don't think I manage.

I am going fuzzy again.

I close my eyes, try to focus my thoughts. "What did you do to her, you . . . you . . ." The words are nearly mush in my mouth.

Although I am fading, I can hear the smile in Marsden's voice.

"Remarkable, isn't it?" he says.

• • •

I am back in the hallway, walking, along with the help of Bok Choy and Olivia. *Chloe,* I think. *She's Chloe now. Not Olivia.* It's hard to think of them as the same person, even though I can tell they are. Same button nose, only less button-like. Same curved earlobes, only bigger.

Chloe.

As I pull out of the fog, I realize that my two guards have been talking.

"You should be kinder to her," Bok Choy is telling Chloe. I think he means me. "She's not so bad."

Beside me Chloe snorts. "When she's unconscious," she replies. But I turn just in time to see the look she gives him when he's not watching. She studies him carefully, a hint of a smile on her otherwise steely face.

"She's been through a lot," Bok Choy replies as he buzzes open the door to what I assume is my cell. "None if this is her fault. Being cruel to her doesn't further our goal."

And Chloe's eyes are soft, watching him. "I'll think about it," she says.

She has her father's eyes.

As Bok Choy deposits me in my cell, I get one last glance at Chloe. She makes some joke I don't catch to Bok Choy, raising a thick, arched eyebrow.

She has my eyebrows.

I rise to my feet, without even noticing the strain in my muscles. Grown or not, altered or mutated or I-don't-care-what, that is still my baby girl. And I'm her mother.

"Chloe," I say—but the door is already shut in front of me by the time I get the word out.

• • •

I do not sit.

I do not pace.

I do not sleep.

I do not weep.

That girl on the other side of the door is my daughter. And whatever the cost, I'm going to get her out of here.

Chapter Nine

WHEREIN OUR HEROINE'S WORST NIGHTMARE (NOT INCLUDING THE ONE WHERE SHE HAS TO PERFORM AN ELABORATE ICE-SKATING DANCE SHE HASN'T REHEARSED, TO THE TUNE OF "SEXY AND I KNOW IT") COMES TRUE

"All right, now. This will be the last sample we take today. Sound good?"

As Dr. Marsden guides the needle under my skin, his voice is as gentle and reassuring as someone who wasn't holding me captive and performing a series of invasive tests on my person.

"You've taken, like, six vials already," I mutter. "I hope you've got a sugar cookie hidden away somewhere."

"We'll make sure you're replenished."

By "replenished" Marsden means more needles—the kind where stuff goes *into* your arm as opposed to being drawn *out* of it.

"I bet people wouldn't mind your taking over the world so much if you guys had sugar cookies."

Marsden chuckles and shakes his head. "I do so prefer you this way," he says, a please-kick-me-in-the-teeth level of obnoxious smile on his face.

"What, you mean lucid?"

"I was going to say 'chipper,' but why split hairs?"

"Quick question," I say. "I mean, not that I'm not enjoying all this blood-taking and awesome bonding time with my baby's kidnapper, because, whew boy, it's been a hoot! But, uh, you mind sharing why you still haven't cracked the secret to hybrid fertility, even after all this time? I thought you were supposed to be a mad genius."

Marsden doesn't seem offended in the slightest. "Even mad geniuses must work through the science to reach their goals."

"So how come I get to have all the needle-pointy fun? Why do the others miss out?" This is my supersneaky way to try to figure out what Marsden has done with my friends.

"Don't worry. Mr. Archer has had his fair share of needle pokes."

So Cole's still alive, and even if they're poking and prodding him, that's a good thing. But . . .

"What about Ducky?"

"Ducky?" Marsden asks. Like I just ordered something that wasn't on the menu. I feel my stomach go icy.

"Donald?" I say. "Floppy hair? Skinny arms? Probably barfed a few times by now?"

"Ah, yes. Your human comrade. He's here. But what use would I have for his DNA?"

I settle down a bit. Ducky's alive. "So Duck gets a free pass from all these good times just for being normal? That hardly seems fair—not that I'm suggesting you start poking him, too."

"I'm looking for an evolutionary breakthrough for a superior species. I don't have time to muddle with apes. And to save you some more sleuthing, your redheaded hybrid friend is alive as well. Her samples are a helpful baseline to compare yours against. So no one's been executed. Does that satisfy you?"

"I suppose," I say. "Unless you're still considering my offer to have you surrender?" The snort from the doorway belongs to Chloe, who has been standing quietly at attention since she brought me here from my cell. I pretend to ignore her, even though what I'm saying is as much for her benefit as Marsden's, if not more so. "You know the Jin'Kai leadership will never understand what you're trying to do here. You could come with us."

"Come with you?" Marsden lets out a snort of his own. "To where? Another Almiri prison?"

"I'm guessing it'd be better than getting sliced up by Devastators, or Kynigos, or whatever the hell you want to call them. Who knows? In time maybe you and the Almiri could work together to find a way to help *both* of you."

"You seem to miss the point of what I'm trying to do here, Elvie," Marsden says. "The point is not to help everyone. It's to help me. My people. I don't care one wit about any of the rest of it, one way or the other. Hybrids, humans, Almiri, it makes no difference to me whether any of you live or die. I will be the savior of the Jin'Kai people. That's all that matters."

"If that were what you really believed," I say, wincing as he pulls the needle out of my arm and slaps a gel patch over the wound, "then you'd be looking for allies, instead of seeing enemies everywhere. You aren't a messiah. Hell, you're not even a patriot. You're a genocidal, racist piece of—"

I don't get to finish the epithet, because that's when Chloe clocks me across the jaw, sending me flying off the exam table onto the floor.

"Shut your filthy mouth, mutt," she hisses at me.

"That's quite enough," Marsden snaps, his voice slicing through the room like a knife. Chloe freezes up and stands at attention.

"Apologies, Doctor," she says. "I only meant—"

"Be quiet. Act out again and there will be punishment. Do I make myself crystal clear?"

"Yes, sir."

Chloe resumes her place by the door, her face sullen and red with shame, and Marsden lifts me up to my feet and guides me back to the table. He holds my head in his hand, examining my jaw.

"I'm fine," I tell him.

"I'll be the judge of that," he replies. He gestures toward Chloe. "You'll have to forgive it."

"'It'?" I say, pulling away from him. "That's my daughter, asshole."

"No, I'm not," Chloe shoots back.

"Look." I wrench my head around on my neck to face my daughter in the doorway. "They may have stolen you away, experimented on you, and filled your head with nonsense, but I *gave birth* to you, dammit. You literally shot out from my down below."

"And thank you so much for the imagery," she sneers.

"You really want to stay here? He just called you an 'it.'"

"I will play an important role in the future of the Jin'Kai

people," Chloe tells me, as if she's reading from a pamphlet.

"Oh, and what role is that? Is there a cheerleading team on this station? Because no daughter of mine is ending up a cheerleader."

When Chloe replies, there is more than a hint of pride in her voice. "I will host a new test subject, one with the engineered potential to save the Jin'Kai from extinction."

That's it. I snap. Snap hard. I'm on top of Marsden, clawing at his face. "You're going to make her a breeder, like you tried to do with me?" I screech. "She's not livestock, you rotten son of a bitch. *I'm* not livestock. We're *people.*"

Marsden easily lifts me away from him, and it's Chloe who roughly slams me facedown on the table and binds my hands behind my back.

"Ah, but that's where you're wrong, Elvie," Marsden informs me coolly. "You were always livestock. Up until now you've just been free-range."

"If you think for a second that I'll allow you to violate my daughter like you did all those other poor girls—"

"No one's violating anyone," Chloe says, spinning me around. "I will be paired with a suitable partner, and I will nourish his offspring."

"Jesus Christ," I spit. "Chloe, don't listen to another word this man tells you, please, I'm begging you." Pain I can handle. Needles? Tests? Do whatever you want to me, Marsden. Just leave my poor daughter out of it. "You don't have to be *paired* with anybody. You should get to be a normal kid. Go ask Bok Choy out for a Coke or something, if he's the one you like, but don't wait for this shit monster to *pair* you."

I can see from the way Chloe flinches that I've inadvertently hit a nerve. Meanwhile, Marsden's too busy looking smug. "I had forgotten your charming nickname for our little friend from the *Echidna*," he tells me. "But don't fear, Chloe. That creature would never be your match. He's far too rudimentary a subject to use for our purposes." He's jotting down notes on his lap-pad, about my samples, I'd wager. Hardly giving either of his "livestock" and our futures any mind. "I hadn't yet analyzed your hybrid DNA when I first started growing that one," he continues. "I hadn't even solved the decay problem at that point."

"Decay?" I say the word, but I can see in Chloe's confused face that the question is on her mind as well. "What do you mean? Bok Choy will . . ."

"Yes, in that first generation of subjects the gene accelerator unfortunately causes their cellular structures to break down fairly rapidly. The life span is far too short to create desirable offspring. Hardly a trait I want contaminating the results of future testing."

When Chloe sees me looking at her, she turns quickly away and wipes at her face as stealthily as she can.

"I'm sorry," I say softly.

"It's all right," Marsden replies. "I corrected the flaw in the second generation. There were some promising results with that round as well, as with the third and fourth. Soon enough I'll have a match suitable for you."

"Me?" I ask, jolted out of my empathetic mother-daughter mind-meld.

"Of course," Marsden says. "You. This one. The redhead.

I'll need all the reusable hosts that I can get. Time is running out, after all."

As Chloe leads me back to my cell, she walks with her head high, staring stonily ahead. But the wetness around her eyes doesn't lie.

Maybe I've found a crack in her armor.

"I really am very sorry," I tell her.

"Shut it," she snaps.

"Marsden's a monster," I tell her. "You can see that, can't you? He's *brainwashed* you, Chloe. You're a whole person, not some sort of breeding sow to be used up and discarded. You're not even Chloe. You know that, right? Your name's Olivia." She squeezes painfully on my arm, but still I keep talking. "We could find a way out of here," I say, my voice low. "There's a way, I'm sure of it. My mother escaped. We can too. Get home somehow."

"I said, *silence*," she tells me, wrenching my arm again.

"If he's so blasé about Bok Choy's life," I gasp through the pain, "what do you think he'll do with you once you're not useful to his research anymore? Or your baby?"

"It doesn't matter," she says. "So long as it's in the service of the Jin'Kai empire."

"You cannot be this stupid," I groan. "Not with half my genes."

She stops dead in her tracks and shoves me against the wall.

"Listen, mutt. The doctor said not to hurt you again, but there's *all kinds* of things that I could do to you that he'd never notice. Understand me?"

She's trying to sound tough, but her voice is trembling. I can feel the hurt coursing through her. *My poor baby*, I think. *I'm so sorry I couldn't stop them from doing this to you.*

"Look, you're confused, I understand, but I'm your mother. I can help you. Maybe if we could get out of here, we could even help—"

"What's going on here?"

We both turn to see Bok Choy standing in front of us, his arms crossed over his chest.

"Nothing," Chloe says, straightening up. "Just returning the prisoner to her cell."

"It doesn't look like nothing," he says. He approaches us and notices the swelling on the side of my face where Chloe hit me. He gives Chloe a harsh glance.

"Chloe . . ."

"Just . . . get out of my way!" she blurts out. Pulling me along, she brushes past Bok Choy.

I don't say anything the rest of the way. In her current state she wouldn't even hear me if I tried.

But I'm not done trying yet, *Olivia*.

"Think, Elvie," I mutter to myself as I pace the room. *"Think, think, think."*

The door lock clicks open and distracts me from what I'm sure was about to be an absolutely brilliant escape plan. I back up against the far wall in a defensive position. What could they possibly want with me again so soon? They just extracted who-knows-how-much genetic-material-slash-unsavory-inside-fluids. I doubt there's anything useful left in me at this point.

The door slides open, and Bok Choy steps into the room. A duffel bag is slung over one shoulder.

"You going somewhere?" I ask him. "Do evil alien commandos get sleepovers?" I look past him into the hallway, but Bok Choy is alone this time. I rub the sore spot on my upper arm. "What do they want now? Don't tell me Marsden's discovered a way to save his species with my spit."

Bok Choy motions toward the door silently.

"What? Come on, speak. I know you can. You've learned quite a bit of English since I saved your life on the *Echidna*."

Again he motions me toward the door without saying a word.

"I'm sorry, sweetie," I say, folding my arms across my chest, "but stubborn crankiness is about all I have left at the moment, so I'm going to have to insist that you convey your evil alien demands to me out loud. I'm in no mood for pantomime."

Bok Choy leans his head back out into the hallway, looking side to side. I notice for the first time that he isn't holding his weapon—it's holstered at his hip with the clip fastened tightly.

"What's going on?" I ask. There's a feeling of anticipation rising in my gut, and I can't tell if it's hope or fear. Either way, it's a good thing they don't feed me much in here, or I'd be ready to yak all over the place. Bok Choy moves to me quickly, a nervousness in his step. He leans in, and for a split second I think he's going to kiss me, which would be all kinds of weird, since it wasn't that long ago that I saw his six-year-old didjeridoo.

"I'm here to rescue you," he whispers into my ear.

I jerk my head back and stare at him. His face is just as terrified as his voice, and his eyes are bulging wide. His chest moves up and down rapidly. It's the first time I've seen one of these superaliens even close to hyperventilating.

"You're here to res—" I start, before Bok Choy clamps a hand over my mouth.

"Shh!" he shout-whispers. "We don't have much time. There's about to be a guard shift in five minutes, and I think we might have a chance of getting you all out of here."

"Why are you doing this?" I ask. If I sound suspicious, it's because I totally am. (Although, to be honest, I cannot fathom what could be in it for Marsden to attempt to trick us like this. He might be a megalomaniacal madman, but mind-dickery just for the sake of it doesn't seem like his style.)

"I don't know a lot," Bok Choy says. "I mean, I'm learning things, but it's all very fast and confusing. I know I haven't . . . been here very long. I know there are things I can't understand yet . . . but there are things I just know. No, that's not the right word. Things I . . . *feel*."

Bok Choy takes the bag from his shoulder and hands it to me. I open it and find a spiffy zip-front sheath jacket. I slip the jacket on right away, immediately appreciating the warmth of the fabric. I hadn't realized how cold I'd been in here.

"It fits perfectly," I marvel, stretching out my arms. "How did you—"

"I've got an eye for sizes," Bok Choy replies with a shrug.

"But"—I switch over to a slightly more important topic of conversation—"aren't you going to get in a lot of trouble for this? Like, the kind of trouble that gets you dead?"

Bok Choy examines the floor as he speaks. "The doctor . . . ," he begins. "He tells us things. How he says things are. I've listened to him, and I've believed him, because, I don't know, I just have? Like there was no reason not to. I had no choice. But the things he's done here, the things he's doing. The things I've helped him with. None of it seems right. But you . . ." And that's when he looks up at me. "You sang to me. You're the only one who's ever done that. You sang to me when I was scared, and showed me kindness. Yours is the only kindness I have ever known."

Who says show tunes can't unite warring nations?

Without really thinking what I'm doing, I reach out and touch Bok Choy's cheek. It's a very motherly gesture, I realize.

Hard to believe you don't have much time left, I think, remembering what Marsden told me about Bok Choy's "viability." But I say nothing. I have a strong suspicion that the poor kid doesn't know.

"I think I figured out what my daughter sees in you," I tell him instead.

Bok Choy cocks his head to the side like a confused puppy. "Huh?"

"Nothing. We should go. Get the others."

Bok Choy nods. "Here." He hands me a pair of nifty Jin'Kai manacles. "This way."

We come out into the hall and make our way quickly down the corridor. I keep my hands crossed in front of me, the cuffs loosely placed around my wrists so that to a passing baddie it'll look like I'm a prisoner being transported. Bok Choy keeps a grip on my arm. When we turn a corner, we both freeze for a split second, hearing footsteps. But whoever the footsteps belong to is traveling away from us, so we continue on.

There are five cells lining the left wall, three of them with a solid red light above the doorway. Doors I've passed at least a dozen times now, wondering if any of my friends might be trapped inside. Sure enough, Bok Choy taps the wall console, and all three cell doors hiss and slide open, their red lights flashing blue. Marnie pops out of the first cell, and if she's surprised to see us, she does a good job of hiding it. I guess in her world there's rarely any time for explanations during life-and-death situations.

"What's going on? How did you get out?" Cole says as he sticks his head out of the far cell and sees us.

The center cell is quiet. No movement. I feel a growing lump of ice form in the pit of my stomach.

"Ducky?" I call. No answer.

I rush past Marnie and ignore Cole as he steps into the hallway, still confused by his sudden emancipation. I clamor down the two steps into the middle cell, expecting the worst. Or worse.

I find Ducky lying stretched out on his side on the hard metal bed slab jutting out of the far wall. He's resting his head in one hand, with the other draped over his hip. He's looking right at me, and the smirk on his face is tight and twitchy, like he's trying with all his might not to burst into a great big moony smile.

"Aren't you a little short for a storm trooper?" he asks, his voice one step away from a giggle.

I could pop him in the mouth, but he's just so happy at the moment that I don't have the heart.

"Ye wretched scamp!" Marnie chastises as she brushes past me into the cell. Ducky rises slowly from the bed, and I can tell he's in pain. They must have done a number on him at some point—doing what, I'd rather not know.

"You okay?" I ask.

Ducky waves me off like he gets tortured by space invaders all the time. "I'm just glad it was you this time," he replies. "The last ten times, the guards didn't think it was funny."

I move to Ducky's side opposite from Marnie, and we help lift him gingerly to his feet. All my friends are alive. I will count myself lucky.

"I don't reckon I'll ever understand yer particular brand of humor," Marnie says, looking at the two of us as we step out into the hallway.

"After the world doesn't end, I've got about a hundred flat pics for you to watch," Ducky tells her.

"Elvie, what's the plan?" Cole asks as he takes my place at Ducky's side, shouldering the brunt of the weight. Cole examines my handcuffs, and then Bok Choy.

"Who's this?" he asks.

"Cole, it's Bok Choy. Little naked boy from the *Echidna*?"

"Holy shit," Cole whistles. "You don't still bite, do you?"

"I, uh, no? Not recently," Bok Choy stammers.

"Can we trust him?" Cole asks me.

"We can trust him. We need to get out of here, see if we can find the ship. Hopefully it's where we left—"

"Halt right there!" a voice shouts at us from down the hallway. Three Jin'Kai guards are running toward us, weapons drawn. "What's the meaning of this?"

"Uh, prisoner transfer," Bok Choy says, reaching to his belt. "I have the order right here."

"Stay that hand, freak," the lead guard says, sticking his weapon right in Bok Choy's face. So I guess the prejudice against Marsden's pet projects extends even to his own loyal men. I can see why he's reluctant to have his superiors see his work before he has acquired the desired results. Bok Choy reluctantly moves his hand away from the blaster at his hip. The guard looks over his shoulder to the other guards. "Call it in. Let's see what Marsden—"

Before the dude can finish, Bok Choy has knocked the gun out of his hand and fallen on him. Cole springs into action immediately, ditching Ducky and leaping at one of the other guards. You can just tell that all this imprisonment has left Cole aching for a good fight, because I don't think he's ever whaled on anybody so enthusiastically. The third Jin'Kai turns his gun on Ducky, who immediately crumples to the floor—which seems to confuse the hell out of the guard. He looks up at Marnie for a split second in his confusion, giving Ducky the opening I *guess* he was looking for. In a move way more bold and coordinated than I ever would've expected of him, Ducky jumps across the floor and tries to leg-tackle his would-be attacker. The guard is thrown off balance for a brief second, and in that time Marnie does a nifty jump-kick move, popping his gun out of his grip and onto the floor. The guard counters with a backhand slap that sends Marnie crashing into the wall, dazed. Then he pulls one leg free from Ducky and kicks him hard in the stomach, eliciting a pitiful yelp.

Cue Elvie's turn to play the hero.

I lean down to reach for one of the fallen weapons—only to realize that the cuffs that I had loosely draped over my wrists have *actually locked into place*, the coiled metal bands giving me less than fifteen centimeters of leeway. My momentary hesitation gives the guard a chance to grab me by the arm and toss me hard at the wall. I land on Marnie—lucky for me but not for her. If she wasn't out cold before, she certainly is now. I decide to pull a classic Ducky and feign my own unconsciousness, which seems to work. Through the slits of my eyelids I see the guard swivel in place, trying to remove Ducky from his ankle.

That's when I spring up, jumping as high as I can and wrapping my manacled hands around the dude's throat. With all my might I pull back, pressing the bands deep into his neck. He jerks back, instinctively reaching for the cuffs in an attempt to pry them away. I press my knee hard into his back, using the leverage to really go for gold. The guard's gagging, unable to get any air, and his whole head goes red, the veins in his forehead throbbing.

It dawns on me in that moment that I am actively strangling another person, with the closest thing to my bare hands that I could get without leaving fingerprints on his throat. And I falter—just enough for the guard to get his fingers underneath the bands. Rather than thanking me for my momentary flash of humanity/mercy/what have you, once the Jin'Kai has a solid grip on the cuffs, he lifts them (and me) up, flipping me over his head and down hard onto my back.

Now I'm the one with the wind knocked out of me. Free from Ducky's grasp, the guard dashes to pick up his gun. But as his hand brushes across the weapon, he is tackled from behind by Bok Choy. Unfortunately for our plucky little gang, the guard is low to the ground, and Bok Choy comes in too fast. The guard easily uses Bok Choy's momentum to slide past him, scooping up the weapon and spinning around to line up a shot.

The crackle of energy sings through the air, and sends the guard flailing from the wound in his chest. I look up from my spot on the floor to see Bok Choy's savior—expecting it to be Cole, or Marnie, or perhaps Ducky (hey, anything is possible). Instead I see everyone in our little melee, including the remaining two Jin'Kai guards, frozen in place, staring at Chloe, her weapon still raised, standing only a few paces away.

The girl sure knows how to make an entrance.

"What are you doing?" one of the other guards asks. Not the most famous of last words, but they'll have to do, because with two more dead-on shots from Chloe, that's the end of our last two adversaries. Well, original adversaries.

"Chloe?" Bok Choy says, hunched in a crouched position amidst the pile of dead Jin'Kai. "Put the gun down, Chloe."

Chloe does not comply. Instead she shifts her aim and points the gun right at me.

"You," she says. Her voice is as still and cold as ice. "If I let you go, you'll take him with you? You'll be able to help him?"

Everyone looks between the two of us. Except for Marnie, of course, since she's out cold. I stand up very slowly. It's still hard to breathe, and I take little gasps in an attempt to build up a reserve of air.

"I . . . don't . . . even know . . . what they . . . did . . . to him," I say. When you've got an unstable person pointing a gun at you, the truth is usually your best strategy to remain unshot.

Chloe straightens her gun arm, making her gun more pointy-at-me'd than it already was. "*Will you help him?*" she asks again.

"What are you talking about?" Bok Choy says. He's edging carefully toward Chloe, probably in an attempt to put himself between the two of us.

"I'll try everything I can," I say. "I can't promise any more than that without being a liar."

"Everything in your power," Chloe presses.

"In my power, and in the considerably greater power of my friends."

Chloe lowers her gun and turns back down the hallway from which she came. "Come on, then. Let's get going."

Bok Choy gives me a curious look, then trots after Chloe. Cole has picked Marnie up off the ground, with Ducky uneasily supporting her head in an attempt to be helpful.

"What was that all about?" Cole asks me.

"Not now, Cole," I say.

"But who does she want you to help?"

"Not *now*, Cole."

We all make it to the end of the hallway, but then Chloe breaks left as Bok Choy heads to the right.

"Wait," Bok Choy tells her. "This way."

"Their ship is up on the factory subhangar," Chloe replies, looking over her shoulder but not breaking her stride. "Marsden gave it to the Governor as payment for my shooting his men."

"Well, at least it's closer than we thought," I say.

But Bok Choy still won't move. "Chloe, we have to get the others," he says.

"There's no time," she answers.

"Wait," I say, stopping dead in my tracks. "What others?"

"There's no time. We have to go now."

"What. Others?"

Chloe harrumphs and folds her arms across her chest in a pretty dead-on me impersonation. At least it would be if she realized she were doing it. She looks at Bok Choy expectantly.

"The other girls," Bok Choy tells me.

The words hit me like a ton of bricks. The other girls. Could it possibly be the girls from the Hanover School? Ramona. Natty. Maybe even . . .

"Where are they?" I ask Bok Choy. "How many of them are here?"

"You're wasting your time with that lot," Chloe says. "It's too risky. Not worth it."

I take a few steps toward her and jab my finger into her chest to emphasize every crucial point. "Now, you listen to me, you little brat. I don't have time to completely deprogram the Jin'Kai propaganda that Marsden's brainwashed you with, but know this—Every. Single. Person. Is. *Worth it.* You follow? A human life—a woman's life—whoever they may be, is every bit as important as those *you'd* risk everything for. *Comprende?*"

Chloe looks at her feet and mumbles something.

"I can't hear you," I snap.

"I said *all right,*" she mumbles more loudly. "Jeez." She turns to Bok Choy. "If we're going to get them, let's get moving already."

"This way," Bok Choy says, and we all follow. I bring up the rear with my bratty-ass daughter.

"Someday you'll understand," I tell her.

"Whatever," she replies.

Teenagers.

Suddenly the floor rocks underneath us, and we find ourselves in complete darkness.

"Now what?" Ducky cries behind me.

As soon as the words are out of his mouth, backup lights illuminate the hallway in a dim, bluish hue. The hairs on the back of my neck stand up, tingling.

"A trick of yours?" I ask Bok Choy.

"No," he says.

"It's like before," Chloe says. "When the other hybrid escaped. She sabotaged the security systems by overloading the power grid. It lasted only ten minutes or so, but that was all she needed. Crafty for a mule."

"Don't call her that," I say, spinning around on Chloe. "That's your grandmother you're talking about. She's not a mule; she's an Enosi. And so am I. And so are you. If you want to call the woman anything, call her 'grandma.' Or 'lying, double-crossing bitch' works too. But never, *ever* 'mule.'"

"Sorry," Chloe tells me, rolling her eyes.

I look around in the dim light. "So who do you think's trying to escape now?" I ask the group. "Besides us, I mean."

"I don't know," Chloe replies. "But if it puts the whole base on high alert, then we're in trouble." She jerks her head toward Bok Choy. "Let's hurry up and grab the ditzes so we can get out of here already."

With Bok Choy in the lead, we make our way to the next detention area over, identical to the one we just left. There are five cell doors along the wall, but only one has a red "locked" light on. I follow Bok Choy directly to the door.

"I thought you said there were girls," I say. "As in plural."

"There are," Bok Choy tells me. "Marsden keeps them all in here."

Bok Choy punches the key code into the wall console, but nothing happens.

"It's stuck," he mutters. "The power, I guess." He grips the door and starts trying to pull it, even though there's no edge to grab. Cole lays Marnie gently down on the ground and lends Bok Choy a hand. Between the two of them, with their other-worldly alien strength, they manage to move the door exactly zero millimeters.

"*Boys,*" I say with a sigh. "Chloe, you have anything that could jimmy this panel loose?"

"Step back," she says. And it's a good thing I do, because before the words are even out of her mouth, she has unslung her gun and fired off one precisely aimed shot to the immediate right of the console, sending sparks flying and blasting a clean hole through the metal plating. I pry the remaining fragments away to create a gap, giving me access to the wiring behind the panel.

"Okay. One second," I say, fiddling blindly.

"Careful," Chloe tells me. "You'll fry yourself." She hands me a pair of thin rubbery gloves from the pocket of her uniform.

"Thanks." I slip the gloves on and resume my work. Chloe slips in beside me, and together we piece through the wiring. I'm happy to learn that in addition to my smart mouth, Chloe has inherited at least a few of my other qualities.

"There," I say as the light above the door surges with a *vwoop!* This time, rather than switching from red to blue, the light blinks out completely.

"Um, Elvie, the door is still locked," Cole says.

"Wrong," I inform him. "The door is still *closed.*"

Chloe and I exchange a glance and push against the door, much as Bok Choy and Cole did before—only, this time the dead door slides, with some resistance, into the wall.

"Voila," I say. "Open sesame, and such."

Inside, the room is completely dark. I peek inside.

"Hello?"

There is some low murmuring. Shadows flicker in the corners.

"It's all right," I say softly. "It's me. It's Elvie. We've come to rescue you guys. One more time, with feeling."

"Elvie?" comes a voice along the back left wall—but it's not said in recognition. It's as if the girl has never heard my name before.

Oh God, I think. *What have they done to these girls?* Because the voice, it's one I know all too well. And the name attached to it is *certainly* not one I'd ever forget.

"It's me, Britta," I say quietly. "We're going." Shockingly, I don't even feel annoyed at the thought that Britta McVicker—world's most obnoxious cheerleader and Cole's former girlfriend—is alive and well. Score one for personal growth!

"Going?" says another voice from the other side of the room.

Another eerily familiar voice.

"Um, yeah," I say. The hair on the back of my neck prickles once more, and I have not yet figured out why. "Come on, guys. Stop hiding back there. It's all right. We're getting you all out of here and going home."

"Home?" says another voice straight ahead of me. Or was that Britta again? "What is home?"

"Give me a light," I call to my friends behind me. The prickling has quickly morphed into nausea, creeping into my throat.

Behind me Bok Choy flashes a small LED lamp, chasing the shadows away with a harsh, cold light. And all at once I have an irrepressible need to puke my metaphysical guts out.

I am standing in a room, surrounded by more than a dozen girls.

And they're all Britta.

Chapter Ten

IN WHICH IT SEEMS EVERYONE HAS SOMETHING TO SAY ABOUT OUR HEROINE'S EX–BOYFRIEND'S BUTT

It's just a dream, I tell myself, eyes shut as tightly as I can force them. *A bad dream. A really, really, really bad dream.*

But when I open my eyes, they're all still here. It's not a dream, or a trick of the light, or some sort of stress-headache-induced hallucination. I am surrounded on all sides by Brittas. At least twelve exact duplicates of my least favorite person-who's-not-actively-trying-to-kill-me in the world. This is a new low, even for a lunatic like Marsden. I mean, homicide? That's bad. Attempted genocide? Not good at all. Imprisoning and torturing innocent young women? Really frowned upon.

But an *army of Brittas*?

The man must be stopped.

"What's the matter, Elvie?" Ducky calls from the hall behind me. "Are you okay in there?"

"Who's that?" a Britta asks, taking a tentative step forward and craning her head to try to see into the hallway.

"Are you taking us for more tests?" another Britta joins in.

"I just had my test," pouts a third Britta. "Please don't make me go back so soon."

Another Britta feels the need to chime in. "Your hair . . . did you make it look that way on purpose?"

"Can't we gag them or something?" Chloe asks me seriously. "Before we get permanently dumber from listening to them?"

Looks like my daughter and I might have more in common than I feared.

"We need to go, Brit—er, *ladies*," I say, trying to reassemble the toppled Jenga tower that is my brain. "We're getting you out of here."

"What's a britterlady?" one asks.

"Why are we leaving?" asks another.

"Who are you?"

"What's wrong with your face? You look like you smelled something bad. Did you smell something bad?"

From there things turn into a cacophony of Britta babble, each of the identical hell beasts bombarding me with questions and accusations that weave in and out of one another so unintelligibly that soon I hear nothing but one long hum of shrill, entitled, and apparently amnesiac voices.

"Look, just shut up!" I finally shout. "We've got to go, like, *now*." You'd think at this point I'd be more adept at explaining to a large group of imprisoned teenage girls why we need to get off a spaceship, but I find myself a tad flustered. And nothing I say stops them from whining at me.

That's when Cole decides to step into the room to see what all the fuss is about.

"Elvie?" he says. "What is going—*whoa*."

"Cole," I say. He's fallen into the same stupefied trance I just found myself in, but we really don't have the time to play out these reactions one at a time. There's still the matter of getting out of here un-murdered. I snap my fingers at him. "Cole!"

Suddenly I realize that the Britta Brigade has fallen silent. And it's not because of my authoritative tone.

"Cole?" one of the Britta's says, the question hanging in the air like a hopeful, half-remembered dream. Every girl is now staring intently at Cole, who manages to close his mouth just long enough for one comically perfect gulp.

"Um, hi," he says awkwardly.

"*Cole* . . . ," another says with a sigh.

And then, in perfect, horrific unison, the Brigade bursts into terrifying, synchronized smiles.

"*Cole-eeeeeeee!*"

As the Brittas swarm around Cole, chattering like Brittas are wont to do, I am reminded of an old recording we once watched in history class of a band called the Beatles trying to escape a rabid crowd of young female fans, who were chasing and pawing at them with unbridled passion. This is exactly like that, only 300 percent more vomit-inducing.

The Brittas engulf Cole like a school of piranhas. I'm half afraid that when they finally swim off, there will be nothing left but Cole's head on top of a cleanly picked skeleton.

"Amazing," Bok Choy says. I didn't even notice him stepping into the room. "They know him."

"Well, he did date her back on Earth," I say. "I mean, one

of them, at least." Then I ask the obvious question. "How are there so many of them? Of *her*?"

Bok Choy winces as the Brigade squeals en masse, having just (re?)discovered how cute Cole's butt is. "The doctor needed . . . a controlled environment," he tells me. "To incubate his experiments. And he found himself with a limited number of hosts."

That's when I notice that one of the Brittas, sporting a thin tank top, has a dark letter *K* tattooed on her right shoulder.

Another sports a *D*.

And yet another, an *H*.

Clones.

"He couldn't have cloned literally *anyone* else?" I ask. "Was Lizzie Borden not available?"

"We have to go," Chloe reminds me, interrupting the shiver that is making its way down my spine. "Either you find some way to herd them, or we leave all their asses here. I won't bother telling you which option I prefer."

As much as I hate to argue for a world in which we actively attempt to rescue a dozen photocopies of my least favorite cheerleader, after my little "Everyone is worth it" speech earlier I don't seem to have much choice.

"Excuse me!" I shout over the din. "Excuse me! Brittas? Hel-*lo*? Hey, dummies!"

But they clearly can't hear/see/smell anything but Cole.

"Cole, flex your butt again!"

"Can I touch your butt, Cole?"

"No, I get to touch it. Cole, let me touch it."

"Cole?"

"Hey, Cole?"

"Cole?"

"Cole?"

Cole.

"Cole!" I call, adding to the din of voices shouting his name. But I guess I manage to break through. Cole whips his head around to face me, completely shell-shocked, and I give him an expectant look. "I think you're the shepherd we need for this particular herd of cats."

It shouldn't surprise me that Cole has no idea what I'm talking about.

"Huh?" he says.

I point down the hallway, in the direction where our ship (pleasepleasehopefully) lies. "Run!" I tell him.

"Ah," Cole replies, finally getting it. And bless his dumb, doofy heart, he makes a break for it, knowing full well that the gaggle of screaming Brittas will follow.

"We're right behind you!" I assure Cole—only to be elbowed in the stomach by a passing Britta.

"Hands off, lardo," she snaps at me. "That butt is *mine.*"

I am too confounded and exhausted to even attempt a comeback.

"Okay," I say to the others as the Britta Brigade pushes its way down the hall like a particularly unsavory hair ball down a drain. "Best get moving."

And that's when I notice that one of the Brittas is still in our midst.

Haggard, harried, dirtier than I've ever seen her, she stands stock-still, staring at the group receding around the corner.

And I am certain, without even checking her shoulder, that *this* is the Britta I've known and hated for so long.

She turns to me and rolls her eyes. "Tell me I'm not that annoying," she says, gesturing toward the others.

I laugh, despite myself. And something escapes my mouth that I never would've expected in the presence of Britta McVicker. "It's nice to see you," I tell her.

She regards me coolly. "Captivity's been *hell* on your complexion," she replies.

So far we haven't passed a single Jin'Kai guard, but I'm not counting on our luck holding out. There's a lot more hallway in this space station than I ever would've anticipated. If you'd told me two months ago precisely how much of my time I was going to spend running for my life through various hallways, I would've asked to see if your medical hallucinogen card had expired.

At least this time the Brittas are keeping things interesting.

"Has your hair *always* been so dreamy?" one asks Cole as we dash past several locked doors.

"Can I touch your biceps again?"

"No, me!"

"It's my turn. You got to touch his butt."

"It *is* a really nice butt."

Chloe is clearly on her last nerve. "I have a blaster," she reminds us.

"Go ahead," says Original Britta, hustling to keep up beside me. "You didn't have to share a room with those chromers."

"You do realize that's *you* you're talking about," Ducky puts in. Then he hesitates. "Isn't it?"

All but the Brittas are silent for a few minutes, perhaps pondering this very question, when Marnie, in Bok Choy's arms, at last begins to stir.

"Oh, thank God," Ducky says. "Cole!" he calls up ahead. "Cole, hold on one sec. Marnie's waking up. We have to make sure she's okay before we— Oh, Marnie, you're awake!"

Marnie blinks several times, as though testing her vision.

"How are you feeling?" Ducky asks her gently.

Marnie offers him a warm smile. "I'm fine, Donald, ye specky goose. I jes' had a bit a the—" Her gaze travels down the hall to the lot of identical blond cheerleaders, all staring directly at her. "I must've hit me head harder 'n I thought," she says. And with that, she's out again.

The floor trembles beneath us, and the emergency runner lights flicker. Sirens start blaring.

And here I thought our luck would give out.

"Crap!" Ducky says. "They're onto us."

"No," Chloe replies, pausing to listen to the muted honking. "Something's . . . off. Those aren't Jin'Kai alarms."

"What do you think it could be?" I ask.

Chloe tilts her head. "Those are station-wide alarms," she says. "Whatever's going on, it's going big."

Which is precisely when one of the Brittas up ahead shouts, "Someone's coming this way!"

"Get behind me!" instructs Bok Choy, passing the still-unconscious Marnie off to Ducky and crouching in a defensive stance with his weapon drawn. Chloe slides into position next to him, her weapon out as well.

A band of Jin'Kai guards comes rushing up the adjoining

corridor, large rifle-size ray guns slung down from shoulder straps in a let's-fuck-shit-up position. I count six of them. No way we survive this. No way.

Except they run right past us. Past all of us. All except the last one, who turns with a confused look on his face.

"What are you doing wasting your time with that lot?" he asks Bok Choy and Chloe, jerking his head toward the Brigade. "Get to your designated battle station. We're under attack!"

"Attack?" Chloe asks. "Almiri?"

"No, the fleet," he says as he runs after his compatriots. *"They're here."*

Well, if that don't put the donkey on the carousel, or some other expression that actually makes sense. (Forgive me, but I'm way too terrified to string words into phrases right now.)

The fleet.

The Jin'Kai invasion force that Marsden warned about.

They're here.

If an armada of Devastators doesn't make you stain your undies, I don't know what in this world will.

Suddenly there's an explosion from up ahead. Screams and gunfire. I race to the front and peer around the corner to get a look. The bodies of five guards lie motionless on the ground, while the sixth is dangling two meters above, held at the throat in a vise grip by a Devastator. This particular Devastator is bigger than the one I tussled with in Antarctica, if that's possible, and wearing full battle armor, a gray, bug-shell-like muscle suit, complete with jagged metal edges at the joints. You know, because apparently its massive claws and spiky exoskeletal protrusions alone aren't enough to eviscerate its prey. Three more

Devastators, similarly armed, stand behind the leader, seemingly unscathed by the firefight. The leader barks something at them, and the three giant uggos run off in another direction.

The remaining Devastator speaks menacingly to the Jin'Kai guard in his grip, in a language that sounds a lot like spoons in a garbage disposal. The Jin'Kai, meanwhile, still alive but wounded and defenseless, whimpers something in response. But I guess his particular mangled spoon response is not what the Devastator wanted to hear, because the creature unsheathes a long, serrated blade from its back and in one smooth motion skewers the helpless guard like a shish kebab. The guard dangles, twitching, on the hilt of the weapon, the blade jutting out of his back.

There's a shriek right in my ear. I turn to see Britta, white with fear, staring at the murder scene, still screaming.

"It's them! Them!" she screams. Like, guess who just arrived at the party.

My initial impulse is to clock her in the head, because *hello*, alerting the freaky monsters to our existence much? Of course, then I remember that Britta has been tortured for who knows how long, and prior to that she actually witnessed a Devastator decapitating her best friend (who was kind of a bitch, but *still*). So, with our own impending head-from-neck removals imminent, I decide, rather magnanimously, not to pile on.

When the monster looks up and roars, a chill of memory washes over me. I really need to start reevaluating my life decisions, I think, given the number of times lately I've found myself face-to-face with monsters who want to kill me.

Unable to quickly dislodge the dead Jin'Kai from his sword, the Devastator tosses his weapon away and charges at us, equipped only with four armored monster arms, endless rows of fang-like teeth, and about half a dozen enormous guns strapped across its heavily protected chest.

I pull Britta back around the bend of the hallway, and the other Brittas, perhaps instinctively, squeeze in to form a protective barrier around us. I'm afraid Ducky's going to go all noodle-boned on us again and collapse, but perhaps because he is holding Marnie, he remains upright, head held high.

Bok Choy exchanges a look with Chloe, who nods in agreement to something that he hasn't actually said out loud. The Devastator comes into view, spinning its head around on its massive neck to spot us. Bok Choy and Chloe open fire immediately, but the blasters leave only harmless-looking scorch marks on the creature's armor and exposed exoskeleton. The Devastator swings upward with its two upper arms, knocking the guns out of Bok Choy's and Chloe's hands, and then it kicks outward with its two heavier middle limbs, ramming Bok Choy and Chloe in their chests and sending them sprawling. The creeper looks up and spots me surrounded by the Brittas—which, I suddenly realize, makes me look a lot more like a valuable target than if an army of clones *weren't* creating a human shield around me.

"Gargle, gargle, kim chee!" it growls. Or something close to that. I left my universal translator in my Comic-Con swag bag.

Even if I don't speak monster, I'm picking up on the Devastator's body language just fine. It pulls yet another nasty pointy sword thing from its side (seriously, how many swords does a giant six-limbed death monster *need*?) and starts plodding toward me. That's when Cole decides to get heroically stupid and leaps with all his Almiri might right for the thing's arm—inadvertently pulling an impressive parallel bars maneuver and flipping right past his attacker into a heap of hurt on the floor.

I'm going to assume that wasn't the plan.

The Devastator clocks Cole with a nasty kick, and Cole is officially down for the count.

"Cooooooole!" the Brittas screech in unison. They all make to run toward their dashing leading man—I swear I hear one sob, "Is his butt okay?"—but then they seem to think better of it (because, one can only assume, of the scary-ass Devastator standing between said hunk and themselves). Together they whirl around and disperse down the length of the hall like cowardly little chicken shits, squealing in terror all the way.

Well, to be fair, some of them faint.

So my protective Britta-barrier has completely crumbled, and now the Devastator looms over me, ready for another shish-kebab-ing. But before I get the pointy end, Bok Choy leaps into the path of the blade.

It impales him, awkwardly, right in the side.

"No!" Chloe screams as Bok Choy cries out in pain. My heart constricts in my chest at the sound of Chloe's wail. She scoops up her blaster and fires at the Devastator.

I feel a tug on my arm and realize that Ducky is pulling me out of the way. As Ducky, Marnie (still unconscious, lucky dog), Original Britta, and I huddle behind a protective pile of rubble the Jin'Kai so thoughtfully left for us during their previous firefight, we can only watch helplessly as the scene in front of us seems to play out in slow motion.

Chloe runs straight at the Devastator, clutching her ineffectual pistol in her fist more like you would a rock than a firearm.

"Chloe!" I scream at my only child. My throat is hot, burning, as I watch her charge headfirst into danger. Britta has to physically restrain me to keep me from leaping after my daughter. (She gets an elbow to the gut for her efforts, but she doesn't let go.)

Chloe literally throws herself at the Devastator, and the creature opens its arms up wide, as if to catch her midleap. She crashes into his chest, and I can practically see the impact rippling through her. The monster's gargantuan arms wrap around my daughter and squeeze. I watch her grimace in pain as the grip around her tightens. The creature opens its massive maw, the strange, jointed teeth flexing in and out on the exposed mouth tendons, and I realize with unavoidable certainty that this beast means to bite my child's head off.

"Smile, you son of a bitch!" Chloe screams. After wiggling her arm free, she reels back and thrusts her fist deep into the Devastator's open mouth, still clutching her gun. The creature chokes and staggers back. Then Chloe flattens her arms against her body, goes limp, and manages to slide out of her assailant's grasp, rolling away as she hits the floor, shielding her face.

And then the Devastator's head explodes.

The headless body collapses to the floor. Without missing a beat, Chloe has flown to Bok Choy's side and cradles him in her lap. He winces in pain when she touches his side. Chloe, meanwhile, doesn't even seem to notice that I'm checking her all over like a prize pig at the fair. "If you ever do something that reckless again, I'll— You're *bleeding!*"

Long jagged gashes snake up Chloe's arm all the way to her elbow, bloody reminders that it can be hazardous to jam your entire arm down a space monster's throat. I fumble in my tunic, for what feels like an eternity, until I am finally able to pull out the ratty cloth Marnie purchased for me. I wrap it around Chloe's arm—the world's least hygienic bandage.

But Chloe will have none of it.

"Get off me. I'm fine." She yanks the rag off her arm and uses it instead to put pressure on Bok Choy's side. He's not looking good. He manages to sit up, but it obviously pains him. "We have to keep moving," he tells Chloe through gritted teeth. "There will be more of them any minute."

"He's right."

To my surprise this voice of reason belongs to none other than Original Britta. Even more surprising, she's busy looting the Devastator's body for weapons.

"What?" she says when she sees my look. "Some of this shit could come in handy."

Uh, who is this chick, and why didn't she take over Britta's body sixteen years ago?

"Hand me one of those knives," I tell Britta, reluctantly leaving my daughter's side. I look around and see that Cole has, thankfully, roused himself, although Marnie is still unconscious. "Cole," I say, "round up the Brittas." Cole aye-ayes and runs off immediately.

"Donald, was it?" Britta says to Ducky.

He gulps. I can't blame him—he went to school with Britta for twelve years, and this is the first she's deigned to speak to him.

"How much can you carry?" she asks him. Then, without waiting for an answer, she proceeds to drape him in supplies from both the dead Devastator and the Jin'Kai guards, making him look like a cosplay enthusiast with no sense of scale.

"I have a question," Ducky says as Cole returns with his flock of Brittas and scoops up Marnie. Britta shoves a blaster into Ducky's hands, and he tries his best not to hold it like you would a dead cockroach. "That Devastator's head just totally exploded."

"Yeah," I say. I'm scooping up my own share of weapons, whatever I can shove safely down the front of my jacket. "We were there, remember? And that wasn't a question."

"True," Ducky replies. "But, um, how, exactly, did that happen?"

"I overloaded the power cell on the blaster," Chloe says, still tending to Bok Choy.

"How'd you know how to do that?" Ducky asks. "Is that part of your training? Evil Alien Weaponry 101?"

"No," Chloe answers. "I just figured it might work."

Ducky smiles broadly at me. "I'd like to think of a clever way to say 'the apple doesn't fall far from the tree,'" he says, "but I think I'm too jacked up on adrenaline and unadulterated fear to be witty."

"Speaking of which," I say, stooping down next to Bok Choy. "If you can move, now'd be the time to show us some of that genetically superior Jin'Kai stamina."

Wincing, Bok Choy allows Chloe to lift him off the floor. "Can do," he says.

We use the sound of gunfire and screaming as an indication of which directions *not* to travel as we make our way through the installation and back to the main ozone plant. Scoring from blaster fire marks the walls our entire way, and whatever security may have been in place before has been completely blown to hell. It seems Marsden wasn't exaggerating about how much the Jin'Kai command would disapprove of his secret genetic tinkering. The ozone plant's backup lights are flickering and fading, and it's clear that whatever forces hit the station, they hit it hard and fast.

We clomp along the high suspended catwalks until we reach a segment that's completely collapsed in what appears to have been a very one-sided firefight.

"Now what?" Ducky asks.

"I could jump down," Cole offers. "Catch you one at a time."

"It's too high," I tell him. "Even for you." I look around, and then my eyes rest on perhaps the worst idea I have had in a long time. Which is really saying something.

"The power's down," I say. "Machinery is offline. These compressors have conduits that lead straight to the loading bay in the hangar, right?"

"You're bat shit," Chloe says. "You want to crawl *through the compressors?*"

"You have a better idea?" I ask.

"Isn't any idea better than going through machinery that houses highly explosive and completely unbreathable gas?" she counters. "Like, literally any idea?"

"The ozone in the conduits is in brick form," I say. "We should be able to climb through without too much trouble."

"Assuming that the bricks are stable," Chloe says. "The temperature is probably already rising with the power off. If the bricks break down, we blow up."

"That sounds bad," Ducky puts in helpfully.

"Look," I argue, "our way is blocked, and there's an army of two-and-a-half-meter-tall space monsters swarming everywhere, just waiting for another chance to cut us to bits. This is the fastest way out. And if the temperatures really are rising, then it's in our best interest to get the flip out of here before the whole place explodes, don't you think?"

"I'm with Elvie."

And spank my tooshie and call me a cab, it's none other than Britta who says it.

"If Elvie says it'll work," she continues while I stare at her, mouth agape, "I believe it. She totally saved all of us on the *Echidna*. Well, *most* of us, anyway."

"Uh, thanks?" I say.

Finding a panel weak enough to jimmy open without using one of the blasters takes a little while, but after we've pried it open with one of the Devastator swords, climbing inside is relatively easy. At least Marnie has the good sense to wake up in time for the trek. I was having visions of tugging her behind us by her shoelaces. To her credit, as soon as Marnie hears that we'll all be crawling through a series of narrow ducts filled with highly unstable explosives, she simply nods and says, "Somethin' fer the songs, yeah?"

The metal ducts that house the conveyors are narrow, but

I'm able to squeeze through by keeping my elbows tucked tightly under my chest.

"Hey, Elvie," Ducky calls from behind me. "Now I know what a TV dinner feels like."

"A what?" Marnie asks from behind Ducky.

"Come to outer space," I join in. "We'll get together, have a few laughs."

Ducky starts chuckling, and I crack a smile myself.

"What in the hell are you two talking about?" Chloe shouts. She's taken the lead, followed immediately by Bok Choy and then myself.

"Don't worry about it," comes Cole's echoey voice. He's holding up the rear, in an effort to herd all of the Brittas as quickly as possible. "You'll get used to those two eventually. They have their own language."

The acrid ozone smell stings my nose, and I squeeze my eyes shut to push the tears away.

"When we're out of here, Chloe," I grunt, squeezing around a difficult bend, "back on Earth, I'm going to have to educate you on the rich dramatic oeuvre of the genre-redefining thespian Bruce Willis."

"If you exercised your tub of an ass as much as you talked, you wouldn't be holding us up back here," says a familiar catty voice. But I can't tell if it belongs to one of the Brigade or to Original Britta.

As we continue—and I do my best to block out the incessant jabbering of the Brittas quizzing Cole about his hair products—I begin to notice something wet beneath me.

"What is this sticky stuff?" I ask. "It's not ozone, is it?"

"I thought if the bricks broke down, we'd go boom," Ducky says.

"Want to get the lead out in front there?" Cole calls. "I'm not super-excited about the 'going boom' part."

"Keep your pants on!" Chloe shouts back to her father. "Some of us are injured."

Ahead of me, Bok Choy says not a word. I can hear him grunting quietly as he moves.

The wetness underneath me is starting to soak through my tunic now, and I'm getting a very bad feeling in my gut. Sure enough, as we pass over a grated portion of the duct, a dim light shimmers through, and I see that the viscous liquid running down my fingers is bright red. Instantly I feel nauseous.

Bok Choy's breathing is slow and labored. With some difficulty I manage to push my arm forward to grab his calf and give it a squeeze. Bok Choy simply pauses for a second. I can see his head dip slightly as a quiet sigh escapes him. He flexes his calf under my hand. I know immediately to stay quiet. Tears are welling in my eyes suddenly, and I realize that they're not for Bok Choy, as sad as his condition makes me. They're for the girl who's in love with him, crawling just ahead of him, totally unaware that he is bleeding out. The girl, I realize with a mixture of guilt and fear, who is helping us all only so that I'll help him.

The last portion of our crawl through the chlorine-smelling pipeline is a sharp vertical drop. Without any real room to maneuver otherwise, we're forced to wiggle headfirst down the tube and slide the rest of the way. After Chloe and Bok Choy lower themselves, it's my turn. I make my way to the edge and look down. Below I watch as Bok Choy lands on a gelatinous receptacle pad no doubt designed to absorb the impact of the ozone bricks sliding through. Chloe swims through the goo to cradle him, and I can tell from the way her face darkens that he's doing even worse than I feared.

"Shit," I whisper, watching my daughter choke on her sobs.

"What's going on?" comes Ducky's voice from behind me. "Don't tell me you're stuck. This is so *not* where I'm dying."

"I'm not stuck," I tell him. I push myself forward and start working my way over the edge. The entire passage is slick with blood now, and I force back the bile that rises in my throat from the sticky-sweet smell. I'm doing my best to shimmy around the bend, my head and shoulders already over the edge and tilting downward, when my right arm slips and, thanks to a luck only I seem to possess, lodges itself at an incredibly painful angle beneath my chest.

"Okay," I tell Ducky. "*Now* I'm stuck."

Groans from the entire length of the duct.

"What's going on up there?" Chloe calls. "Hurry up! We've got to get to the ship!"

"Just . . . hold . . . *on*," I grunt, trying out various uncomfortable contortions to try to pull my arm free. But no luck. The worst part is that I can feel the pull of gravity on my body, and the sensation is giving me a Ducky-size case of vertigo. As the blood rushes more quickly to my head, I really begin to panic. Is this how I finally die, as a clog in a drain? Is this how we *all* die?

That's when I hear Ducky thumping forward in the passage behind me. I feel pressure on my feet and soon realize that he's nuzzling my boots with his head.

"Duck?" I ask as I feel him parting my feet slightly with his noggin. "What are you doing?"

"I'm sorry," Ducky says, and I can tell he means it. But what in the world is he—

"Ducky!" I scream, jolting up and hitting my head on the top of the duct. Ducky has slid my feet to the edges of the narrow tube and is currently *crawling headfirst between my legs.*

"Sorry!" he says again. "I'm so sorry! Really! Sorry!"

The repeated exclamations of apology do very little to allay the incredibly uncomfortable situation that we find ourselves in.

"What are you *doing?*" I say again. Broken records, the two of us.

"We've got to get you moving," he says. "I can't move my arms. This is the only way I can . . ."

And then, with no further warning, my best friend in the whole world has the top of his head pressed squarely into my butt.

"Sorry!"

"It's working!" I cry as I feel my body slide a few centimeters. "Keep it up, Duck!"

"Donald!" Marnie calls from behind him. "Careful, love! I'm quite fond of that head of yers."

Two more bumps, and my elbows have cleared the edge, joining my head and shoulders in the very downward dog position. Gravity finally grabs hold of me, and now I slide slowly along until I'm completely upside down and falling toward the receptacle bin.

I pop out like a gumball from a candy dispenser and

come down with a squishy *plop* into the bin. Bok Choy and Chloe have climbed out already, but Chloe's too busy comforting her friend to help me clear the edge as I slip and slide on the Jell-O-like padding.

"He's hurt," Chloe says, rather needlessly, when I land beside them on solid ground.

Bok Choy shakes his head. "There'll be time to deal with it later," he tells her. But the rag, sopping wet with blood, seems to imply otherwise.

Ducky flops down into the gelatin bin behind us. He climbs out and lands next to me, his face all different kinds of red. "Again," he mumbles. "Sorry."

The others follow, one by one, and we find ourselves in the loading bay for the factory's private hangar, where the bricks are gathered, tagged, and loaded onto the ships that will deploy them into the atmosphere. Bok Choy gathers his strength and leads us, as quietly as you can move with a bunch of confused and genetically- and intellectually-challenged clones, up a large, wide flight of stairs to the control room between the loading bay and the hangar.

The control room is long, probably twenty-plus meters across, with a transparent aluminum window panel looking out over the hangar. Cole edges up to the window and peeks down over the edge.

"Well?" Marnie asks.

"Shit," he says.

I creep up alongside him, hoping to embellish his commentary with a little more detail.

"Shit," I add helpfully.

Below us the smoking wreckage of dozens of small ships litters the deck. At first I wonder if the Devastators targeted the hangar with some sort of ship-to-ship missile, but the damage is too specific, with ships lying in useless fiery heaps while the cargo loaders and flatbed trolleys remain untouched— presumably because the Jin'Kai determined that it's difficult to escape into outer space on a forklift.

"Careful," Marnie says from beside me. "They're still wandering around down there." I spot roughly a dozen Devastators on the floor. They're all hovering around one ship, the sight of which fills me with excitement and dread both at once.

"That's our ship!" I cry.

"You came here in that thing?" Britta asks. "How did you expect to fit us all into that little tin can?"

"I didn't," I snap back. "If you want, we can leave you here."

Ducky's comment is slightly more helpful. "It looks like they didn't blow it up or anything."

"They're probably right confused about why it's there," Marnie says. "It's not Jin'Kai or human. They might be tryin' to find out if there's an Almiri presence aboard the station."

"Well, our ship's in one piece, so that's good," Cole says. "But I hate to point out that it's also crawling with those things."

"That's not all," Bok Choy says, grimacing. Chloe offers a concerned hand to steady him at the console, but he shakes her off. "They've attached something to the ship. Some sort of docking clamps. It'll take me a while to disable them."

"You start fiddlin' with those, and they'll know we're here," Marnie says.

"Not if we distract them," I say. I flick on the console next to Bok Choy and bring up the inventory screen for the loading bay.

"There's more than two thousand ozone bricks sitting in here waiting for a stack and pack," I say. I turn to Chloe. "You feel like setting off any more fireworks?"

"You can't detonate those bricks," Ducky warns. "If we can't get the ship to fly, you'll block our only way out."

"If the ship doesn't fly," I point out, "then we're all dead anyway." I hold out my hand to Chloe, who smirks and drops a long, pointy blaster into my grip. "Bok Choy, you work on those clamps. Cole, you and the others take the Brittas—" At the sound of their name, all of their perky blond heads turn to me in unison. "Wait down in the access corridor until the coast is clear. Chloe, let's go shoot this place to hell."

Chloe and I make our way back into the loading bay. A floor console stands near the front loading gate that connects the bay to the hangar. I activate it and initiate the loading sequence. Immediately, shielded panels begin sliding open on the three walls, frosty mist rolling out from the refrigerated storage compartments. Inside each compartment, rack after rack of dark purple bricks begins to automatically extend into the bay, where normally a loader would be waiting to install them on a deployment craft. The bricks themselves are actually quite pretty. They look like a cross between colored quartz and grape-flavored Popsicles.

"Okay. We're only going to get one chance at this," I say.

"Well, now's not the time for cold feet," Chloe says. She positions herself in front of the loading gate and cocks two big guns, one in each hand, like the little Rambolina I always dreamed of rearing. "Open sesame."

I tap in the commands, and the gate groans and creaks open, rusted metal screeching against rusted metal.

"That got their attention!" comes Bok Choy's voice over the comm in the control panel. "They're sending two your way."

"Well, they're going to love this, then," Chloe replies. As soon as the gate is fully open, the two Devastators come into view and see her. Before they can react, she opens fire. "Die, you sap-suckers!" she cries, unleashing unholy hell on them with their own advanced firearms. The two giant creeps stagger backward under the barrage of fire. From behind them enraged voices fill the air.

"Here they come!" Bok Choy warns.

Chloe runs back inside the bay, sending random fire toward the gate, being careful not to shoot anywhere near the bricks. I hightail it back up the stairs toward the control room and crouch by the door. Chloe races my way.

"Now!" she says.

Not yet, I tell myself. I square up my gun and balance it on my knee.

Once Chloe reaches me, she spins around, looking back down at the empty bay below us. "What are you waiting for?" she asks.

"This," I say.

As the Devastators come barreling into the bay, I take aim and fire my weapon, straight past the aliens, at the stack of bricks at the opposite end of the room. The bricks explode one after another in a chain reaction, cascading around the room from one stack to the next. The concussive force knocks both me and Chloe to the ground, but the Devastators on the floor are completely engulfed by the maelstrom, and they wail in pain. Still, blaster fire seeks us out as we scramble on our hands and knees back to the control room. The door slides shut behind us as soon as we're inside.

I'm pretty sure mani-pedis would've been a more stress-free form of mother-daughter bonding.

Bok Choy is still working intently over the docking controls.

"Are the others aboard?" I ask.

"They're at the ship," he informs me. "They're under fire from a few stray hostiles."

"What about the docking clamps?"

"I need another minute."

"We don't have a minute!" Chloe shouts.

Bok Choy doesn't look up from his work. "Just get to the ship," he says. "Stick close to the left wall there. You'll be able to flank them and create cover so the others can get aboard."

"What about you?" Chloe asks, her voice strained.

Bok Choy pauses for the first time and looks up at her. "I'll be with you soon," he tells her, then immediately returns his focus to the control panel.

"But . . . ," she starts, but she can't get any more words out. I grab her arm and tug her toward the exit.

"Chloe, we have to help the others," I say.

Chloe reluctantly exits with me, but she keeps her gaze on Bok Choy as we move. He never looks up.

I can hear the blaster fire as we move quickly along the

left wall, weaving around the rubble that was once a small fleet of crappy fliers. As we zoom around a long block of loading equipment, I make out Cole and Marnie exchanging fire with the Devastators from behind the ship's loading ramp, while the others use the ramp as cover. There are three baddies returning fire. Our vantage point creates a triangle among all three parties; we're slightly behind the Devastators but still obscured by debris.

Without a word between us, Chloe and I open fire. As soon as we do, the Devastators pivot and discover us, sending a return volley before retreating to cover. This gives Cole, Marnie, and the others a chance to scurry up the gangway into the ship. Once everyone else is aboard, Cole and Marnie emerge halfway back down the ramp and fire again at the Devastators' position. Pinched between two sets of foes, the Devastators can't line up any good shots, and Chloe and I are able to make a dash for the ship, the Devastators' fire clearing wide of us and exploding harmlessly against the hull of a ruined ozone flier.

"Get in!" Cole says, waving Chloe and me past him into the main hold.

I run inside to find Ducky trying to calm the Brittas. "We're fine," he tells them. "You're all fine. Remember how cute Cole is? His, uh, butt and everything? Just concentrate on that."

The Brittas, rattled like a group of puppies during a thunderstorm, settle slightly at the thought of Cole's posterior. Well, save one.

"I hate every last one of you," Original Britta tells her gaggle of clones.

Ducky spots me as I come up the ramp. "Elvie, thank God," he says.

"We've got to get this tub in the air," I say.

"We can't leave yet," Chloe says, shadowing me to the cockpit. "He's still back there. We're not leaving without him."

"Of course not," I tell her. I slide into the pilot's chair and begin the takeoff sequence. "Go back out there and help Cole and Marnie hold those scumbags back."

Chloe doesn't look wholly convinced, but I give her a good mom-glare, and she retreats back to the ramp.

"Ducky!" I shout back into the hold. "Get your ass up here!"

He runs in at breakneck speed. "What is it?"

"I know you don't know how to fly this thing, but I need a co-pilot."

"What about the Brittas?" he asks.

"Let Britta handle the Brittas."

Ducky slips into the seat next to me without further hesitation.

"Check that our thrusters and stabilizers are all online while I fire up the engines," I tell him. And when he gives me a *Wha-huh?* gaze, I elaborate. "Think *Tech-a-Mecha Revolutions 3*. Heroic mode."

"Now you're talking my language," Ducky says. He begins deftly flicking through the touch screen controls. But after just a few seconds he lets out a low whistle. "Um, hey, Elvie? What is this?" He flicks the display toward me, and his screen slides onto my display. At first I think that Ducky has accidentally accessed some weird redundant system, but when I give it a second look, I realize what it is.

"Jesus, Mary, George, and Ringo," I gasp. "Bricks. A full load of ozone bricks. At least a hundred."

"On this ship?"

"The Governor's men must've had the ship retrofitted after Marsden handed it over," I say, cycling through the system. "They've installed a launcher into the aft section too."

"A ship this advanced, and they use it like an ordinary junker?" Ducky asks. Then a troubling expression washes over his face. "The bricks can't blow up once they're loaded," he says. "Right?"

I don't bother answering, because I think we both realize how dead we're all about to be. The Governor's men—who, in my very brief encounter with them, didn't strike me as overly careful about their work—have done a really, really shitty job of installing the new system into our ship. Try as I might, I can't get the rear repulsors to light up on my board.

Bust out the label maker and mark us BONED.

"Bok Choy, are you there?" I say, patching into an open channel on the comm.

"I'm here, Elvie," comes his voice. It is weak and shaky. "The clamps are disabled. You should be able to start the take-off sequence."

"That's the thing," I tell him. "I can't. The back repulsors are offline. I'm not going to be able to get her off the deck."

"Can't we just start up the engine and slide out?" Ducky asks.

"With a half ton of explosive ozone in the hold?" I say. "We'll light up like a Girl Scout campfire before we've moved half a meter."

"So, that's a no, then."

"Elvie!" Cole screams from behind me, racing through the gauntlet of Brittas. "There's more of them coming. We need to get out of here!"

"What do I do?" I ask Bok Choy into the comm.

There's nothing but silence on the other end for several seconds.

"Bok Choy?" I repeat, growing more and more frantic. "What do I do?"

After what feels like a century, I hear Bok. He exhales a long, drawn-out sigh, one that sounds almost like relief.

"Bring up your ramp," he tells me.

"What?" I reply. I must've misheard. "How will you—"

"Bring it up," he interrupts. "Set your ignition cycle on standby and put all of your power into the aft dampeners."

"But why . . ." But I know why. I stop asking questions and start following instructions. Behind me I can hear the ramp rising.

"Elvie?" Ducky asks.

I ignore him. "Do you want me to tell her?" I ask Bok Choy.

There's another slight pause.

"Thank you," he answers.

Outside in the hangar the red alert lights begin strobing just as the launch siren rings.

"What are you doing?" Chloe says as she barges into the cockpit. "Lower the ramp. Now!"

"Sit down and hold on tight," I tell her, finishing the preparations Bok Choy gave me.

"Did you hear what I said?" she shrieks, her voice shrill.

"I heard you."

"What's happening?" Marnie asks as she enters, stepping up next to Ducky.

"Bok Choy is decompressing the hangar," I say. "Strap yourself down if you value your unbroken bones. Cole, go help the Brittas."

"*What?*" Chloe screams. "*No, no, no.* Lower the ramp. I said, lower the ramp. We're going to get him."

"Please sit down, Chloe," I tell her as calmly as I can.

In response Chloe raises her gun and points it at my head. "Lower that ramp," she instructs me again.

I stand up slowly and turn to face her. "Marnie," I say, and without another word Marnie slides into the pilot's chair and resumes where I left off.

"Open that ramp right now," Chloe says, tears streaking her cheeks, "or I'll kill you."

"Chloe," I say. *Calm, Elvie. Your baby's crying. Channel your calm.* "He has to do this. For you."

"I swear I'll shoot you right now," Chloe says, but her gun shakes in her hands. "You know I will."

"Chloe," I say one last time. Then I knock the gun from her trembling hands, and it crashes to the floor. Chloe takes a swing at me, which I deflect—but her second strike catches me right on the nose. I grab hold of her wrists and push her backward. Chloe falls hard into a chair behind the pilot's seat, me on top of her. She pulls me toward her, and I smack my mouth on the back of the chair, cutting the inside of my upper lip against my teeth.

But I don't let go.

"I'll kill you!" she wails.

I wrap my arms around her tightly, linking my hands together behind the seat.

"He wanted me to tell you."

"I'll *kill* you!" She is nothing but sobs now.

I close my eyes and squeeze my daughter as tightly as I can, swaddling her like in those first few weeks before I lost her.

"I love you," I tell her.

She kicks, scratches, bites, sobs. Still I hang on.

The main hangar door slides open, exposing the hangar to the vacuum of space. The ship shakes violently and rolls, shuddering each time a loose piece of wreckage slams into us as it is blown out into space.

"Hold on!" Marnie shouts.

When I feel my stomach go into my throat, I know we're upside down. We're off the deck and spinning like a top toward the door. I slide back and forth, my grip tight on the chair, pressed against Chloe. There's so much turbulence that I don't initially understand that the high-pitched sound in my ear is my daughter. I can feel her arms clutching my back, and I squeeze her even closer as we continue spinning toward the void.

"I love you," I tell her again. Soft in her ear. "I love you."

Chapter Eleven

WHEREIN IT BECOMES CLEAR THAT OUR HEROINE'S FRESHMAN GUIDANCE COUNSELOR WAS TOTALLY WRONG ABOUT PLAYING VIDEO GAMES NOT COUNTING AS A "LIFE SKILL"

"We're na' clear yet!" Marnie screams. The ship has stopped spinning, and I can feel the engines kicking into full burn. We haven't exploded or anything, so I count that as a plus.

Chloe pushes me away from her. Her face is streaked and her eyes are red and raw. But right this second I can't worry about consoling her on the loss of her would-be love.

Right now they're trying to shoot us out of the sky.

The ship shudders with a *crack!* and Marnie veers sharply to one side, trying to avoid the next volley from whoever or whatever is behind us. As we come about, I can see one ship out of the corner of the front viewport bearing down on us.

"Just one ship? I'm insulted."

Marnie coughs and points to the tactical display.

"Oh," I say. "Four ships. Well that's . . . more like it?"

"Hold on," Marnie barks. "They're lookin' to cut us off!"

The only sounds that follow are the engines straining and

the Brittas moaning. Then another *crack!*—this one harder than before.

"What are they hitting us with?" Ducky screams. His eyes are darting around the copilot console, the confidence he had only a few moments ago now lost in the panic of an actual spaceship chase.

"Ducky, move it," I command. Ducky bolts out of his seat like it's covered in spiders, and I slide in and bring up the environmental scanners.

"Looks like they're using some sort of particle cannons," I say. "Assuming I'm reading this right."

"Well, what do *we* have?" Ducky asks.

"This isn't a combat ship," I reply.

"What? I thought this was an Almiri attack ship. Where are the phasors? The photon torpedoes?"

"We stole a shuttle, Duck, not the *Millennium Falcon*."

"I'm very scared right now, so I'm going to overlook your franchise conflation. This time."

"Elvie, can ye get our stealth field up?" Marnie asks me. "I dunnae if we'll be completely invisible to whatever sensors they've got, but we might be able to lose 'em."

"No go," I say. "The shield is still charging. Apparently our fancy new ozone system is leeching energy from the same cells, so it can't . . ."

"Elvs?" Cole asks as I trail off. "What is it?"

"Marnie," I say slowly, "I need you to straighten out."

"They'll have a clear shot lined up if we do that!" she screeches in response.

"Just do it. And get ready to break when I say."

Marnie straightens out our course, although there's a stream of what are obviously Scottish obscenities escaping from under her breath as she does so.

"I sure hope you know what you're doing, Elvs," Cole says.

"Me too. This is my first space battle."

"Two of 'em on our six," Marnie tells us. "Three thousand meters. . . . Fifteen hundred meters. . . . They're locked on!"

I slap the release button on our new shipment of ozone bricks. The clumsy gears grind and groan, but thankfully within seconds the display reads *Payload deployed.*

"Break now!" I cry.

Marnie pulls up on the controls, pushing us all back hard into our seats. A split second later the ship shudders more violently than ever before.

"They're hitting us again!" Ducky shouts.

"No," Marnie says. She glances from the tactical display over to me. The look on her face can only be described as dumbfounded respect. "Tha' wasn't us. It was them. Two ships destroyed."

"What happened?" Ducky asks. "Are they crashing into each other or something?"

"At these speeds," Marnie tells him, "the impact of a few hundred bricks a ozone was enough to blow 'em to kingdom come."

"To be fair," I say, trying not to gloat in the middle of the crisis. "I thought at best it would distract or disable them."

"There are still two more of them out there," Chloe chimes in from her seat behind us. It's the first time she's spoken since takeoff, and her voice is so low and even that I get a chill up my spine. "Unless you think they'll fall for that again, I think this bucket is out of tricks."

"And out of bricks," I say. A shot across the bow jolts us, and I wince. "At least we're less likely to explode if they hit us square in the ass."

As if on cue, another shot rocks us. I scan the navigation charts. "Marnie, take us to these coordinates," I say, tapping the screen to bring up the course I want and sliding the screen over to her display.

Marnie looks at the screen like I just sent her a mash note asking if I "like-like" her. "Elvie, there's not a chance in bloody hell we'll survive a run through that," she says.

"Through what?" Cole asks.

"There's a lane filled with derelict stations, ships, and other space junk," I explain. "A lot of clutter, but it's the shortest path out of the Rust Belt headed back to Earth."

"It's called the Gauntlet," Marnie says. "And they call it that fer a reason. It'd be suicide."

Another blast smacks into us.

"We're losing hull integrity," I say. "We don't have time to debate this, Marnie. With any luck they won't bother to follow us in there."

"We fly in there, and they won't need to," Marnie replies, on the verge of yelling now. "We'll be smashed to smithereens!"

There's a bright white flash in the viewport, coming from behind us. The ship swings around, and I see what remains of the space station, combusting like a giant goldfish at high altitude.

"Holy Moses," Ducky gasps. "Did they just blow up the entire station?"

"Take us into that run now!" I shout at Marnie.

"Elvie, I cannae fly us through all that," Marnie says. "I'm no fighter pilot. I've flown maybe two transports in me whole life."

"Give me the controls," I say. Marnie obliges, with only a "Saints preserve us" as she slides the flight protocols to my console.

As soon as I have control, I turn us toward the Gauntlet, keeping the Devastator ships on the display in the corner of my eye.

"They're closing in fast," Ducky says.

I put the engines into full burn and use the thrusters to zigzag us jarringly around. "Time to put those hundreds of hours of *Jetman* to good use," I say.

Our readout shows several energy blasts coming from the Devastators, but none of them land. The only casualty of my daredevil piloting is Ducky's stomach. Squeals of disgust shower down from the Brittas. It's all doing wonders for my concentration.

"Marnie's right," Chloe says, staring at the heads-up. "You'll never be able to clear all that." And it's true that our path is filled with more junk than a Macydale Black Friday sale. As we enter, I manage to avoid several large hunks of disintegrating hull fragments, only to collide with several smaller floaters, which scrape and scratch as they drag along the top of the ship.

"You ever fly something like this?" Cole says. And it takes me a second to realize he's asking our *daughter*.

"Cole, she's, like, a month and a half old or something," I point out.

"I think I can figure it out," Chloe replies. She takes the other pilot's seat from Marnie, who follows Ducky's barf trail to the main hold, presumably to care for her weak-stomached paramour. Or perhaps to smack all the Brittas into silence— either one would be fine by me.

"I'll focus on steering," I tell Chloe. "I need you to fire the thrusters when I say. Got it?"

"Stop telling me what to do," Chloe snaps.

"Chloe," I say, forgoing an eye roll only because I need to focus on the field in front of us. "I know you're going through a major growth spurt and everything, but now is a poor time for teenage sass."

"You're not the boss of me!"

"Actually," I say, "that's *precisely*—"

It's Cole who breaks in. "You've got this, Chloe," he says calmly. "I know you can do it."

"I can do it," she repeats.

Despite my best efforts to outmaneuver the Devastators, their ships are too fast for our little shuttle. The only weakness that I can see is that they don't bank well. However, given enough open space, they can easily correct for any overshots, making up the distance in a matter of nanoseconds. Up ahead the junk is clearing somewhat, offering us a safer path, but it also means fewer obstacles for the Devastators to work around. And soon I see the reason for the sparse debris field—an old L.O.C., similar class to the *Echidna*, maybe slightly bigger. Years of bouncing around in the debris field has punched several enormous holes through the hull, leaving it a massive floating skeleton.

"What are you doing?" Chloe asks as I turn us onto an intercept course. "There's a clear path directly to port!"

"Well, at least we know you've got your nautical terms down," I say. "I'd hate to think this was a wasted learning moment."

"You're crazy," Chloe says.

"Get used to it, sweetie. It's genetic."

I pilot us directly into the wreckage of the cruiser's hull, hoping that its interior is as worm-eaten as the outer hull suggests.

The Devastators remain in pursuit.

"Stern thrusters now!" I shout. "Port! Stern! Port!"

Chloe follows each command instantly, lurching the ship to and fro as I thread the needle.

And then, suddenly, our path is blocked. I don't have time to call out for thrusters. There's an open gap to our right, and I put my whole body into the turn. We're all sideways in our seats like we're on an old-timey sci-fi television show. The bottom of the hull scraping against metal sounds like a million forks being drawn slowly across a million china plates. We clear the ship, just barely, and fly out into the clear. The ship shudders slightly.

Chloe looks at the tactical display. "They're toast," she says. "Both hostiles are down." She turns to me, her face stoic. "Nice flying. For a maniacal, heartless nut."

"Nice copiloting," I reply. And call me mature or something, because I only *think* the *for an immature, snotty brat* part. "Couldn't have done it without you," I say instead. Something dangerously close to a smile nearly creeps across Chloe's face.

"Guys," Cole says. "I hate to interrupt this touching mother-daughter moment, but . . ."

Chloe looks at the tactical again. "*Rikslamma,*" she spits, in what I can only assume is the foulest of Jin'Kai epithets.

I don't need the tactical to summon my own swear words. Through the viewport approximately *eighty bajillion Devastator ships* come into focus, ranging from what look to be single-pilot fighters to enormous juggernauts three times bigger than the largest orbital cruiser I've ever seen, forming a blockade between us and our home planet.

"Does it count that I got us *pretty close* to not being dead?" I ask.

"It looks like they're already engaged," Chloe says, eyes on the tactical. "I've got readings on two unique power signature types coming from that fleet."

"Byron," I say. "I didn't think the Almiri built that many ships." Cole shrugs.

"They've spotted us," Chloe cuts in. "Three bogeys are breaking off and are in pursuit."

"Didn't we just play this tune?" I mutter. I come about and try to make a break for it, back into the belt, but these ships are bigger and faster than the ones that had been tasked primarily with taking out a defenseless space station.

"They're right on top of us!" Chloe shouts.

Which, actually, I'd already pretty much figured out, because now our ship is rocking under a constant barrage of fire. The tactical and heads-up displays go dead—and just like that we're flying blind.

"Port thrusters gone!" Chloe informs us. "Secondary engine offline!"

"This is it, then," I say. I turn to her. "Chloe, I just want you to know that I love you and—"

"Cut the sap and look straight ahead!" Chloe screams, pointing. Through the viewport a ship is materializing right before my eyes. It's easily twenty times as big as us.

It's also awfully familiar.

Two large turrets on either side of the hull open up a barrage of fire, visible only as brief blue muzzle flashes. The shots fly right past us, clearly intended for someone else. I turn the ship as best I can to get clear of the cross fire, and as I do, we all get a view of the Devastator vessels exploding silently in the void. The comm crackles to life on the console.

"Elvie? Is that you, dearheart?"

"Daddy?" I screech. I'm sobbing and laughing at the same time, barely able to form words.

Beside me Chloe snorts. "*Daddy*," she mutters.

I clear my throat. "Dad, don't tell me you're flying that thing?"

"Well, technically, your grandfather is," my father replies. "And you have Oates to thank for the fireworks display. I suppose you could say I'm the resident science officer aboard."

"Dad, I found Chloe. Olivia. Long story. But the Devastators are chasing us."

"I know, dearheart, I know. The Almiri and Earth military forces are already engaged with the enemy."

"The military?" I ask. Stunned murmurs pop up around me. (Well, except from the Britta Brigade—they're still busy complaining about Ducky's puke on their shoes.)

"A lot has happened while you've been away," Dad tells me. "Crazy, world-altering stuff. Someone could write a doozy of a novel about it someday, perhaps. We can cover you out of the fire zone. I'm sending you coordinates now."

"Our tactical computer is offline."

"Then I'll give you the coordinates over the comm and you can dock with us. Don't worry. We'll get a head start on these sons of guns."

"Where are we going?" I ask.

"Elvie, dearheart, we're going to Mars."

Chapter Twelve

IN WHICH OUR MERRY BAND OF MISFITS GET THEIR ASSES TO MARS

"Dearheart!" Dad shouts, waving like a madman as Chloe and I walk down the shuttle's ramp into the hangar of Byron's command ship like we just returned from a two-week vacation cruise, as opposed to a daring and intestine-twisting escape through a debris field in space. A team of three Almiri passes us and makes its way up into our (okay, technically *their*) ship, pulling a hover cart loaded down with fancy alien doozy-whatsits.

"Where are they goin'?" Marnie asks as they brush past her, Cole, and Ducky at the top of the ramp without so much as a "Pardon me."

"They're going to take a look at your hyperdrive," Dad says.

"Oh. Well, then, Harry, I think I'll join 'em an' get a better jog o' how this girl's wired, if it's all the same t' ye."

"I'll join you," Ducky says, his face still green. "Just as soon as I make use of the facilities one"—he pauses midsentence for a seriously rancid burp—"more time."

I look at Cole, who's just standing there, and the look I give him must say, *Why are you just standing there?* because he smirks and nods at my father.

"So, this is my granddaughter?" Dad asks, examining Chloe like he's inspecting a new motherboard for his computer.

"I'll babysit the Brigade for a while," Cole says. "Holler if you need me."

Chloe glares at my father, squirming her face away when he touches her cheek. "*This* is my genetic lineage?" she asks, grunting. "Human. Ugh. Let me guess—your knees give out all the time, or something equally ridiculous."

Dad looks from Chloe to me. "Quite the resemblance," he says.

"There will be time for the family reunion later," I say. "Dad, tell me what's going on. The short version, please. I don't have any patience for exposition at this point."

Dad clears his throat. "Come with me," he says ominously.

Dad leads me and Chloe out of the hangar and down a tight corridor. While the bones of the ship's interior are unmistakably alien and advanced, there's also no question that this is Byron's personal flagship, with all of his decorating flair on display. Hung between access panels and computer node stations is a series of familiar oil paintings, mostly of dogs, that clash terribly with the otherwise clean white metallic décor. Just as I'm about to make a crack about Gramps's Achilles heel for lousy art, we pass by a large mural of—literally—Achilles.

Note to self: when you're not so busy fighting for your life, remember to check if you're related to Achilles.

As we walk, Dad takes his best stab at explaining to me

what's been going on Earth-side as of late. "Shortly after you, ahem, *parted ways* with us," Dad begins, "Byron and Oates and the rest of us rendezvoused with the surviving Almiri leadership. Byron and Oates were able to convince them that current circumstances dictated a change in policy regarding the Enosi resistance and their sub rosa relationship with the rest of mankind."

"*This* is the short version?" Chloe mutters.

"Dad," I say. "Cut to the chase, will you? Earth, happenings, you guys, Mars. Just tell me how this all ties together."

Dad nods and continues. "A little more than a week ago, the Jin'Kai invasion force entered expanded satellite range—which, as you can imagine, made it a perfectly horrible time for the Almiri to reveal to the United States government that the president and several key members of the cabinet weren't technically human—"

"Wait," I interrupt him. "President *Holloway*?" Then I pause a moment and consider the leader of the free world's perfect single dimple. "Okay, yeah, that makes sense. Move on."

"Despite the unfortunate timing," Dad continues, "the Almiri's 'coming out' to most of the world's governments has thus far been largely without incident." He grins. "I like to think that I played a crucial role, given my unique position as a human with intimate understandings of the Almiri. I maintained the position—agreed upon by our elected leaders, I might point out—that our only hope in the days to come is to postpone any public revelation about aliens among us, and the inevitable fallout, in the hopes of coming together to valiantly repel those who would destroy us. It was a most inspiring bit of captaincy on my part, and a riveting story that I will tell you about in full at a more appropriate time—"

"Please tell me that being long-winded isn't genetic," Chloe cuts in.

"Good for you, Dad," I tell him. He is still grinning, clearly pleased with himself. "Now skip to the part where they're reenacting the act-three space battle from Return of the Jedi over New Jersey."

Dad nods. "Yes. I was getting to that. As you already know, the Almiri have been developing advanced offensive and defensive technologies for some time, in the hopes of slowly doling them out to the rest of us in a way that felt organic to our own technological growth. Some of these technologies had already found their way into the military, thank goodness, seeing as your grandfather's attack fleet consisted of only about one hundred small to midsize vessels. When the Jin'Kai invaders arrived on the horizon, Byron's force was deployed to repel them, along with any human-built ships that might be remotely up to the task. So the fleet you saw back there, engaged with the Jin'Kai? It consists mostly of human orbital military craft."

"Which aren't going to be able to survive in a sustained conflict," I surmise.

"Precisely," Dad agrees. "On a positive note, from what little evidence I've been able to gather so far, the Almiri ships have a decent edge in maneuverability over the enemy."

I nod at that. "We found that out for ourselves."

"Up until now the Almiri have been losing roughly one ship for every twelve enemies neutralized," Dad says. "An excellent win-loss ratio. Unfortunately, simply due to

Jin'Kai numbers, we're bound to lose in a war of attrition."

We come to the end of the corridor, and Dad flicks a security card to open the door blocking our path. The door *swooshes* open to reveal the bridge. Unlike before, now not all of the bridge crew are Almiri. There are several men and women wearing American and French military uniforms running their stations side by side with their alien counterparts.

"Cool, huh?" Dad asks.

It is, but I've got other things on my mind. "So why Mars? If things are going so badly, then what are we doing running off to the red planet?"

"Isn't it obvious?"

It's not my father who says it.

The command chair swivels, revealing the cool, confident star of *East of Eden*, wearing a tight red uniform so covered in shiny baubles that he looks like an extra from Hansel Wintergarten's Christmas video "Hey Girl, I'm a Tree, Come Decorate Me . . . as a Friend."

"Mars holds the key to rescuing the world!" Byron says dramatically.

"And this," I say to Chloe, "would be *my* grandfather. Hey, Gramps. Long time no see. Sorry about, you know, stealing your ship and stuff."

He does not look mad. Byron rises from his chair and walks over to me, reaching out his arms in a super-awkward gesture to hug me. I hesitate perhaps a moment too long, and he starts to pick up on it, so finally I just rush over and wrap my arms around him. Byron gives me two hard claps on the back, which I can feel reverberating throughout my skeleton.

"It's good to see you," he says.

"You too," I say. I pull away and clear my throat. I point toward Chloe, who is hanging out in the doorway, observing the entire scene with about as much emotion as you'd have watching a yogurt commercial. "This is Olivia," I tell Byron.

"Chloe," she corrects me. Her voice is harsh, but she's shifting her weight uncomfortably from foot to foot, splitting her gaze between us and the floor.

"Chloe, right," I say, turning back to Byron. "Long story. She's your great-granddaughter."

"Is she now?" he says. He walks over to Chloe, staring at her intently as he does, making her visibly more uncomfortable with each approaching step. Standing directly in front of her, Byron raises his hand and offers it to her.

"Hello, young lady," he greets her. "Welcome aboard."

"Whatever," Chloe replies, self-consciously hugging herself while admiring the fine welding work on the floor plating. "You were saying? About saving the world?"

Byron adjusts a shoulder bauble as he explains. "Ah, yes, that. You see, a hundred years ago I was doing research for an epic poem I was writing."

"Dammit, it *is* genetic," Chloe says, more astonished than anything else.

Byron appears not to notice. "I had in mind a poem that focused on the Almiri's early days on Earth. A heroic retelling of how we came down to live among a species bursting with potential yet held back by their rather quaint grasp of the universe."

"And you thought somebody was going to want to *read* that?" Chloe asks.

"The intention was to perform it aloud," Byron continues, undeterred. "I was trying to 'unearth,' if you'll pardon the pun, the earliest records we had of our journey through the cosmos—landing, making first contact, et cetera, et cetera. Records that should have been contained in our primary historical data bank. However, when I tried to access these records, I found none. I tried employing the assistance of our archivists, but they could not—or would not—help me. Through some sleuthing on my own over the next several decades, I was able to recover data entries whose time codes put them at or near the dawn of our arrival on Earth. The entries, however, were badly damaged. The damage appeared to be the result of energy surges and environmental corruption. Accidental in nature."

"A little *too* accidental," Dad chimes in.

"Exactly, Harry," Byron says. "Upon further investigation it became clear to me that these entries had been intentionally destroyed. But why would anyone want to erase the most momentous event in the history of our race?"

I'm finally beginning to see where all this is headed. "They had something to hide," I venture.

"Precisely," Byron agrees. "From that discovery I launched into a nearly thirty-year long endeavor to recover anything that I could from the records. I was mostly unsuccessful, until just recently, when I was able to avail myself of your father's rather impressive faculty for computer wizardry."

The fact that Lord Byron/James Dean/his father-in-law just gave Dad the ultimate compliment is giving Dad's ego a near pornographic level of stroking. His goofy grin appears to be lifting him several centimeters off the floor.

"So what mysterious secrets did you discover?" I ask. "And what does this have to do with Mars or the Jin'Kai or anything? I mean, not that I don't love superlong stories about history and poetry, but the thing is that I *really* don't."

"We weren't able to glean much. But what we did find was telling. Geographical references to the colony ship's initial landing site, fractured descriptions of the landscape, climate. None of these meshed with the commonly held beliefs of the Almiri, or the history passed down in our Code. And then we found a single instance of the name of the host planet."

Dad cuts in like a kid who can't keep from revealing the punch line to his older sibling's joke. "Barsoom!" he cries. And I swear he squeals when he says it.

"What the crimson crap," Chloe says, "is a Barsoom?"

I am clearly better versed in pre-turn-of-the-century sci-fi pulp novels than my daughter, because I recognize the forgotten nickname of the familiar planet immediately.

"Mars? You mean the Almiri didn't land on Earth originally? Why? And why bother to go to such great lengths to change their history?"

"Perhaps they were ashamed," Byron says. "From what I can gather, the Almiri were quickly repelled by the indigenous resistance. I wouldn't be surprised if my ancestors wanted to keep the defeat under wraps. We're not exactly known for being great losers."

"This is all purely speculation at this point," Dad reminds me.

But I'm stuck on another tiny detail. "Hold up. Did you just say 'indigenous'?" I've met all sorts of alien creatures over the past several months, but for some reason the existence of *martians* is what's threatening to blow my circuits.

"The point is," Byron says, gazing at me like *I'm* the one who's getting us off topic in this conversation, "it appears that someone or some*thing* convinced the Almiri to abandon their originally designated host planet, and the circumstances were such that my forefathers thought it best to erase all evidence of the fact and create a false history for my people."

"And if there was something powerful enough to chase off the Almiri," I say, slowly putting it all together, "you think this something might be useful against the Jin'Kai."

"It is a desperate shot in the dark, I will readily admit," Byron says. "But at this point it's all we have left in reserve. The alliance of Almiri, human, and Enosi fights bravely against unimaginable odds, but our time is quickly running out."

"How quickly?" I ask. "It will take us weeks to get to Mars. Not to mention the time it's going to take us to convince the martians—I repeat, *martians*—to let us use their superweapons."

"With our hyperdrive engaged, we should be there in a matter of hours," Byron tells me. "We should have an adequate head start on the Jin'Kai, even if they are in pursuit. And as to the planet's inhabitants," he says, "as far as we can discern, Mars was long ago abandoned."

"Then why the hell are we going there?" Chloe asks.

"The planet is devoid of *life*. Not artifacts."

"And how could you possibly know a thing like that?" Chloe asks.

"The Ares Project," I say, queen of the obvious realizations. "You've had your people searching for weapons for a while."

"Well, not *weapons* specifically," Byron says. "Not until recently. But remnants, yes. Pieces of the puzzle. And all the pieces we have point to one very particular spot. We will be landing at Terraforming Station 1-1-3-8. Prior to being evacuated, the team there had reported unusual power readings below the surface. They'd been in the process of tunneling toward the source."

"And you think these power readings will lead us to some sort of Jin-Kai-killing deus ex machina?" I ask.

"We can only hope."

"And here I'd always thought poetry was a complete waste of time."

"Don't go knocking old Byron's verses, now, miss," comes a sturdy voice from behind me. "A man needs something to occupy his mind during long trips to the loo."

I spin around and embrace Titus Oates, who wraps me in a massive bear hug.

"I'm so glad you're okay!" I say, squeezing him. He squeezes back.

"I should say the same," he tells me. Then he leans back to look me in the eye. "In the future, Miss Elvie, if you could refrain from absconding with any vehicle that isn't expressly yours . . ."

I hug him again. Chloe leans over to my dad and stage-whispers.

"Don't tell me that's my great-great-uncle," she says.

• • •

As we make our way down to the surface of the planet, it's weird not being behind the controls. But I don't think Lord Byron was particularly keen on having his granddaughter behind the wheel.

"You're coming in a little hot," comes Oates's voice over the comm. He's still up on the command ship, tracking our landing. Our dinged-up little jalopy is coming in blind, since the terraforming stations' systems have all been powered down to avoid detection by the Jin'Kai. "Bring her up a titch and start firing your front thrusters."

"How exactly does one quantify 'a titch'?" I ask Dad nervously. Dad, ever the champion of precision, simply shakes his head in dismay. Our descent has been bumpy enough that Ducky has been in the bathroom since we disembarked, and the entire Britta Brigade hasn't missed an opportunity to *eeeewwwww* after each upchuck.

"Fret not, Elvie," Byron says jovially. "Oates and I speak the same language. Look! Down below! You can see the station."

Indeed, as we approach the ground, the station comes more clearly into view through the sandstorm that has kept us blind till now. The station itself is fairly small and nondescript: from this altitude it almost looks like a metallic wedding tent, although I know that in reality it's a prefab building with living quarters and an engineering bay. What stands out is the atmospheric generator that towers above the station. It's an enormous orb, with intricately crosshatched paneling running down its sides, making it look something like a baseball the size of a baseball field. Along the top runs a series of vents from which the generator—dormant now—would pump the gaseous cocktail necessary to start the process of transforming Mars from an "uninhabitable rock" to a "prime real estate opportunity."

"You look like you can handle things from here," Oates chimes over the comm again. "If you won't be needing us any further, we'll be off. I hope you find what you're looking for, old sport."

"I do too," Byron says. "Be safe, my friend."

"Good-bye, Miss Elvie," Oates says. "I'll be seeing you before long."

"You be careful," I say, my eyes welling up against my will.

With that, the comm cuts out, and Byron begins our final descent. Ducky enters the cockpit, wiping his mouth and looking very much the worse for wear.

"I still don't see why they're taking the ship with all the guns," he says drearily.

"They're needed back in the fray," Byron says. "*The Albatross* is our fittest fighting vessel. They'll buy us the time we need."

"You hope," comes Chloe's cheery answer.

"He could have at least taken Britta and the rest with him," Ducky moans. "As if puking weren't bad enough, I have to do it with an entire cheerleading squad listening in."

"Truly you've suffered above all others," Chloe says. Ducky starts to respond, but a jolt of turbulence sets him off again, and he rushes back out of the cockpit without another word, holding his hand over his mouth.

"Eeeeeewwwwwww!" comes the chorus of Brittas.

"We're coming in for a landing," Byron says. "Elvie, Archer, Harry, you're with me."

"I think I should stay behind to look after the repairs, don't you?" Dad says. "We've got the hyperdrive working again, but if the Jin'Kai show up, I'd sure like to have that stealth field operational."

"You're my resident computer wizard, Harry. How am I supposed to access any foreign systems we come across without you?"

"I can't be in two places at once, and I've got more time under the hood with these babies than anyone else here other than yourself. Besides, with a totally foreign system, you'll need someone with a more intuitive feel than I have. In which case, Elvie's your woman," Dad says. I nearly choke on my surprise. "What?" he says. "You know I've always been extraordinarily proud of your acumen."

"I know," I say. "I've just never heard you say I was *better* than you."

"I have every faith in your abilities," Dad tells me.

I think my cheeks are burning.

"You'll need help," I say.

"Donald and Marnie can stay to assist me."

There's a pang in my chest at the thought that I won't be sharing my first martian experience with Ducky. But if Dad actually approves of him as an assistant, I know that will be a good consolation prize in his eyes.

"Fine," I say. "But then you have to keep the Brittas as well. I'm not going anywhere with that lot."

• • •

After activating the station's environmental systems and giving them enough time to pump the station full of breathable air, Cole, Byron, Chloe, and I head down inside. With caution we step into the station via the long entry corridor, which, if my love of schematics and my more-than-decent memory are correct, leads directly into the living quarters — a sparsely furnished area for the initial terraforming crew to sleep and eat in while not operating the massive machinery at the heart of the base. Byron takes the lead, clearly anxious about what we'll discover.

I'm on Mars, I keep having to remind myself with every step. I always dreamed I'd be a part of the Ares Project one day. This isn't exactly the way I envisioned it, but hey, dreams change.

Up ahead Byron comes to a doorway. "Archer, give me a hand with this, would you?" he asks. Cole runs over to his superior, and the two of them attempt to pull the unpowered door open. I stand with Chloe behind the two as they grunt and strain, and Chloe mumbles something under her breath.

"What was that?" I ask.

"I said I don't even know what I'm doing here," she says.

"Well, we're trying to uncover . . . ancient martian secrets . . . that will . . . do something. We hope. Or not."

"It's pointless. Even if you find something, the Jin'Kai are the superior race. They'll win this fight precisely because of their superiority."

"Superior, my occasionally bruised behind," I say. "They might be all burly and, okay, occasionally covered in a slimy impenetrable exoskeleton, but they are *totally* evil."

"Your morality is subjective."

"I don't think it's subjective morality to say you shouldn't steal young girls and use them like cattle."

"The Almiri do it," she says.

"Well," I start. "That's different." She gives me a look, and I swear it's like looking into a mirror. A really judgy mirror. "Okay, it's not different. But that's one of the things we're going to change."

"I should be with them," Chloe says.

"Them?" I ask, dumbfounded. "'Them' who? The Jin'Kai? Marsden? The ones who stole you from me, messed with your DNA, brainwashed you?" After all this time, I cannot believe that she'd still consider those intergalactic dickheads as her preferred team.

"They didn't brainwash me. You keep treating me like I'm some stupid little kid."

"You're, like, two months old!"

"I have my own mind."

"Yeah, well, tell me when you decide to use it."

Instantly my brain locks up. Because those aren't my words streaming out of my mouth like some uncontrollable verbal diarrhea.

They're my mother's. The one person in the universe I swore I would never be like.

"Look," I say, trying to reset. "I know you don't like me all that much. But trust that I want what's best for you. You are the whole reason I'm doing any of this. Not for the Almiri. Or even the Enosi. Or even flipping mankind. It's all for you, kiddo. So that, when all this is over, nobody gets to decide your fate but you. I'd lay down my life for you, annoying brat that you are. Bok Choy *did* lay down his life for you."

I can see from the clenching of her jaw that I may have just pulled the last stable Jenga peg out from under her wavering reserve of restraint.

"*He* didn't lay down anything," she says, sharply enough to cut my heart out in one fluid swipe. "*You* left him." I feel air escape from my lungs, but I can't form any words. My vision goes blurry, and I realize that my eyes are filling with tears. "And *you're* trying to decide my fate right now!"

"Th-that's not true," I stammer. "I . . . tried . . . with Bok . . . I *tried* . . ."

"That's enough!" Cole shouts suddenly. He storms up to Chloe, getting right in her face. "I don't want to hear another shitty thing out of you, or so help me, I might just put you over my knee. That is *your mother*, do you understand? Your mother, who carried you for nine months, who gave birth to you, cared for you under unbelievably hard circumstances, and when you were stolen away from her, stopped at nothing—*nothing*—to get you back. Now, we're all sorry about what happened to Bok Choy. He was incredibly noble and brave. But don't you dare crap on what both he and Elvie have done for you."

"She could have waited," Chloe says, suddenly crying. "She could have—"

"She could have done jack shit. He was already dying, Chloe. He was bleeding out from his gut. And if the stab wound didn't get him, all that messed-up weird science Marsden played with his DNA would have. You know that. He knew what he needed to do, and that was save you and your mother, because he loved you. The way we love you."

Chloe is a ball of tears now. She takes a halfhearted swing at Cole, only to fall into his arms without resistance. As she sobs into his chest, I wipe my own tears away and take in the lovable doofus whom I've been so hard on the past year. It's as if he's suddenly blossoming into an honest-to-goodness father right in front of me.

"It's okay, sweetie," Cole tells Chloe in a hushed tone, rocking her gently. "It's okay. I mean, it's not, because we're all probably going to die soon, but you're okay."

Ah, Cole.

"We need to keep moving," Byron announces. He has jimmied the door open far enough that we can all fit through. "The strange power sources were reported down this way. The crew was excavating the area when they were recalled."

Cole guides Chloe as she slips through the doorway after Byron and starts down the stairs. I tap Cole on the shoulder, and when he turns around, I surprise him with a big hug.

"What's that for?" he asks.

"You're going to be a great dad," I tell him. "Check that. You *are* a great dad."

Cole grins. "Guess my paternity suit had to kick in sometime."

I pause, mentally accessing my Cole-to-English translator. "Cole," I say slowly. "Did you by any chance mean 'paternal instinct'?"

He nods. "Yeah. That thing."

And with that, Cole squeezes his way through the doorway. I follow closely behind.

The stairs spiral downward for several dozen meters before

they disappear and give way to a red, ashy rock path.

"We must be getting close," Byron says. He carries a sensor pad in front of him, much like the tracker we used to find Chloe back on the ozone station. "The readings are getting . . . for lack of a better term, weird. There's definitely a power signature down here, and it's not one of ours."

"So, did these guys find something underneath their station by sheer dumb luck?" I ask.

"No," Byron answers. "Each station was positioned in an area that seemed likely to have supported life at some point in the past. While the surface of Mars had been lifeless for eons when we first began the Ares Project, it seemed reasonable to assume that if there had been a native species, that species would have developed a subterranean civilization. And the most likely starting points for building such a system would have been below where the native species had lived prior to the environment's becoming uninhabitable."

"Of course," I say, vowing never to ask for explanations from an epic poet again. (Seriously, there's a reason the guy never took up haiku.)

"Here," Byron says. We are facing a large rock front.

"Are you sure?" I ask. "The path continues down this way."

"The signature is coming from behind this wall." Byron pockets the sensor pad and exchanges it for two wonky-looking pistols. He hands one to Cole.

"Concentrated pattern, Archer," Byron says. "Let's try not to cave the whole tunnel in around us."

I flinch at the sound of the weapons echoing through the corridor as Cole and Byron fire into the rock face, zigzagging their shots from the ceiling down to the floor. The rock crumbles away more and more rapidly, and after a few moments they stop firing to let the dust settle.

"Wow," Chloe says as the results of their labor come into focus. "More rock. Great job, guys."

"Wait," I say. I step forward. It's true that the surface looks nearly identical to the rock that was just cleared away. But something seems . . . off. I place my hand on the surface. It's cool to the touch, but the longer my hand stays in place, the warmer the surface gets. I place my other hand on the rock, and suddenly a low humming begins to emanate from the rock.

"Incredible," Byron says.

"Well, what do I do now?" I ask. "Say something in old Elvish?"

Where's Ducky when you need someone to laugh at your hilarious nerd jokes? Not a peep from these guys. Nothing.

But soon I've stopped caring that my humor goes unappreciated, because the rock begins to slide apart down a middle seam, and it becomes clear that it isn't a rock wall at all but a door. It parts all the way, revealing a large circular room crafted out of more red mineral, similar to the door. We step inside, our footsteps echoing in the empty space.

And then the wall/door slams shut behind us.

"Shit," I say. I place both hands on the door again, but nothing. There's no visible seam to work either.

"So here we are, in a pitch-black cave, under Mars," Chloe says. "Now what?"

As if in response to her question, the room springs to life. Lights flash along the sheer walls without any hint of a source.

It appears as if the rock itself is illuminating the space. Along the curved walls, large sections begin to flicker with strange, scrolling symbols.

"Did I do that?" Chloe asks in a whisper.

Cole is more direct. "Helllllloooooo?" he calls loudly. "Who's there, please?"

I place a hand on his arm. "It's not a who," I tell him, amazed. "It's a what." I point at the scrolling imagery around us. "It's a screen. This is a computer."

"Then what's that say?" Cole wonders, tracing a few of the gibberish symbols with his finger. "Is it Martian?"

"I don't think it's a language, per se," I reply, slowly examining it. "It looks more like code."

"Very astute, Earth child."

The voice is so otherworldly that even Byron jumps at the sound. We all look around the room frantically but see no one.

"Who's there?" I ask, not even bothering to feel silly for pulling a Cole Archer.

"There is no one there, Earth child. It is simply me. The 'computer,' as you put it. Here. Perhaps this will make for a more fluid exchange of data."

The center of the ceiling begins to glow, and a cone of red light shoots down to the floor and begins spinning around. After a few moments the light takes shape as a tall, humanoid form, almost like a regular person but thinner, hairless, and with large, oblong black eyes.

"Greetings, travelers. You have come very far. I am Merv. How may I assist you?"

Chapter Thirteen

WHEREIN, IF YOU THOUGHT THAT THERE WAS NOTHING FURTHER TO LEARN ABOUT ALIEN LIFE, YOU WOULD BE WRONG. SOOOOOOO WRONG.

"You seem confused by my appearance," Merv says as he looks at each of us in turn. Well, not looks, I guess—I'm assuming this room-slash-computer has camera sensors recording our every move, embedded somewhere unseen, along with the magically appearing monitors, but the holographic projection is doing a good imitation of "looking" with its massive dark eyes as it registers our movements.

"What's to be confused about?" I say. "You're a computer. This is what martians looked like. End of story."

"Ah, yes, 'martians.' Perhaps I should clarify—"

"I said *end of story*. There are too many different alien species to keep track of already. We're kind of on a tight schedule here, and I honestly don't care anymore. So, you're a martian. Let's move on."

I don't know if holographic representations of AI can get offended, but apparently they can *look* offended. Merv's eyes widen in what I'm assuming is a martian expression of indignation.

"*Very well,*" he says at last. "*Tell me, then. What is your purpose here?*"

"Well, like you said, we're from Earth. But we're not all, strictly speaking, earthlings. This here"—I point at Byron—"is my grandfather. He's what's called an Almiri."

Byron is staring, mouth agape, at Merv. "I've waited a very long time for this," he tells the holograph earnestly.

"*Accessing . . . ah. 'Almiri. Long-range colony seed ship, planetary arrival 2656.8 cycles ago. You have taken the name of your vessel. When your kind arrived here, you called yourself Klahnia.*"

"That's correct," Byron replies. He seems pleased that Merv knows so much about his people.

"*Why have you returned? Doing so violates our pact.*"

"Pact?" Byron asks. "We come seeking help. Earth is under attack."

"*Activating external sensors . . . Accessing . . .*" Merv seems to stare blankly at the far wall for several moments. "*Yes, it appears that Earth is indeed under attack,*" he says as he refocuses on us. "*I am detecting three distinct engine signatures. Two are significantly more advanced than the other.*"

"Those are our ships helping the humans," Byron explains. "The aggressors call themselves Jin'Kai."

"*Analysis suggests they are Klahnia.*"

"Yes," Byron admits. "It's a long story."

"*Your female companion does not care for long stories.*"

"And yet that's all I ever seem to get," I mutter.

Merv turns back to me, his eyes rotating upward slightly. *"You are not Klahnia."*

"Good eye."

"You are not human."

"Two for two. Want to cash out now, or try for the Kia?"

"Your query does not compute. However, it appears hybridization was a success."

That jolts all of us, even Cole, who has been way more focused on the flashing lights than the conversation with the sentient computer.

"You know about the hybrids?" I ask.

"Yes. Shall I explain? Or do you prefer again to rest on assumptions?"

"Explain away."

"I could use pictures and small words if that would help."

"When did *you* get so snarky?"

"I am programmed to adapt my interface to communicate more readily with the user."

"Score one for the ancient computer guy," Chloe mutters.

"Right," I tell Merv. "So, speaking of adaptation?"

"The Klahnia ship Almiri *arrived on Barsoom expecting to find a primitive peoples they could easily conquer and use for the purpose of procreating their species."*

"Conquer?" Byron starts. "We would never—"

"There will be time for baseless indignation after I have completed my expository. To continue, the Klahnia did not find this to be the case. The society they intruded upon was a flourishing and advanced species, considerably more developed in many regards than themselves. The attempt to subjugate the

native population was drawn-out, bloody, and fruitless."

"So you guys defeated the Almiri?" I ask. Dreams of martian superweapons once again dance in my head. "Do you still have the weapons you used to beat them?"

"There are no large-scale weapon systems left operational on this planet. If this is what you came seeking, then may I suggest you . . . Accessing Earth cultural databases . . . 'Go Fish.'"

Well, that's that, then. As nifty as this history lesson has been, it's all been for nothing. No martian weapons. No answer for the Jin'Kai fleet. No hope.

"Please do not exhibit an outwardly defeatist attitude. Your problems would not be solved by finding weapons here."

"Is that a fact?" Chloe says. Merv considers her, his eyes rotating like when he was looking at me earlier.

"Our conflict with the Klahnia had no victor. Neither side had definitive technological superiority, at least where the arts of war were concerned. After a time neither side had the ability or desire to continue. A treaty was agreed upon, including several stipulations. First, that the Klahnia would depart, never to return. In exchange, we would provide them with an alternative home suitable to their needs."

"Earth," I say. "So if you got the Almiri to leave, why aren't there any martians running around? What happened?"

"The planet was determined unsuitable for the further development of the species, and so it was abandoned."

"Where did they go?" Cole asks.

Look who just started paying attention.

"My programming does not include this information."

My wheels are spinning. "But I thought there were only

six species in the galaxy that the Klahnia could use as breeding hosts," I say. "That was the whole point of the six colony ships, wasn't it, Byron?"

"That's what we've always believed," Byron says.

"There are more than six galactic species compatible with the Klahnia's breeding requirements."

"And humans just happened to be one of them, sitting right next door to you martian folks?"

"No."

I scratch my head. Cole apparently feels head-scratchy too.

"Okay, I'm lost," he says. "I know this comes as a shock."

Merv's eyes twist in his head again, and suddenly one of the monitor displays pushes away from the wall and hovers in three dimensions in front of us. A stream of data scrolls over the screen, and maps that appear to be star charts arrange themselves around the edges of the text.

"My information banks contain the histories of 4,672 sentient species throughout the known universe. We have been observing and studying other worlds considerably longer than the Klahnia — or Almiri, as they now refer to themselves. Of these known species, one in ten exhibit the genetic markers that would make them suitable hosts for the parasitic breeding cycle of the Almiri."

"You're saying there are more than four hundred species out there that they could be breeding with?" Chloe asks, sounding as incredulous as I feel. "Marsden doesn't know that. I'm sure none of the other Jin'Kai do either."

"More than four hundred viable species, yes. However, there was never any intention of offering up another defenseless species to the fate the Klahnia had intended for us."

"What do you call siccing them on the humans, then, huh?" I ask.

"*Earthlings were chosen with a different purpose in mind.*"

"And what purpose would that be?"

"*The Klahnia were a brutal, violent, unpredictable race. They were also, colloquially speaking, not great planners. If they were to succeed in their goal of finding a suitable host species, because of the nature of their procreation cycle, they most likely would have exhausted their potential hosts within a few hundred years, thereby forcing themselves to move on to another planet, and then another, and another, leaving nothing but husks in their wake.*"

"Sounds familiar," Cole says.

"*While not a perfect match for Klahnia breeding, humans appeared*"—Merv emphasizes the word "appeared," even raising his holographic eyebrows—"*on many levels to be exactly that. So much so that the Klahnia were fooled into believing humans could indeed be used to help spawn future generations of their species. However, given enough time, the dominant species' genetic traits would surely exert their will. And the strongest evolutionary trait in all the universe is the ability to adapt.*"

"Hybrids," I say. I feel like I've been struck by lightning, my body vibrating as the current runs across my skin. "You sent the Almiri to Earth because you knew that they'd start producing hybrid children. The mutation that produced the Enosi didn't come from the Almiri. It came from humans."

"Yes," Merv says. "*The will to adapt and survive is stronger on Earth than on nearly any other planet recorded. If environmental factors threaten a species, that species simply adapts to the new variables to continue to thrive. Failure to do so leads to extinction."*

"But humans aren't stronger than the Almiri, or the Jin'Kai," Chloe argues. "They're weaker, slower. They live a fraction as long."

"And yet they survive. The enormous dinosaurs of Earth's past were more powerful than any other species within half a million light years. Yet when disaster struck the planet—literally—those who could not adapt perished. And what mighty animal took their place? The chicken. Do not mistake the strength of an individual as indicative of the strength of the species."

Beside me Byron lets out a bemused chuckle. "'*Veni, vidi, vici,'*" he says, shaking his head.

"Who's Vinny Vidivici?" Cole asks.

"It's Latin, dear boy, from one of our forbearers. 'I came, I saw, I conquered.' It's all so terribly ironic now, isn't it? First we were gods. Then kings, emperors, conquerors. Then we discovered science, the arts, social justice. All the while, we thought we were influencing mankind. We thought ourselves their betters. But it was man who changed us." Byron strikes a pose, one arm crooked, hand resting on his hip, while the other arm shoots out dramatically in front of him. "'How happy is the blameless vestal's lot! The world forgetting, by the world forgot.' How cruel that this wondrous revelation comes to us at the twilight hour of our story."

"Is he always like this?"

"As long as I've known him," I tell Merv.

"What I don't understand," Cole says, "is why our ancestors didn't just wipe humans out completely, the way they tried on Mars, the way the Jin'Kai have done over and over again?"

"*For a time we kept watch. Envoys were sent periodically to make sure that your people upheld our agreement and followed the Code.*"

"You wrote the Code?" Byron asks. He's surprised, sure, but almost giddy at the revelation. More fodder for the poem, I suspect. "All of our laws, all of our dearly held beliefs, found their origin here?"

"*It was necessary to ensure that your kind did not over-populate too quickly. The mutation would need adequate time to spread organically through human-hybrid mating.*"

"I don't think time is going to be a luxury afforded us by the Jin'Kai," I say. "With their numbers they'll make the entire planet infertile within a single generation."

"*That is impossible. The mutation has already achieved biological dominance. The movement toward the new species is now inevitable. Human parents or Klahnia parents, the major-ity of births will be the same. Hybrid. The unification of all. It cannot be avoided.*" Merv pauses. "*It appears we have more visitors.*"

"Visitors?" Cole asks. "Who?"

"Who do you think?" I reply, looking at the display. "Jin'Kai. Devastators. Three ships landed right outside."

"The others will be sitting ducks out there!" Cole cries.

I examine the sensor readout—the martian systems turn out to be quite intuitive—but I can't seem to find our shuttle anywhere.

"Dad must have gotten the stealth shield activated," I say. Byron looks over my shoulder. "If the Devastators are scouring the area, it won't be long before they find the ship, stealth shield or not."

"You're right," I agree. "We've got to get them in here before the Jin'Kai discover them. Merv, open the doors so we can get our friends."

"*I'm afraid I cannot do that,*" Merv says.

"What? Why not?"

"*The new arrivals appear to be very aggressive. My preservation protocols prohibit me from willfully allowing such forces access to my data banks.*"

"My father's out there, you stupid holographic twit!" I yell. "And my best friend, and his girlfriend. And . . . a bunch of annoying cheerleaders. But they're people too, and if you think I'm going to let you—"

"*I'm sorry. The entrance must remain sealed.*"

I watch the display helplessly as the motion sensors pick up several signals spreading out in military formation outside the entrance to the terraforming station. The Devastators are dangerously close to where our ship is most likely sitting, cloaked. It's only a matter of time.

"I can't sit here and just watch," I say.

"Don't worry," Cole says. "The Jin'Kai will probably follow the same power source we did. Maybe your Dad and the others can take off safely while the Devastators attack us here."

"Very comforting, Cole," I tell him. Damn. We were so close. I could practically taste the deus ex—

"*Pardon me, but would you like me to activate this installation's defensive systems?*"

We all turn and stare at Merv, mouths agape.

"I thought you said there were no weapons left on the planet!" Cole screeches.

"There are no weapons that you could use off-planet in a conflict. However, this installation is fortified with energy shielding, several direct-energy turrets, and—"

"Yes. Yes! Activate them!" we all shout.

"Very good. Shall I transport your friends on the stealthed vessel inside before raising the shields?"

"You have *molecular transporters?*" Byron asks. "I'm most impressed."

"Could have used that information *before* my heart attack, Merv," I say. "But, yes. Beam them up, Scotty."

"I am not sure I understand the command. Accessing . . ." Merv's eyes twist in his head for several seconds. *"Ah, yes. 'Scotty.' Charming. There is interference from the rudimentary stealth field. I cannot ascertain if they are all friendlies. There are more than a dozen life-forms aboard. Perhaps these 'Jin'Kai' have already boarded?"*

"No, that would be our in-house cheerleading squad," I say. "They're not exactly friendlies . . . but I guess you'd better beam them all in anyway."

Beside me Chloe lets out a groan. And I can't even blame her.

"Very well. Initiating transport."

There is a flickering light in the center of the room, and forms begin to take shape. At first they're transparent, but as the shimmering light around them fades, they become more solid. But something's wrong. Only a handful of them are standing up. Most of them are lying flat on the ground. As they come into focus, it looks like all of the Brittas are out cold on the floor. Then I spot Marnie, also unconscious. The hairs on the back of my neck prickle.

"What the hell?" Chloe asks.

Standing next to the unconscious girls are three people — Dad and Ducky, wearing some sort of hooded suits, and behind them . . .

"You just won't stay dead, will you, Doc?"

Marsden looks discombobulated. Which I guess is to be expected when you've just been de- and re-molecularized.

"What is this?" he asks. His muscles are coiled and his eyes wide. Then, as though it's the only logical move, Marsden swiftly grabs Ducky and pulls him into a headlock, brandishing a weapon and pointing it directly at Duck's noggin.

"Easy with that thing," I say. The blood in my veins runs ice cold, but I try to explain things as calmly as I can to the madman with the ray gun. "You're on Mars. Or, well, under it." He still seems confused. "Lemme guess," I continue. "You hid on the shuttle when we blasted our way out of the Rust Belt, like a rat leaving a sinking ship."

"Such a way with words," Marsden says, quickly returning to his usual evil-scientist-in-charge shtick. "You wouldn't believe that I always forget that." He makes a quick survey of the room. "Weapons. All of them. Kick them over."

Reluctantly Byron and Cole take the blasters they used to carve the rock face and slide them across the floor toward Marsden.

"What did you do, Marsden?" I ask. "Are they all dead?"

"What, the cattle?" Marsden asks, darting his eyes down

toward Marnie and the Brittas. "No. The plan was to gas every-one and then commandeer the ship."

"Donald and I were outside doing repairs," Dad explains, pulling his shielded hood back so that he can be heard. "When we reentered the ship, we found the girls unconscious and our friend here trying to start up the engines."

You'd think I'd be insanely pissed about this new devel-opment. But the fact that I don't have to listen to a bunch of Brittas prattle about Cole's butt in this tense moment is less-ening my rage.

Marsden's still got my bestie in a headlock, though, so there's that to deal with.

"Mind telling me what is going on?" Marsden asks. And given the gun and all, I'm inclined to answer him.

I point to the hologram who's been taking in our standoff with fascinated detachment. "This is Merv," I explain. "He's kind of the resident record-keeper here on Mars. We came here looking for a superweapon to blast your buddies to smith-ereens with, but what we found instead was a big old truth bomb. It's all pretty long and convoluted, but the short version is: You're done. It's all over. Your experiments are based on bad science, Doctor. You let your prejudice blind you to the truth. The mutation responsible for the Enosi hybrids does not originate in the Almiri but in man."

Marsden slits his eyes at me. "That's impossible," he says. "The mutation appears in the gestating Almiri fetus."

"See for yourself," I say. I flick through the screen in front of me. "Merv, put the pertinent info up for the good doctor to read, would you?"

"This has been the strangest day," Merv replies, but he follows orders. The data streams on a holographic display in front of Marsden.

Marsden's eyes scroll over the text, and you can practically see his conviction melting away with each line he reads.

"This is impossible," he repeats.

"It doesn't matter how many times you try to graft your own DNA onto any of us," I tell him. "The stronger species will always win out. And humans are the stronger species. So suck on that until it tastes like candy."

"I am not in the mood for games, Elvie."

"Neither am I. The writing is literally on the wall, Doc. So maybe you should just put down the gun and go to your Devastator buddies out there for an honorable beheading, or whatever."

"Speaking of which," Merv interjects. *"The encroaching aliens have come into contact with the first line of turrets. Shields at ninety-three percent. Analysis suggests defensive systems will hold for ten minutes."*

"They're here?" Marsden asks, his face going white.

"Dearheart, what exactly is going on?" Dad asks.

"Same old stuff, Dad. Aliens. Revelation. Drama. Put the gun down, Doc."

Marsden ignores me, staring intently at the genetic analysis scrolling in front of him. "My work . . ." I've got to give it to him, the man sounds truly gutted. "If all this is true . . . If we had known, we never would have come to your backward planet."

And there it is. The cartoon lightbulb going off above my head. "I guess you wouldn't have, would you?" I say. I turn to my new buddy the hologram. "Merv, maybe you can help us out after all."

"*As I mentioned previously, there are no weapons systems left on the planet that would be of use to you in a planetary conflict.*"

"We don't need to beat the Devastators," I say, thinking things through out loud. "We only need to make them realize how pointless beating us would be."

Byron shakes his head. "I don't follow," he says.

"What are you getting at, Elvie?" Marsden asks. His grip on Ducky has not loosened in the slightest.

"The whole point of this stupid invasion is for the Jin'Kai to find a new source of baby mommas, right? But if we could get a signal out, share the info about the mutation, let them see that hybridization is an inevitable and systemic thing at this point, and there's no reason to stay . . ."

"Then they'll just exterminate the whole planet," Marsden says.

"That sounds bad," Cole puts in.

"They wouldn't waste their time with extermination if they have somewhere better to be," I say. "Heck, this might even save *your* bacon, Doc."

"Elvie . . ." Ducky starts to ask. But Marsden squeezes more tightly, and he shuts up.

"Merv," I say, attempting to keep my cool. A *plan, Elvie. All you need is a plan.* "You said there are, what, four hundred some species out there compatible with the Klahnia? I'm assuming they're pretty far away, right? I mean, seeing as the Almiri never found them before."

"The species are a considerable distance from this system, yes."

"And you have broadcast capabilities, right? If I wanted to transmit a message on an open frequency, the Jin'Kai fleet would be able to pick it up and understand it?"

"That is correct."

"So if they're so desperate to start making babies, there'd be very little reason to stay here and fight before they left. If we could send them coordinates . . ."

"It is against my programming to allow you to expose a vulnerable species to an aggressor."

"Yeah, that makes sense," I say. "Do you have a user interface I can operate manually?"

"Yes, but—"

"Can you activate it, please?"

"It is against my programming to—"

"I got that part. Just open the goddamn interface."

"Very well." Merv's eyes widen and spin, and a three-dimensional holographic keyboard panel appears in front of me, complete with a monitor. But when Marsden retrains his gun on me, I take a step back from the keyboard, arms raised.

"What are you playing at?" Marsden asks.

"I'm not playing, Doc. What you're seeing here is a last ditch effort to keep us *all* alive."

Marsden appears very unsure—an unusual look for him. His gun arm relaxes ever so slightly, which I take to mean that I momentarily have his attention. I move back to the keyboard. The cryptic martian code scrawls in front of me.

"I slept through Beginners' Martian freshman year, Merv," I say, already furiously scrolling through the data in front of me. "Mind throwing a universal translator my way?" Cole and Chloe crowd around me as English appears on the screen. "Show me star charts for the nearest compatible species." Merv complies.

Embedded in the charts are data about each inhabited planet, detailing varieties of plant and animal life, sentient species (some planets, remarkably, have more than one), and levels of technological advancement. It's pretty much the most astounding discovery in history, but I'll have time to contemplate it later. Hopefully. In the present I need coordinates. The *right* coordinates.

"Elvie, don't," Byron says. "This is wrong."

"He's right, Elvs," Cole says. "You can't just shove the Jin'Kai off onto some other unsuspecting race because it's convenient."

For his part Ducky makes a gagging noise that I take as agreement.

"Look, I don't know about you all," I say, "but I just met my daughter, like, a week ago, and for most of that time she's been a real bitch. No offense, sweetie."

"None taken."

"I'd like a little more time to get to know her better, and worldwide annihilation would seriously get in the way of that. I mean to survive this. I mean for us all to survive."

"If we were to sacrifice another planet's freedom to save our own skins," Byron warns—and I swear I will knee him in the groin if he starts in on the poetry right now—"that would make us no better than the Jin'Kai."

"He's right, dearheart," Dad says gently. "While I cannot

contemplate oblivion, I find it a sweeter fate than that of being an accomplice to mass genocide."

"All right. That's just about enough, I think." It's Marsden who says it. When I look up, his gun is trained steadily on me, his forearm still firmly pressed into Ducky's windpipe.

"Doc, this will work, I swear. You just have to—"

"Trust you? I think not." He takes a step back toward the sealed door. "You are all quite convincing, but I'm not about to be hoodwinked by a half-assed ruse concocted by the Almiri and their pets."

"This is the only way, Marsden," I plead, doing my best to stay calm. "What do you think you're going to do, just walk out there and fly away happily with the monsters who want to kill you?"

"That's exactly what I intend to do. But they won't lay a finger on me," he says, throwing his glance to Chloe. "Not once I have her."

My heart does a nosedive straight to the pit of my stomach. "Forget it, Doc. She's with us now. You burned that bridge when you revealed yourself as the cold, calculating prick that you are."

Marsden trains the gun on Chloe.

"I don't care if I have to carry her out in pieces. She's coming with me."

"This may not be the best time," Merv interjects, *"but the intruders have crossed the first threshold and have engaged the secondary turret position. Shields are at sixty-seven percent."*

"I don't think you've thought this through, Doc," I say. "Taking my daughter with you won't change any of the facts that we've learned here today."

"This is not your daughter," Marsden says. His tone is so matter-of-fact that it sounds like a smirk.

"What do you mean?" I feel breathless. "Of course she is."

"Your troublesome mother took your mewling infant when she abandoned my facility weeks ago," Marsden tells me. "This one is of my making."

Chloe and I lock eyes with each other, and I'm not sure which of us is more terrified.

"A clone?" Cole asks. His voice is weak, nearly defeated. It's a tone I don't think I've ever heard from him.

"But the tracker . . . ," I say. "It led me right to her. It . . . it *beeped*."

"The tracer is genetic," Byron offers. His voice is gentle, as though he knows that what he's about to explain will gut me. "If Chloe is really a clone, it's possible the tracer could have been transferred into her DNA as well."

I spent all that time rescuing my baby girl, and now I've lost her all over again. And my mom has her? Where? Are they safe?

No. No time for this. You're in a cave underneath the surface of Mars, Elvie Nara. You have an evil alien doctor holding you at gunpoint. The lives of your father, your friends, and yes, even the clone of your daughter, are at stake. Push it down. Push it deep down and save that worry for later. Right now you have to save the world.

"Marsden," I say. "You're a putz."

"Not your best insult, Miss Nara, but given the circumstances I'll let it slide."

"Taking Chloe won't help you one bit."

"It is my fifth attempt at splicing your offspring's hybrid

DNA with the superior Jin'Kai code, and the only one to survive this long," Marsden says. "My best shot at creating a sustainable breeding population lies in her cells."

"Marsden, haven't you listened to a single thing that I've been saying?" I snap. "Your DNA *cannot overwrite the hybrid gene*. This was all by design. You lie with Enosi, and Enosi is all you're going to get."

"*Lies!*" Marsden booms. "I will unlock the secret! Make it viable. We will never need to depend on an inferior race again. We will be eternal!"

"*I should point out,*" Merv butts in, "*that the intruders have engaged the final line of turrets. Shields at twenty-nine percent. If this room is breached, I will be forced to terminate life support.*"

"Do you plan on being a complete racist idiot the rest of your soon-to-be-very-short life?" I rage at the doc. "There's still a way for everyone to walk away from this!"

"You know, Elvie, now that I think about it, I don't find you all that charming anymore. Perhaps your particular brand of snark has grown old." He tightens his grip on his gun. "Maybe it's time that we shut you up once and for all."

"Stop!" Chloe shouts. She looks at me for a brief second, then turns to Marsden, her mind made up. "I'll go with you."

The surprise is written all over Marsden's face, as I'm sure it is on mine.

"I'll come without a fight, all right?" Chloe tells him. "Just don't hurt anyone."

"I'm not in the mood for tricks," Marsden warns.

"No tricks. You leave them be, and I come with you. You

don't, and you'll have to extract the DNA you need from your ass, 'cause that's where my foot will be."

"Chloe," I say, suddenly choked up. "You don't have to do this. There must be some other—"

"If there's one thing you taught me, it's that I have the right to choose my own path," she says. "So. This is my choice. Besides, I'm not even really your daughter."

"I might not have given birth to you," I say. "But either way, you're my daughter. That foot-up-the-ass remark seems to prove it."

I get a slight smile out of her with that. "I hope you find your real daughter," she tells me. Then she turns back to Marsden. "We have a deal?"

"We have a deal," he says.

Chloe walks slowly over to him, her hands raised. As soon as she gets close to him, Marsden shoves Ducky away and grabs hold of her, pulling her against him into the same headlock.

"Of course, you realize I can't just leave them here to continue what they're doing," Marsden says, raising the gun toward me again, his finger on the trigger.

"And of course you realize that you should have checked me for a weapon," Chloe says. Her hand flies into her tunic and she squeezes. The blaster shot sizzles through the loose fabric on her back and catches Marsden in the ribs. "How's that free will taste, scumbag?"

Marsden cries out, stumbling back a few steps. Chloe tries to pull the gun free to get off another shot, but Marsden kicks her squarely in the face, knocking her out cold.

"Chloe!" I scream, rushing to her on the ground.

That's when Cole and Byron make their move on Marsden. The doctor gets off a shot that hits Byron in the shoulder, sending him sprawling. Cole collides with Marsden, whose gun falls to the ground, and Ducky makes a beeline for it, nearly over-running the weapon, fumbling it, and kicking it ahead of him as he stumbles, bent over. Even Dad tries to get in on the fisticuffs, grappling with Cole and Marsden, but one well-placed kick into his bad knee, and he crumples to the floor in agony. Marsden turns over and rolls Cole into a choke hold. Cole's face turns purple, the veins throbbing in his throat and forehead.

"I expected a little better after our first sparring match," Marsden tells him.

"Stop it!" I cry. I'm cradling Chloe's head in my lap on the ground, tears streaming down my face. "You're killing him!"

"That is the general idea," Marsden says.

"Let him go. Now."

Marsden turns to see Ducky training his own gun on him. Ducky's sweating and trembling. I want to tell Duck to step back, that he's too close to Marsden, but before I can open my mouth, the doctor reaches out and snatches the gun right from Ducky's hands. He flings Cole to the floor, where he gasps desperately for air, unable to move.

Marsden grins at me as he trains the gun on Ducky. "Perhaps I'll let you watch me kill everyone you love before I get to you," he says. "How would you like that, Elvie?"

"Please," I whimper. "No."

Dad has crawled over to me and is wrapping me and Chloe in a protective embrace. Ducky looks at me wistfully and smiles.

"Elvie . . . ," Dad whispers. "Listen."

That's when I hear the humming sound. Marsden hears it too—a split second too late. Ducky drops and covers his face just as the blaster explodes in the doctor's hand, flinging him across the room, where he crashes into a bloody heap on the floor. The blast knocks Ducky in the opposite direction and throws me and Dad back on the floor as well. The ceiling is spinning above me, until I focus in on the red hologram staring down at me.

"*Are you badly injured?*" Merv asks, blinking.

"I don't think so," I say.

"*Good. I just wanted to inform you that shielding will fail in approximately ninety seconds. It's been nice getting to know you.*"

"Don't write me off just yet, Merv," I say, rising unsteadily from the ground. "Show me that manual interface again."

"Did you see that?" Ducky asks a little too loudly. His ears are probably ringing even more than mine are. "Elvie, did you see what I did? I did it! I totally did it." He tries to stand up too quickly, and winces, holding his shoulder.

"I saw, Ducky," I say without looking away from the display. "Great job."

"I overloaded the pistol, just like Chloe did before." He's still beaming with excitement. "I tricked him into grabbing the gun, and then it blew up right in his hand!"

"Like I said, I saw. Cole, make sure Chloe is okay."

"I hope that guy stays dead this time," Cole mutters. His voice is hoarse, and he rubs his throat as he makes his way over to Chloe. As if in answer, a moan emanates from Marsden's slumped mass, and the doctor shifts slightly on the ground.

"Oh, come *on!*" Cole says. "Are you kidding me?"

Merv considers Marsden. *"This one is badly damaged. Disintegrated limb. Ruptured internal organs. Heavy blood loss. He will be deceased in moments."*

"Good," Ducky says, but then he stops himself. "I mean, not 'good,' but . . . I never killed anyone before." He looks at me. "I don't think I like it, Elvie."

"How . . . do you think . . . I feel?" Marsden manages to flip himself over, and the sight of him is enough to make me sick. The left side of his face looks *melted,* and his left arm has been blown off past the elbow. His stomach is a mass of leaking organs, and his shirt is so slick with blood that I can't even remember what color it was originally. Upon looking at the doctor, Ducky immediately barfs on the ground.

"Done in . . . by a human," Marsden croaks.

"Just die already," I say. "I'm so done with you."

"He really does seem like quite the anal orifice," Merv remarks.

So I guess there's a little tweaking needed in the AI's colorful metaphor subroutine.

"Elvie." Dad puts his hands on mine, halting my typing. "Stop, dearheart. It's over."

"I really wish I had time to debate this with you guys, but I don't. You're just going to have to trust that I know what I'm doing." I put the last touches on the info packet. "Merv, prepare to upload the packet."

"While I am impressed that you have managed to override the considerable safeguards in my programming in such a short amount of time, I still must protest this course of action."

"Listen to the ancient artificial intelligence, dearheart."

"I just need a few more seconds," I say through gritted teeth.

There is a sudden blast from outside. The lights momentarily flutter, and red dust falls from the ceiling. The unmistakable sound of blaster fire can be heard, each shot sending another shudder through the room.

"*Shielding has failed*," Merv states. "*The door will hold a few seconds only. You have my sympathies, truly.*"

"Elvie, enough!" Byron grabs me and pulls me away from the keyboard. "Look at what we've learned here today. My species believed that they were a benevolent, enlightened people who bestowed their goodness on mankind. Our forefathers buried the truth about how we really came to live as we do, and that arrogance has lead to our undoing. Let the cycle of madness end here. Do not sentence another people to our fate."

"You're forgetting that the martians pushed the Almiri off onto Earth in the first place. They didn't have a problem making their problems our problems. So it's not just you who's getting boned here." I struggle against his grip, but he's too strong.

"They did so in an effort to change us for the better. They were motivated by something greater than mere self-preservation. They had a plan. You can't do something as reckless as this without thinking it through! You don't have a plan."

I stop struggling and look Byron dead in the eye.

"I'm Elvie Nara. I *always* have a plan." I turn to Merv, who is watching our struggle with detached curiosity. "Merv, send the info packet."

"Don't do it!" Byron shouts.

"*I am sorry,*" Merv says, "*but she has overwritten my programming.*"

Merv's eyes spin in his head.

"*The packet has been delivered.*"

Suddenly an enormous blast shakes the entire room, and the door crumbles away in shards of red ore. An entire squadron of decked-out Devastators bursts through, weapons at the ready. They train their weapons on us and bark indecipherable commands at us in their own language. They seem slightly confused by the pile of Brittas lying, unconscious, on the ground, not to mention the pile of Marsden.

"We surrender!" Ducky cries, hands in the air.

I simply grasp my father's hand and squeeze. "We were so close," I say.

"I love you, dearheart," Dad replies.

I feel someone take my other hand. I look down. It's Chloe. She smiles at me and shrugs, and I can't help but laugh. It seems to confuse the lead Devastator. He charges toward me and picks me straight up off the ground with one monster claw, despite the protests from my friends. The Devastator barks something at me, its long dagger right in my face.

"*Excuse me?*" Merv says. The Devastator turns and glares at him. "*I have an incoming message from the alien fleet.*"

Suddenly Merv's image disappears, and in its place stands a tall, imposing Devastator wearing some sort of cape. The death squad immediately stands at attention. The image barks at them for a few seconds, and the lead Devastator responds, his tone confused-sounding (well, as confused-sounding as mangled spoons in the garbage disposal can get). The answer he receives sounds incredibly angry, even by Devastator standards. Then the image blurs once more and Merv reappears.

"The transmission has ended."

The Devastator with the kung fu grip on my throat looks at me and narrows his yellow eyes. His jointed teeth ripple in a cascade from one side of his mouth to the other, a sort of disdainful Jin'Kai sneer, I suppose. I feel his putrid breath on my face and prepare myself for the worst. Then, without warning, the gnarly creep drops me roughly to the ground. He barks a command to the others, and to my great shock, they all turn and head out of the room.

"What are they doing?" Dad asks. "Is that it?"

"The package was received and acknowledged. The intruders have received orders to fall back immediately."

"Then it's done," Byron says glumly.

"That's it? The invasion is over?" Ducky asks. "We won?"

"No . . . you . . . can't . . . *leave* me," Marsden gurgles from the floor. "It's a trick. . . . Don't . . . a trick . . ."

Most of the Devastators head out of the room without acknowledging Marsden in any way, but as their leader pulls up the rear, he turns and spits a nasty alien loogie right on the expiring villain. With that, the last of the baddies disappear through the hole in the door. All that's left of our would-be executioners is the sound of their footsteps plodding toward the surface.

Merv's eyes spin in his head. *"It appears that the encroaching fleet has broken off their attack on Earth and is falling back. The 'Devastators,' as you call them, are preparing for immediate departure to the coordinates contained within the data packet."*

"I don't even know what to say," Ducky says, shaking his head. "But didn't that feel . . . *extremely* too easy?"

"The hard part will be living with what we did here," Byron says, staring grimly at the star maps. "You realize we have blood on our hands now," he tells me. "You've doomed an entire planet to a fate of enslavement."

"Have I?" I say. "Or did I just send the Jin'Kai coordinates to a dead moon that could take them hundreds of years to get within sensor range of?"

"What?" Cole asks.

"*Accessing . . . Hmm, yes. Very clever. Very clever indeed. You have a deft hand for programming. The alteration to my data is seamless. I have only been able to detect it by comparing it to the file redundancy.*"

"The code couldn't have fingerprints on it," I say. "It had to look like the original data entered years ago."

Dad is the first to catch on, the lightbulb slowly illuminating over his head. "So they think they're headed to an inhabited planet," he says. And if he doesn't sound proud of his only daughter, then I'll be a clone's mother. "When in fact they're off on a wild goose chase."

"The best way to lie to someone is to give them ninety-nine percent of the truth," I reply.

From the corner Marsden laughs weakly. We all turn to look at him.

"Oh right," I say. "I forgot that you aren't all the way dead yet."

"You're too clever by half, Elvie Nara," Marsden says. "You may have fooled them for a time. But what do you think will happen when they realize you tricked them? They might easily discover another viable planet on their own, or simply realize they were duped. In either case, what's to stop them then from coming back and finishing what they started?"

"When that day comes, we'll be ready for them," I say. "A few hundred years is a good head start on anybody."

"I would be happy to provide your peoples with any information in the depository that may be of use to them."

"See that?" I say. "We even have Merv on board."

"You will fail," Marsden spits. Blood speckles his lips. "You cannot deter my brethren with smoke and mirrors. We will come for you. We are strong."

I kneel down next to Marsden and look him in the eye.

"You are a dinosaur," I say. "I'm the chicken." And I get right in his evil bastard face then, before I let out a triumphant, *"Ba-cawk!"*

The hate rises in Marsden's eyes as he looks at me. He can't move, but his body trembles with rage. He starts to cough, and blood sprays from his mouth, flecking my face. The hate in his eyes clouds over, and his gaze goes blank as his death rattle escapes from his lungs. And then . . . that's it. I stand up and move to Chloe, slip an arm around her waist, and rest my head on her shoulder. To my surprise Chloe offers me a small hug in return.

It's over. Dr. Marsden is finally over.

Murmurs from across the room inform us that the gas Marsden used to dope Marnie and the Britta Brigade is wearing off. Slowly the girls rise from the ground, rubbing their eyes and whining about bed hair. After a few seconds the first of them spots Marsden, which sets off a chain reaction of shrill shrieking and gagging.

"Wha's all this, then?" Marnie says, rising off the floor.

"You missed it!" Ducky says, rushing to her.

"Missed what?"

"Elvie totally saving the entire world. Of course, she couldn't have done it without me. You should've *seen* me with Marsden." Marnie gives Ducky a enormous squeeze of a hug, and he flinches away in pain. "Careful with the ribs," he says. "Most likely they're broken."

"Well, then I guess I best be kissin' ye instead," she replies, and that said, she plants a fat, wet kiss on Ducky, smack on the mouth.

And Ducky, bless him, he doesn't flinch or turn red or anything. He kisses that girl right back.

I look at everyone standing around me. My adoring, adorable father. My pretentious, centuries-old grandfather. My best friend in the whole world. His way too worldly and awesome girlfriend. A young woman who is as much a part of me as if I'd given birth to her myself. And my Cole.

Well, not *my* Cole. But Cole. He offers me that trademark lopsided grin, and it releases any pressure that might still have been lingering in my shoulders. Now that I'm relaxed, I can allow myself to admit that I'm tired. And I need to rest. But not just yet.

There's one more thing I need to do.

Chapter Fourteen

IN WHICH OUR HEROINE CONFRONTS HER PAST AND RECOVERS HER FUTURE

"So, this is the place, huh?" Cole asks, looking around. "I expected something a little more, I dunno, secret-y."

"This is the place," I tell him. The smell of the sea is a refreshingly salty alternative to the stale, canned O_2 I've been breathing lately, first on New Moon and then on Mars. The sun is just starting to poke up over the horizon, sending a cascade of shimmering orange and purple lights across the ocean's surface. The early spring breeze is still bitingly cold, but it feels revitalizing more than anything else. We walk along the sandy beach—me, Cole, and Chloe—our spaceship parked in stealth mode farther down the beach next to the boardwalk, which is completely deserted so early in the season.

"You're sure they're here?" Chloe asks.

"Trust me," I say, glancing at the tracker in my hand. "They're here."

Ahead of us lies a large groyne, rocks held together by

concrete, forming a jetty that juts away from the beach and into the water. I can just make out the silhouette of someone at the edge of the groyne, but I don't really need to get up close to know who it is.

Leave it to my mother to escape from outer space and hightail it directly to *New Jersey*.

We climb up onto the rocks and start the long walk to the edge. Zee sits cross-legged with her back to us, looking out at the waves, rocking back and forth. Sitting next to her is a small radio, and I catch snatches of a low, garbled news report as we approach. I can't quite make it out, but I can guess what they're talking about. Since the Jin'Kai ran off and the Almiri came out publicly to the world, that's pretty much been dominating the news cycle. World news. Local politics. Postulations about how this will impact the tenuous real estate market in "high alien" population areas. The only reason the news anchors ever take a break to talk about March Madness is because Villanova's starting backcourt can trace their ancestry to the other side of the galaxy.

As we get closer, I catch the tail end of the report.

"*. . . the only known survivor of the doomed space station, single-handedly slowing the alien invaders as they made their way toward Earth. So stay tuned for our exclusive interview with Huxtable, the hero of New Moon.*"

Seriously, who *is* that guy?

"Elvan," Zee says without turning around. "I knew it would be only a matter of time before you caught up with us."

It's hard to know exactly how to greet the woman who gave birth to you, faked her own death, let you grow up motherless, then snuck back into your life only to steal your daughter from you. "Hi, Mom!" just sounds like you're repressing things that will boil over at Thanksgiving ten years later. "Hey, you deceitful, double-crossing bitch"—while perhaps appropriate—seems a little too vulgar. So I decide to go with a classic.

"Put your hands up where I can see them."

"May I stand?" Zee asks, rising without waiting for an answer.

"I said hands *up*. These Almiri ray guns don't have a hammer to cock or anything, so just imagine a dramatically slow 'click' and use it as motivation to do exactly as I say."

She raises only one hand. "I'm not trying to be difficult," she says, turning slowly. "It's just that my hands are presently occupied."

"*Olivia!*" I screech. I immediately forget that I'm supposed to be pulling a calm, cool, collected badass-cowboy impersonation and run, elbows flailing, toward my baby girl, who is curled up in the crook of Zee's arm.

"Is she okay, Elvs?" Cole asks. His gun is still firmly trained at my mother's head. "Please tell me she's okay."

"I'd hate to have come all this way just to shoot my pseudo-grandmother in the face," Chloe adds. "I mean, it'd be a nice topper, but . . ."

Zee doesn't even fight me as I scoop Olivia from her.

Oh God, she's so warm. So beautiful. She's grown since I've seen her. Not grown enough to be an ex-Jin'Kai youth cadet or anything, but the appropriate amount of development for the time we've been apart. I begin laughing and crying, both at once, snot shooting out of my nose in disgusting bubbles. I don't care. Who cares? She's back. She's here. After all this time, missing her, thinking I'd found her, then realizing I hadn't and missing her triple, I've finally, finally got my baby girl back.

"She looks good," I tell Cole. "Come see. Doesn't she look good?" I check her all over. Ten fingers, ten toes, two ears. Nose fine.

And then I get to the stomach.

"What?" Cole asks in a near panic when he sees the fire hydrant's worth of tears that come pouring out of me. "What is it?"

"Oh, I wasn't—" I begin, trying to explain the tears. But I am becoming quickly hysterical. I hold up our daughter so he can see for himself.

I ♥ Momy!

It's still there, the smeared remnants of the message Cole scrawled on our baby's stomach in indelible marker, all the way back in Antarctica, a few dozen lifetimes ago.

"I told you that marker was permanent," I say, laughing. More snot shoots out of my nose. Olivia lets out a tiny giggle and reaches a fat arm out for me, clenching my hand in hers.

"Aren't there two *m*s in 'mommy'?" Chloe asks.

"Oh God, I'm just so glad you're okay." I squeeze Olivia as tight as I can without damaging her precious internal organs. I may just keep squeezing until she leaves for college.

"I wanted to show her this spot," Zee tells me softly. "While I still had her. It's very special. Your father proposed to me right here. Did you know that? Right here on the rocks."

"You *kidnapped* her," I snap.

"Stop being dramatic," Zee says, waving a dismissive hand. "You should be thanking me for rescuing her from Marsden and his thugs."

"Are you really that delusional?" I ask in disbelief. "You're the one who turned her over to Dr. Marsden in the first place!"

"You want me to shoot her now?" Chloe says. "Or is there something we're waiting for?"

"No one's shooting anyone, Chloe," I reply.

Suddenly a look of horrified realization spreads across Zee's face. "What is *she* doing here?" she demands, eyeing Chloe up and down like she's some sort of infectious disease. "What's going on?"

"Chill out. Chloe's not with Marsden anymore," I tell her. "No one's with Marsden anymore. He's perma-dead."

"She's not even real, Elvan. She's a, a . . . a *thing*." Zee can hardly get the words out. She's gone from calm and collected to unjustifiably morally outraged in the span of ten seconds.

"She's been there for me a lot more than you ever were," I say.

"They grew her in a test tube. They pulled the DNA from your daughter, corrupted it with their own filthy genes, and created an abomination. You can't trust something like that. She's not a real person."

"Hey, watch it," Cole says. "That's my daughter's clone you're talking about."

Chloe takes Zee in, a wicked smile spreading across her face. "You're starting to sound a lot like my old boss," she says. "And by the end he and I *really* didn't see eye to eye."

"I'm just trying not to laugh at the idea of you thinking

someone *else* is untrustworthy," I tell my mother, rocking Olivia gently in my arms as she coos.

"I did what I thought was best for our people. My mistake was believing that the Jin'Kai would be any different from their Almiri cousins. I won't make that same mistake again." She takes a few steps toward me, and instinctively I back away. Cole is immediately beside me, a hand on my shoulder, and Chloe flanks me on the other side, her gun trained directly on Zee.

"Elvan, there's still time. Come with me."

"Come with you?" I ask. "Come with you where?"

"There's an Enosi enclave not far from here. People will be gathering, making preparations. It will be safe there."

"Safe? Haven't you been listening to that radio of yours? The war's over. It's the dawn of a brand-new day."

"You're being foolish. The real war has just begun."

"Do you, like, *ever* have a cheery thought?" I ask. "You should be overjoyed. The mere existence of hybrids has saved the entire planet from annihilation. Dad and Byron are even cowriting a poem about it. They're calling it 'The Defeat of Devastation.'"

In my arms Olivia wiggles around. She wants a better view of her daddy. When she sees him, she breaks into a broad grin. *She smiles now,* I realize. *I missed her first smile.*

But at least I get to see the rest of them.

"Oh, everyone's happy now," Zee says. "The humans are more than willing to accept the presence of a people that have been exploiting them for millennia, and the Almiri are more than happy to receive that acceptance. But how long do you think it will last? How long before they both start seeing the existence of the hybrids as a threat to their respective species?"

"Wow," I say. "I feel really sorry for you. I know you've been out of the loop for a little bit, what with hiding under a rock—I'm guessing somewhere in the Rust Belt?—so let me fill you in. We discovered life on Mars. Well, a computer on Mars, at least, with records of life there. And those records told us a lot of things. Like how we—you, me, and now Olivia—aren't some accidental mutation but a planned evolution of not one but two species. We're the future now."

"And just how do you think they'll react to that, huh? Any of them. You think mankind has a real capacity to accept something so new and different? You think the Almiri will stand for sullying their perfect race?" She gestures back toward the radio. "The news already has stories of protests in the cities, of Almiri ships taking off to find another home separate from the 'lower' species. How long before unrest and disdain lead back to the path they always take—fear and loathing? How long before the Almiri's solution—extermination—is back on the table?"

Zee takes another step toward me. This time I don't shrink away. She puts a hand on my arm and looks me in the eye.

"There's still time. You can come with us. We won't be on the sidelines anymore. We'll be prepared for whatever comes."

"What makes you so sure we *can't* all live harmoniously?" Cole asks her. "How can you possibly know that we can't live together in peace?"

"Because I *know!*" Zee is shouting now, enraged. "I've *seen* it. Don't you understand? Elvan, your daughter's place should be with her own people. That's who she can trust to protect her. Come with us, and I can help you raise her, the way I should have raised you."

"You had no idea we'd find you," I say, the realization suddenly hitting me. Olivia gurgles and grips my thumb, squeezing it tightly. "You weren't waiting for us here, in this place. You were going to take Olivia, go underground. Teach her to be a distrusting, paranoid crazy person, just like you."

"Elvan—"

"She's not your daughter. *I* am your daughter. At least I was." I turn and walk back toward the beach. Chloe falls into place beside me, giving Zee a sarcastic good-bye wave as we go. Zee starts after me, but Cole blocks her path.

"You're being stupid, Elvan!" Zee screeches at me. "This is the only way! You're making a mistake, and it's your daughter who'll pay for it."

I spin around and glare daggers through my mother. I want to shout a lot of things at her, especially about how she shouldn't exactly apply for a guest lecturer position in the field of How Not to Suck at Motherhood. And I'd like to illustrate my point with some of the choicest curse words I've ever had the good fortune to come across. But I steel myself, try to reach some inner calm, or at least lower my blood pressure to normal levels. This is not about me anymore, I tell myself. It's about Olivia.

"You know," I say calmly. "You're right about one thing. There *are* Almiri leaving. There are definitely some who don't want to see the big picture, still think they're the big cheese. And so they're leaving. And you know what? They'll die. There are humans who are scared of change, scared of something different. But you know what? They'll adapt. And guess what else, Zee? There are Jin'Kai already turning themselves in, surrendering to authorities, willing to pay the price for their crimes. Because they want in on the 'grand experiment.' They understand the stakes of the game, a lot better than you. I've met some Almiri who are real douche bags, and I've met some who are extraordinary heroes. I've met Jin'Kai who wouldn't think twice about killing just to prove a point, and I've met one who died to protect the girl he loved. I've met Enosi I would trust with my *life* . . . and I've met you. Your problem, Zee, is that you can't get past where people come from, when all that really matters is where they're headed."

"Don't come running to me when your brave new world disappoints you," she spits at me.

"Well," I say. "I've met you. And I've met the world. And I think I'll put my faith in the world."

And with that, I turn again, and walk off with Chloe by my side. Zee is shouting something while Cole holds her back, but the crashing of the waves against the rocks drowns out whatever hollow protests she might be making.

"So, is that it?" Chloe asks. "You're done with her?"

"It would appear so," I say, trying to keep the tears welling in my eyes from spilling down over my cheeks. Olivia makes a high cooing sound and stares with wonder at Chloe. Chloe makes a sort of fish face, and Olivia giggles, and I can't help but laugh.

"But you never know," I continue. "Sometimes people can surprise you."

EPILOGUE

"We're here," Dad says as he pulls the car into the private lot. "Donald, I trust you'll feel better with a little fresh air."

"I'm okay, Mr. Nara," Ducky says, not entirely convincingly, as he opens his door and exits the car. I begin to fiddle with the straps on Olivia's car seat, a ridiculous contraption that Dad researched and purchased and insists on using whenever we drive the baby around in the old car. It takes me five minutes, minimum, to figure out how to dismantle the many redundant belts and harnesses every single time we go anywhere.

"Need a hand?" Cole asks. He sits on the other side of Olivia, playing the "spinning finger" game that seems to amuse him more than it does her.

"No," I say. "I've got it. Why don't you help them with the bags?"

Cole gives me an awkward half smile and obliges. I feel a

little bad for blowing him off when he's just trying to be helpful, but right now every reminder of what he *could* be doing is making me more and more miserable.

It's not that I still love Cole. At least in a romantic sense. I don't. It took me a while, but I've come to a definite conclusion on that front. But that doesn't mean I won't miss him when he's gone. After all, not being in a relationship with your child's father is one thing. Having him blast off into space on a dangerous mission with no end point is something else entirely.

When I finally get Olivia free from the Dad-approved safety seat, I lift her out of the car and make my way with Dad, Ducky, and Cole across the lot and toward the flightport that will shuttle us to the takeoff site for the *Nautilus*, the spanking new deep-space craft they'll be trekking on. Waiting for us at the shuttle stop are Marnie and Chloe, engaged in an animated conversation.

"Hey, you two," I say. "Everything cool?"

"It's fine," Chloe says. "Just a disagreement on the best way to incapacitate an attacker. I still say it's the groin."

"Not if ye dinnae wanta be seen comin' from a light-year off," Marnie replies. She grabs Chloe's shoulder and makes to jam her heel down on the top of Chloe's foot, in a weird slow-motion demonstration. "Ye go fer the instep, always," she insists.

"Right," I reply. "Obviously." Chloe and Marnie have gotten to be fairly close as they've prepared for their journey into the cosmos. I guess being the only two women aboard, they've decided that they should form some sort of alliance.

"Well, will ye look at tha'?" Marnie coos, calling off her

assault demonstration and bringing her face down to meet Olivia's. "She's learnt to wave already! By the time we get back, she'll be flying her own ship, and tha'."

"Olivia won't be flying any ships until she's at *least* two," I reply. And I don't tell Marnie, but I don't think Olivia's waving so much as flapping her hand in front of her face in an attempt to land it in her mouth. I've been watching her carefully for signs of supergrowth, but as far as I can tell, all Marsden did was extract her DNA. Thank goodness. I plan to be along for every milestone, big or small, from here on out.

I can see Chloe focusing on the baby with that poorly veiled intense stare that she's developed whenever we're together.

"Would you like to hold her?" I ask, already knowing exactly the response I'm going to get.

"Well, um, sure, if your arms are tired," Chloe answers, straining to sound completely uninterested.

"Oh, *exhausted*," I say, smiling. Chloe eagerly accepts the wriggling baby and rocks her gently in her arms. As always when being held by her doppel, Olivia focuses in on Chloe like her gaze is laser-guided, her brow crinkled in wonderment, her mouth pursed into a perfect little o.

"So, I haven't decided what she should call you when we communicate," I say. "I mean, if we're able. Do you want to be Aunt Chloe, Cousin Chloe? I guess 'sister' would be the closest thing to true, but that might raise too many questions too soon."

"Whatever. Like I care," Chloe says. Her eyes dart up at me quickly before falling back down onto Olivia. "Aunt Chloe's fine."

"Great, then it's settled."

Chloe's mouth goes thin. "You're not going to be one of those moms who sends vidcaps, like, every twenty seconds, are you?" she asks. But even with the rehearsed disdain in her voice, the way she bounces Olivia like an old pro undercuts her apathetic posturing. "Like, 'Here's the baby farting!' 'Here's the face she makes when she smells mustard.' 'Here she is at—' Wow, did you see that? She went right for my nose! *Such a strong grip, Wivvie. You're such a strong girl!*" She stops herself when she realizes we're all staring at her, smirking, and she blushes sheepishly.

The shuttle pulls into the stop, the doors slide open, and we all step inside to be whisked toward the takeoff pad.

"You don't even need the vidcaps," Cole tells Chloe, smiling and cooing at the baby just as big as everyone else. Olivia really is a happiness magnet. "You already know she's going to turn out exactly like you."

"Well, probably not *exactly* like me," Chloe replies. She bounces the source of her genetic material on her hip. "Nature versus nurture, and all that."

"Just *when*, precisely, in your two-week growing-up period did you have time to learn about nature versus nurture?" Ducky cuts in.

Chloe rolls her eyes. "It was an exhaustive course," she explains.

"Olivia may not be *exactly* the same as you," I tell Chloe. And I offer her a genuine smile. "But she sure could do a lot worse."

Chloe blinks and turns her face to the floor.

"This is, like, the weirdest, sweetest thing ever," Ducky says.

The shuttle comes to a halt, and the doors swing open onto the launch pad. The rest of the crew of this crazy mission is standing at attention, waiting for us. Oates tips his cap to us politely as we disembark and start toward the *Nautilus*.

"Ladies, gentlemen. Shall we?" he says in that wonderful British lilt.

"Just promise me to come back not-blown-up," I say, looking at each of them in turn. And goddamn that lump in my throat. "That goes for all of you."

"I shall do my utmost, miss," Oates tells me.

"Are ye sure ye cannae join us?" Marnie asks. "I woulda thought ye'd be jumping at the chance, an adventurer such as yerself."

At that, I snort. "Flying off into the great unknown? Keeping tabs on the entire Jin'Kai fleet while avoiding capture? Trying to find clues as to where the ancient martian civilization scampered off to? All in a ship too small to transport a varsity soccer team? No thanks." I let Olivia grab my finger. "I just saved the planet," I tell Marnie. "The universe can manage without me for a little while. Besides"—Olivia giggles that perfect, heartwarming laugh of hers, as if on cue—"there's another tiny matter that requires my attention at the moment. I mean, *someone's* got to make sure she grows up in the spirit of interspecies cooperation. We'd hate for her to take after her grandmother. *Wouldn't we, Wivvie?*" I tickle her chin, and she blows a spit bubble out of the side of her mouth in reply.

"You shall be with us in spirit, miss," Oates puts in.

"Oh, you'll have so many badasses on board, you won't even miss me," I say. I grin at Oates. "I mean, any killer whales out there, I *dare* them to get by you guys. And Cole here"—I punch his arm playfully (when was the last time I did *that?*)—"I think he's proven he's more than just a cute butt."

Cole wrinkles his nose at me.

"Okay, sorry," I say. "I take it back. You *are* just a cute butt."

"No." He shakes his head. "It isn't that. I . . ." He blinks at me. "I'm not going. On the ship. I'm staying here. I . . . I thought you knew that."

Perhaps I shouldn't be, but I am flabbergasted. "You're staying here?" I ask. The action hero star? "But . . . why?"

"Why?" he repeats. Now it's his turn to look confounded. "I thought that would've been obvious." He glances down at Olivia, who returns his warm smile.

Oh yeah. The baby. *Cole's* baby.

Dur.

"We're a family," Cole tells me. "I plan on having it stay that way."

For one of the very few times in my life, I'm utterly speechless. To think, I once worried I'd have to raise this little girl all on my own, and now here the little squirt has a whole *family*.

"But . . ." A new worry has popped into my head. "I mean, I just want to clarify . . . I, like, don't plan on getting back together with you. I mean, we can be Olivia's family without . . . It's not that I don't *like* . . . I just don't have *romantic* feelings . . ." I stop babbling when I realize that literally everyone is staring at me.

"Wow," Ducky puts in. "Maybe your dad and Byron

should write an epic poem about you sticking your foot in your mouth."

Cole just smirks. "No worries, Elvs. I know I can be slow on the uptake, but I think even I've figured out that I like you better when we're not a couple."

Call the fire department, 'cause my face is burning. "Uh. Good," I say lamely. "Just, uh, don't get back together with Britta or anything. Any of the Brittas."

"You're not the boss of me," he says.

"Seriously, Cole, last I heard from them, they were legitimately considering forming a band called Britta and the Brittas."

"I promise nothing," he says with that perfect smile of his. I smile back, suddenly overjoyed to know that I'm not losing my ex-boyfriend to the dark reaches of the outer cosmos.

But then I remember something.

"Wait, then what was with all the suitcases in the car?" I ask.

"They're mine," Ducky says.

The words hit me so quickly and so sharply that I feel like someone just fired a carving knife into my heart using some sort of high-powered knife-propelling device.

"*You're* going?" I ask, incredulous.

"Well, don't sound too surprised," he says. "After all, who took out Dr. Marsden with his quick thinking?"

"But you're not a space commando!" I protest.

"Not yet, maybe," Ducky says. "But I'll get there. I want to be the hero of my own story, Elvie. No more sidekicking. I'll be the first man to barf in multiple solar systems!" We laugh at that. "Besides, I won't be alone. I'll have Marnie looking out for me. And Merv, of course."

Right. Before departing from Mars, the AI construct requested that he be brought back to Earth with us, now that his duties in the alien data depository were no longer needed. Dad and I figured out a way to transfer him from the martian computer system onto the world's biggest memory drive (thank goodness for Almiri high tech), and he's been integrated into the *Nautilus*'s computers to serve as the only "crew" member with any firsthand knowledge of the mysterious race they'll be seeking out.

"Trust me," I say. "A few days with Merv up there, and you'll be trying to swim home."

"I dunno," Ducky says. "We've already discussed programming our own *Jetman* game to pass the time."

There's no point even pretending that I'm not going to be all weepy about this, so I just let the waterworks burst forth as I wrap Ducky in an enormous hug.

"I love you *so much*," I say, crying into the crook of his neck. "Like, bonkers sauce."

"I know," he says. I can feel his own tears on my cheek.

"I'm sorry if I ever made you feel like a sidekick," I say. He pulls me back, and we look at each other through weepy girly eyes, the both of us.

"Hey, you never did that. I'm doing this for me. It's the opportunity of a lifetime. I just hope that you'll understand, and be proud of me."

"I'm already proud of you, you dumb idiot," I say, and we fall back into another big, soppy, wet hug.

. . .

Standing at the base of the ship's ramp, Chloe is the last to say good-bye before boarding. She shuffles her feet awkwardly, not looking at me or Cole but instead focusing all her attention on Olivia, who rests comfortably in her arms.

"It's so weird," she says. "She's, like, older than me, but not."

"Of all the weird crap over the past year, you holding your infant self is definitely in the top five," I agree.

"I'm glad we were able to get her back," Chloe says. "I'm glad at least one of us will get to have a childhood. Make it a good one, all right?"

"Cross my heart and blah, blah, blah," I say. "We'll do our very best. And when you come back—"

"*If* I come back," she interrupts.

"*When.* We'll be here. And you can make sure we did everything right for your 'niece.'"

"I know you will. You're a great mom."

She leans in close to my ear, so only I can hear. "Not every twenty seconds," she tells me. "But a vidcap every now and then probably wouldn't be the worst thing."

"I promise," I say.

She carefully hands Olivia off to Cole, and to my surprise she pulls us all into a Cole-Elvie-Olivia-Chloe sandwich.

"You guys aren't the worst," she says.

"Thanks?" Cole replies.

She disengages from the family group hug, turns, and, just like that, walks up the platform and disappears inside the ship. I wonder if it's the last I'll ever see of her.

. . .

276

The start-up sequence is mostly a blur to me. A haze of tears. I'm mildly aware of Cole settling Olivia back into my arms, and of her clinging to my arm, blowing cute little raspberries at my cheek. At some point Dad and Byron wander over to me. Dad sets a hand on my back, and Cole moves in closer too. Together we watch as our friends and family shoot off into the great unknown.

"You going to be okay, dearheart?" Dad asks me softly.

I sniffle, watching the ship dart higher, higher, *highest* into the atmo. It is quickly less than a speck, leaving a trail of vaporized exhaust in its wake. Then it's gone. I look down at Olivia. Her beautiful face. "I think so," I reply.

We are silent for a while, all of us watching the empty sky, until a horrifying thought occurs to me.

"Do I have to go back to high school?" I ask. "'Cause I'm not sure Lower Merion is going to transfer my credits from the evil alien academy."

"Your grandfather and I were discussing that," Dad says.

"Really?"

"Well," Byron says with that rakish grin of his, "I know it's always been your dream to join the Ares Project someday."

"You're going forward with the terraforming?" I ask. "You think people will still want to colonize the surface even after the discovery of an underground martian civilization?"

"I'm optimistic that the terraforming and archeological interests will dovetail together nicely," Byron says. "Now, you're not really in a position to join the team right now, of course, but seeing as the provost of the Armstrong School is a personal friend of mine . . ."

"The Armstrong School?" I gasp. "Really?"

"What's the Armstrong School?" Cole asks

"Only the single best and hardest-to-get-into aeronautic engineering program in the world!" I gush. I turn back to Byron. "You know the provost?"

"I should say so. I did save his life during the Franco-Prussian War. If you want to go, there's a spot for you in the fall class."

If my jaw dropped any lower, I'd need Olivia to scoop it up and push it back into place.

"You cannot be serious."

"And yet I am."

My dad is grinning too. "Great news, right?" he says, rubbing my shoulder.

"What about Olivia? Cole?"

"We can place Mr. Archer in a position nearby, if he likes," Byron replies. "And my great-granddaughter will not want for care."

"Wow, I just . . . Wow," I say. It's like getting exactly the Christmas present you asked for, immediately after learning that Santa is an old man in a fat suit. But I have to slow down, think everything through.

"Can I have some time to think about it?" I ask.

"Dearheart?" Dad says.

"I'm not saying no," I tell them. I shift Olivia on my hip. "God, I'm not saying no. It's just . . . I've been thinking . . . well, I guess I've come to realize lately that, despite everything, I've lived a very fortunate life, and that there are a lot of people who haven't. That ozone factory that blew up—there are hundreds more places like it, and maybe millions of people living lives that until recently I couldn't even conceive of. The kind of poverty I saw there, that was more alien to me than any pretty boy Almiri or monster-looking Devastator. I think . . . I think maybe I'd like to help people the way I've had people help me. Maybe that still means Ares. Maybe more. But I need a little time to think. Like what you were talking about on Mars. 'The world forgot' and all that."

"Yes, about that," Byron says. "Maybe don't mention to Alex that I was quoting him. It'll go straight to his head."

When I look back up, my father is beaming. "You're a wise woman, Elvie," he says. "That's for sure."

I lean my head on his shoulder and snuggle my daughter closer into my side. Cole wraps an arm around the two of us, and together with Byron we go back to watching the sky. In the upper atmosphere I think I catch the glint of something shining briefly, and then disappearing the next moment. Perhaps it's the flash from the *Nautilus*'s hyperdrive, pushing my loved ones into the final frontier. Perhaps it's a satellite for HBO. Regardless, my friends are beginning their greatest journey, just like I'm about to embark on mine. Who knows what lies around the bend, what calamity we'll have to deal with next? How will we handle all the unknown perils our new life has in store for us?

In my arms Olivia giggles—the kind of sweet, charming, delightful baby giggle that travels all the way through you. I kiss her head.

"You're right," I whisper to my daughter. "Whatever comes, we'll adapt."